APOCALYPSE

APOCALYPSE

J. DANIEL HAYS

C. MARVIN PATE

GRAND RAPIDS, MICHIGAN 49530 USA

ZONDERVAN™

Apocalypse
Copyright © 2004 by C. Marvin Pate and J. Daniel Hays

Requests for information should be addressed to:
Zondervan, *Grand Rapids, Michigan 49530*

Library of Congress Cataloging-in-Publication Data

Hays, J. Daniel, 1953-
    Apocalypse/ J. Daniel Hays and C. Marvin Pate.
      p. cm.
    Includes bibliographical references.
    ISBN 0-310-25355-1 (softcover)
      1. Church history—Primitive and early church, ca. 30-600—Fiction.
  2. Bible.   3. N.T. Revelation—Fiction.   I. Pate, C. Marvin, 1952-   II. Title
    PS3608.A983A66 2004
    813'.6—dc22
                                          2003026921

Interior design by Michelle Espinoza

Printed in the United States of America

04 05 06 07 08 09 10 /❖ DC/ 10 9 8 7 6 5 4 3 2 1

CONTENTS

1. Assassins 13
2. The Scroll 21
3. Ephesus and Julia 33
4. The Imperial High Priest 43
5. The Beast and His Mark 59
6. Family, Friends, and Faithfulness 75
7. A Walk with Friends 89
8. The Synagogue 101
9. Horsemen in the Night 109
10. The Followers of Balaam 121
11. The Beast Arrives 129
12. The Parting of the Ways 141
13. Lukewarm Laodicea 151
14. The Guild 165
15. Looking East 173
16. Who Are the Ones in the White Robes? 179
17. Hiding the Apocalypse 187
18. Decisions 201
19. The Sword of the Enemy 211
20. The City of the Beast 229
21. The Bride 239
22. Martyrdom or Escape? 247
Postscript: Historical Aspects of the Novel 263

LIST OF
CHARACTERS

Antonius—a young man residing in Laodicea; son of Gallus and
    Cassandra; unofficially betrothed to Monica

Apollinarius—scribe of John the apostle

Archelaus—president of the Wool Merchants' Guild in Laodicea

Caecelia—wife of Isaeus; servant/friend of Gallus and Cassandra

Caius—high priest of the Imperial Temple in Ephesus; father of
    Plautus

Caligula—Antonius's dog

Cassandra—wife of Gallus and mother of Antonius

Creon—Greek scribe who makes copies of the Apocalypse

Demetrius—chief steward of Senator Flavius

Domitian—Caesar in Rome

Epaphras—pastor of the church in Laodicea

Ephraim—rabbi of the synagogue in Laodicea; father of Simeon

Flavius—Roman senator; husband of Sabina and father of Julia

Gallus—famous Roman centurion, now retired and a wool merchant
    in Laodicea; husband of Cassandra and father of Antonius

Heron—Greek captain of the ship *Orion*

Isaeus—servant of Gallus and Cassandra; husband of Caecelia;
    friend of Antonius

John—exiled Christian apostle who writes the Apocalypse

Jonathan—elder in the synagogue in Laodicea

Julia—beautiful, unmarried daughter of Senator Flavius and Sabina

Juba—retired Roman legionnaire; Berber from North Africa; husband to Vivia and father of Monica, Marcellus, and Mardonius; friend of Gallus

Marcellus—twin brother of Mardonius; son of Juba and Vivia; brother of Monica

Mardonius—twin brother of Marcellus; son of Juba and Vivia; brother of Monica

Maximus—member of the Roman praetorian guard

Miriam—young Jewish woman in Laodicea; daughter of Jonathan

Monica—young woman residing in Laodicea; daughter of Juba and Vivia; unofficially betrothed to Antonius

Nathan—Jewish banker in Ephesus

Plautus—son of Caius; high priest of the Imperial Temple in Laodicea

Polukarpos—young pastor of the church in Smyrna

Quintus—former proconsul of the Roman province of Asia, replaced by Sulla

Sabina—Roman wife of Senator Flavius; mother of Julia

Severus—cousin of Flavius; wealthy resident of Ephesus

Shabako—elder in the Laodicean church; retired legionnaire from Ethiopia

Simeon—young Jewish Christian friend of Antonius

Sulla—new proconsul of the Roman province of Asia, replacing Quintus

APOCALYPSE

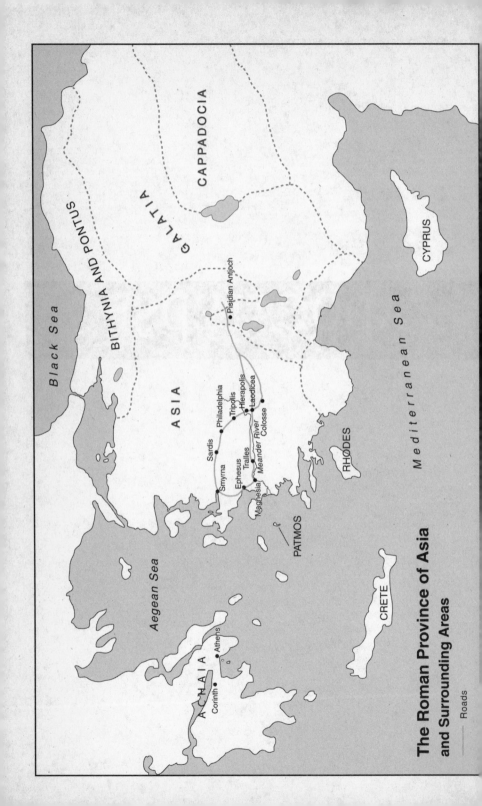

The Roman Province of Asia and Surrounding Areas

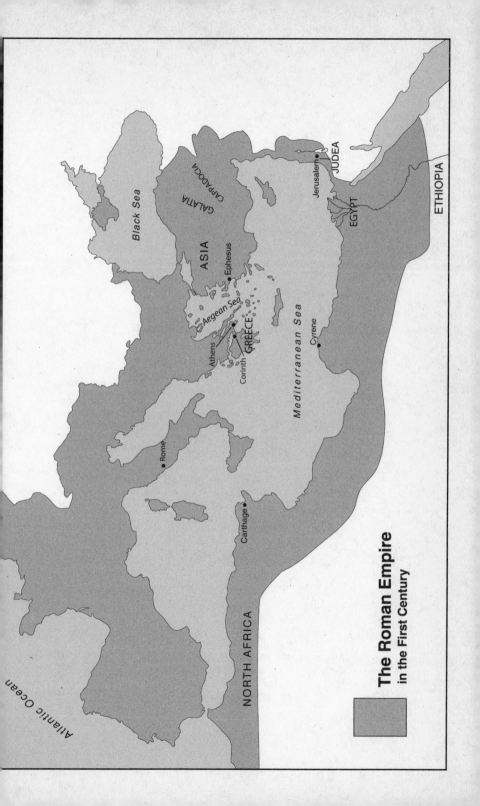

Atlantic Ocean

Black Sea

GALATIA

CAPPADOCIA

ASIA

Ephesus

Aegean Sea

GREECE

Athens

Corinth

Jerusalem

JUDEA

EGYPT

ETHIOPIA

Cyrene

Mediterranean Sea

Rome

Carthage

NORTH AFRICA

The Roman Empire
in the First Century

chapter one

Ἀποκάλυψις Ἰησοῦ Χριστοῦ ἣν ἔδωκεν αὐτῷ ὁ θεὸς δεῖξαι τοῖς

ASSASSINS

δούλοις αὐτοῦ ἃ δεῖ γενέσθαι ἐν τάχει, καὶ ἐσήμανεν ἀποστείλας

The sky had grown gray and angry, but no rain had yet fallen. The wind shifted to the north and gained velocity, causing the sails on the two short masts to flutter limply for a moment and then pop tight again. The ship groaned and creaked, then began picking up speed. Standing by the dual rudders at the stern, the captain, known simply as Heron, cursed under his breath and turned the ship slightly to the south, putting the wind behind him.

Heron, a Greek, had been on the sea since childhood. His matted curly hair and beard had once been the color of pitch, but now was more gray than black. He stood slightly stooped and his face was lined with wrinkles, proof of the harsh years he had known, both on the sea and in port. He was missing the first two fingers on his left hand, a stark reminder of his brawl with a Thracian sailor over a harlot in Corinth three years earlier.

Heron gave a shout, and the five-man crew sprang to life and began to pull down the mainsail and shorten the leading sail. The waves were growing larger by the moment, and one of them suddenly crashed against the back of the fleeing vessel, covering the captain with cold spray and foam. His curses grew audible. He lashed the rudder into place and quickly surveyed his ship.

The *Orion* was a medium-sized ship—not a giant like one of the monstrous Roman grain transports, but not a small coastal lugger either. She had two masts, one now naked in the wind and the other with a shortened but tight sail, straining against the gusting storm. She sat low in the water with a heavy load of Athenian wine, but she was a seaworthy vessel and she rode the big rolling waves well. The storm did not look serious. The captain was concerned not about safety but only about his schedule and the unpleasant task that lay ahead.

His two passengers were stirring, the older man walking slowly toward the bow and the young man hurrying nervously toward the captain. As the youth approached a wave crashed into the stern again, spraying both of them.

"Mother of Zeus!" cursed the captain.

The young man adjusted his wet cloak, wrapping it tighter around him to minimize the effect of the cold wind driving into his body. He was slightly taller than the captain, with green eyes and pitch-black hair, which was now blowing wildly in the wind. The captain knew only that the lad was a merchant's son, returning to Ephesus from delivering a load of wool to Athens. His father must be a fool, mused the captain, to send such a youngster by himself on such a mission. He found himself wondering whether the young man might have a bag of silver coins somewhere underneath that wet cloak.

"Captain," the young man said, "I am not a seafaring man, but is it not a bit early in the season for storms?"

"Yes, lad, it is early, but this is not enough of a storm to worry about, although it may delay us a day or two. The *Orion* has been through many a storm much worse than this. But mind you pay attention and don't get washed overboard." *At least not with your money still in your bag.*

The captain eyed the lad, sizing him up. He was big and appeared strong, but with a babyish face. How old could he be . . . eighteen, nineteen maybe? Marcus and the others should have no trouble with him, if it comes to a fight, Heron concluded. And the boy may even have some real money—a bonus he hadn't originally counted on.

No, it was the other one—the senator—that Heron was worried about. He glanced at the balding, middle-aged man at the front of the ship, apparently deep in thought and oblivious to the storm. He didn't look like much of a fighter. Still, a Roman senator! The gods were with Heron today. The senator was traveling alone, without slaves to attend him (or protect him). Another foolish man! And the storm was a stroke of luck. Passengers get washed overboard. It happens—who can prevent it? Besides, as far as he knew, no one was aware that either passenger was aboard this particular ship. No one had been at the pier to see them off in Athens—a boy returning home alone after a business trip and a fallen politician trying to sneak away quietly to the provinces. And the senator, no doubt, also had money with him. Even in his flight, he would take a considerable sum with him, wouldn't he? So with the boy's money and the senator's money and the one hundred pieces of silver that would be paid if the distinguished senator should happen to disappear on this voyage, it should be a very profitable trip indeed, not even counting the Athenian wine.

"Captain," the youth asked, "who is the other passenger, if I may ask?"

"Ask all you want, boy," Heron growled, "but I am not inclined to tell you. Ask him yourself who he is."

Ignoring the captain's rudeness, the lad continued. "I can't get any response out of him. I tried to engage him in conversation earlier, but all I got was a polite morning greeting."

The wind seemed to be picking up, and the captain looked at the sails on his front mast. Amused, the captain could not resist playing with his young passenger. "What do *you* make of him, boy?"

"As far as I can tell, he is not a merchant, or at least not a typical one. He appears to be Roman. His Latin is without accent. He bears himself as one noble born; yet he travels without an attendant. His clothes are expensive, but practical, made for travel. He also looks sad and weary."

"You see much, boy," muttered the captain. *It's a shame,* he thought, *that the boy had to be here. He seems a decent lad. Still, it can't be helped. Business is business.*

The captain's attention was drawn suddenly to the front of the ship, where the Roman stranger was growing animated, walking back and forth and peering off to the left, trying to see something out on the waves. The captain noticed a dark object out on the waves as well, probably a small boat, but he couldn't make it out for sure.

The Roman stranger walked quickly to the stern, his cloak flapping madly in the wind. Ignoring the young man, he approached Heron and said calmly, "Captain, there is a small fishing vessel struggling against the storm there in the distance to the left. They appear to be in some trouble. Perhaps we should draw near and see if they require assistance."

"We don't stop for fishermen," the captain answered with disgust. "They can look out for themselves."

Having secured the ship to weather the storm, and seeing the Roman senator walk to the stern, the five men of the crew now likewise approached the captain and the two passengers. All eight men now stood in a circle at the stern of the ship in awkward silence. The wind continued to whistle through the empty rigging of the main mast. The Roman stranger looked anxiously out toward the fishing boat, which was slowly drawing closer. The youth had grown more alert as well, but his alarm was over the appearance of the five sailors. They were a rough-looking group, especially the big Greek known as Marcus and the stocky Cretan with the disfigured ear. The young man noticed that Marcus had a wooden club in his hand that he was trying to keep hidden from the view of the stranger. The stout Cretan also held a club. The others had their hands inside their cloaks. The young man tensed instinctively, slowly loosening the tie on his cloak and then moving his right hand cautiously inside.

The Roman broke the silence. "Look, Captain, the fishing boat is floundering! We must help them."

The captain glanced briefly at the struggling boat. Its sails were torn from the mast. Someone on board appeared to be frantically struggling with the oars, trying to bring the bow of the boat around to face the waves.

"They are not fishermen," the captain said. "They're idiots. Any fisherman would have been able to see the signs of the storm coming. No one in his right mind would take to the open sea before a storm in such a small craft. And they handle the boat poorly. Idiots." A large wave crashed over the front of the small boat.

"They're doomed. But it is not our concern. It is the will of the gods if they die. I am not stopping." *And we certainly don't need any witnesses on board.*

"Captain," the Roman said sternly, "I am a Roman senator, and I command you to assist the people in that boat before they die. Disobey and you will answer to the proconsul at Ephesus—a good friend of mine."

"I know who you are, Senator Flavius Lucius Domitilla," sneered the captain. "But you are hardly in a position to command anyone. Our great lord and master Caesar Domitian has just executed your brother and banished your sister-in-law to Britain for their heretical worship of this new god and for their treason against Rome and Caesar. Everyone knows this. You yourself are fleeing the wrath of Domitian, hoping that by running to the provinces you can save yourself. You have more enemies than friends, most honored Senator, and I doubt if the proconsul is impressed with your credentials anymore. Anyway, you certainly have no authority on the open sea to command me, the captain of the *Orion,* or my esteemed associates."

With a devilish grin on his face, Marcus, the biggest of the five mariners, took a step forward, pulling out his club for all to see. The young man stepped back, eyes wide in shock at hearing who the stranger was, and in alarm at the rapidly developing turn of events. In the distance thunder rumbled.

"Captain," said the big sailor, "let's take them now. No sense in waiting. We have this nice storm. Let's get it over with and throw them overboard."

The senator drew back. "Treachery," he muttered. "I expected as much. Let the lad live, Captain. He is not part of this."

"No, my most-honored Senator," the captain answered, "the boy became part of this when he bought his passage for this voyage. It is the will of the gods and his misfortune. He will keep you company during your swim down to the depths to visit your new lord, Neptune. Every Roman senator needs at least one servant to attend to him."

All five of the crew members smiled at the joke and slowly advanced toward the senator and the young man, both of whom had backed against the outer railing of the ship. The three sailors without clubs drew short knives out of their cloaks.

"I am sorry, son," the senator said softly to the young man. "I should have seen it coming."

Suddenly the big sailor raised his club high, let out a blood-curdling shout, and charged the senator. At the same instant, a blinding flash of lightning lit the sky, followed immediately by a deafening crash of ear-splitting thunder. The sailors jumped at the flash and the roar, instinctively ducking and looking up at the sky for an instant. Next came another cry—a scream this time—and as they looked back toward their victims they saw in horror the young lad with his foot elevated on the chest of Marcus, pulling the blood-covered blade of a short sword out of the astonished sailor's chest and then pushing him away with his foot. Marcus fell backward and landed on the deck with a dull thud. He lay on his back, very still, face pale, eyes wide open, air and foaming blood oozing out of his chest with each tortured gasping breath.

διὰ τοῦ ἀγγέλου αὐτοῦ τῷ δούλῳ αὐτοῦ Ἰωάννῃ, ὃς ἐμαρτύρησεν

THE SCROLL

τὸν λόγον τοῦ θεοῦ καὶ τὴν μαρτυρίαν Ἰησοῦ Χριστοῦ

"Who's next?" demanded the young man with the sword.

He no longer had the look of an inexperienced youngster. His cloak was discarded, lying on the deck behind him. His tunic was short and tight, with minimal sleeves, allowing all on board to glimpse the impressive size of his upper arms and chest. In his right hand he held a Roman infantryman's short sword. He stood in a soldier's stance— left foot slightly forward, knees slightly bent, right arm slightly extended. Lightning again lit the sky and reflected off the glistening upper blade of the sword, highlighted by the bloodred tip.

His mouth was taut and his eyes burned intently, with no trace of fear. "Come, you scoundrels! My sword is drawn. Let's finish our business together."

The senator had drawn out a small, elegant, gold-hilted dagger, and he stepped up beside the young warrior. "I'll cover your back, son."

"We can still take them!" shouted the captain. "They are but two, and we are still five. Forget the sword. He was just lucky. He is just a wet-eared, scared boy who thinks his sword makes him a man. Kill him and let's be done with it. He can't get all of us; let's rush him."

The sailors were slowly backing away. "By all the gods of Crete," swore the stout Cretan sailor with the disfigured ear, no longer grinning. Traces of panic showed in his eyes. "Captain, you promised that the senator would be alone and unguarded. By the gods, he looks well-guarded to me. Look at Marcus! Mother of Neptune, he's dying right here on the deck! And look at that lad's bloody Roman sword! This is a Roman soldier, Captain, and you are a lying dog. Rush him yourself, if you want him so badly."

Despite the wind, an awkward silence followed. The sailors' cloaks flapped and their hair blew in their faces. The captain and his four crewmen stood still, staring at the steel-eyed young man, trying to decide what to do next. Their indecision was interrupted by Marcus, the would-be assassin lying wounded on the deck, who rolled onto his side and began coughing up blood. He then gave a wretched whispery gasp, slowly closed his eyes, and went limp. Any fighting spirit that may have lingered in the hearts of the sailors ebbed and vanished with Marcus's awful last breath.

The senator took charge. "You four go forward and prepare to pull in the men from the fishing boat. You, Captain, move quickly to the rudder and steer us over to those struggling people before they perish. And no tricks, or you shall join in the chorus that your colleague here on the deck has been singing. But first, throw those daggers and clubs over the side. Now! Move!"

Slowly and with visible reluctance, the captain and crew tossed their daggers and clubs overboard. The crewmen headed forward while Heron walked to the very back of the ship and unlashed one of the rudders. Another wave crashed into the stern at that very moment, and the captain caught the seawater right in his face. With his wet sleeve he wiped the water from his eyes and muttered inaudible curses about the senator's ancestry. But he altered course, and the ship now pointed in the direction of the struggling fishing boat. The gap between the two vessels closed quickly.

"And you, son," the senator said as he turned to address his new comrade-in-arms. "What blessed name do you go by, lad?"

"Antonius Marius Amulius."

"Well, Antonius, why don't you stay right here on the deck with your terrible sword in your hand to ensure that no one has a change of heart about us. And . . . by the way, thank you very much. No doubt you saved my life."

"Uh . . . yes, sir. And thank you, sir. I'll stay right here."

"Pretty work you did on this big sailor, eh?" The senator glanced down at the lifeless Marcus. "But just a bit high with your thrust, weren't you? Into the hard ribs instead of the soft stomach. That's a soldier's sword in your hand, but you are not really a soldier, are you, Antonius Marius Amulius?"

"No, sir. I am a merchant's son. We export black wool. But you've a keen eye for combat, sir. I intended to thrust lower, but as I drew my sword I was also trying to cast off my cloak, and for a brief moment my arm was entangled. I freed it only at the last instant, and to be honest, sir, I panicked a bit and struck quickly and my aim was not proper. But I struck hard, sir, and the sword went through the ribs and did not glance off them."

Antonius looked down at Marcus's blood-spattered corpse. The rush of the battle was quickly fading, and as his heartbeat slowed, his head began to clear. He forced himself to stoop next to the dead sailor and wipe the blood from his sword on the sailor's tunic. He stood slowly and methodically returned his sword to its sheath. His face, however, had grown pale. He walked to the edge of the ship, trying to retain his composure. His knees felt weak and he placed a hand on the deck railing to steady himself.

The senator watched. "Get control of yourself, Antonius," he urged quietly. "We do not want our new enemies on this ship to see you get sick over this. They need to remain convinced that you are a trained killer."

"Yes, sir. I know. I will be all right. Let me get a breath or two." Antonius stared out at the rolling seas for a moment, holding the railing firmly, and slowly regained his composure. The color began to return to his face. He turned back and glanced down at Marcus. "This is the first man I have actually killed. The others have been only straw dummies. And ... well ... this is different than I thought it would be. And although I have been trained to use a sword, I am not one who seeks violence. In truth, I envision myself as a man of peace."

"You did the right thing, son. You were both brave and bold. And if you had hesitated, we would both be dead and at the bottom of the sea. Because of your action, we may be able to rescue those poor fishermen before they drown. So you have saved more than you have killed."

The wind was growing stronger, and the waves seemed to be increasing in size. The sailors had quietly collected the gear needed for a rescue. Two of them stood at the front of the ship with a rope attached to a wooden float. The other two stood farther back and were lowering a rope ladder over the side. The senator looked back at the captain, who scowled at him but kept the ship on course, pointed toward the fishing boat, now only about three or four hundred paces in the distance.

The wind continued to howl around them. Antonius shivered. He retrieved his wet cloak and wrapped it around his shoulders. As the young man straightened his cloak, the senator asked him, "Where did you get that infantryman's sword, and who taught you how to use it?"

For the first time a slight smile broke the serious look on Antonius's face. "My father taught me how to use the sword. He was a Roman legionnaire. This is his sword. He presented it to me as I departed on this trip."

"And quite a sword it is, too. And today you have honored it—and your father—greatly. No doubt your sword will be forever known in your family by what you have done with it today, fighting off six wretched and dangerous sailors on the open sea, and saving a Roman senator from a certain death."

"Oh no, sir, begging your pardon, but today's events can hardly add to the honor of *this* sword. I merely killed one unsuspecting scoundrel, who was armed only with a club. But *this* sword . . . with this sword my father cut through the entire barbarian army in the forest of Athanel to rejoin his general Sulla and the Roman army on the banks of the Elbe."

"Your father was in the forest of Athanel?" the senator asked, incredulously. "No wonder you fight like a demon."

"Then you have heard of the battle, sir? Some have tried to tell me that the story is merely a myth—a fabrication of old, retired soldiers."

"No, Antonius, the battle is hardly a myth. The incompetent Sulla made an incredible tactical blunder, allowing a force of one hundred Roman legionnaires and two hundred Berber auxiliaries to be surrounded by several thousand German barbarians. Then, adding cowardice to stupidity, he refused to march to their rescue because he feared he was outnumbered. Instead, he withdrew to the Elbe to await reinforcements, thus sacrificing them. The abandoned legionnaires and Berbers, however, fought through the heart of the barbarian army, and miraculously, twenty of them, including their centurion—the 'Bloody Centurion' as he is known now in army marching songs—survived to return and report to Sulla, to the general's great shame and embarrassment. The great coward Sulla never officially reported the battle, and he and his top officers vigorously deny it ever happened. But the army knows. The legionnaires know. They tell this story around campfires at night to the new troops."

"I've heard the story often from my father's friend Juba, one of the Berbers who fought with him. But he has never explained how the unit came to be separated and surrounded. And I have never heard the details about the general Sulla before. How do you know all of this, if I may be so bold as to ask?"

"My older brother—may he rest with the Lord in peace—was in command of the reinforcement column that Sulla was waiting on. It is a small world, Antonius, and I am honored to know you. Incredible! I've been rescued by one whose father fought with the Bloody Centurion in the forest of Athanel."

"No, sir. And begging your pardon, sir, but my father *is* the Bloody Centurion. And this is his sword."

The senator looked at Antonius with astonishment and opened his mouth to say something, but hesitated. Another wave crashed over the back of the *Orion* and the cold spray brought the two men back to the present. The fishing boat was now only seventy-five paces away, pointed into the oncoming waves and toward the approaching rescue ship.

"Look, sir!" Antonius said. "There is only one person aboard."

All aboard the *Orion* could now make out the lone occupant of the smaller vessel. He was struggling desperately with the oars, frantically trying to keep the boat pointed squarely into the towering waves so that he might have some chance of staying upright. A huge wave crashed over the small craft, and all of the boat but the bare mast disappeared momentarily from view. As the wave rolled on, the craft bobbed back into view, but everyone could see that it was now totally swamped.

"He's done for!" shouted the captain.

"Stay on course!" ordered the senator. "Be ready with those ropes! Steady at the helm, Captain. Don't run over him."

The captain only glared.

The occupant of the small craft looked up, and for the first time, noticed the *Orion* approaching. However, he could no longer control his floundering craft—now completely full of water. He stood up with a large bundle under his arm and jumped into the water just as his craft turned sideways into the next wave. The crashing wave caught the side of the boat and capsized it.

"Will we reach him in time, sir?" Antonius asked.

"If he can swim for a few minutes, he'll have a chance," the senator replied. "I hope whatever he has in his arms floats."

All on board the *Orion* fixed their eyes on the small speck in the water. He was visible for a moment on the crest of a wave, and then gone from view as he slid into a trough. Antonius's heart pounded. *He's gone under!* But then the man bobbed to the surface on the crest of the next wave. They were drawing close.

Antonius could see that the man's hair and beard were nearly white and that his face was covered with wrinkles. "He's an old man!" Antonius shouted. "He can't last long. We must hurry!"

"The old relic should drop that bundle," the senator muttered. "It's not keeping him afloat; it's pulling him down. See how he struggles with it." Then he shouted, "To the left, Captain! More to the left!"

"We cannot turn sharply into the waves or *we* will be swamped. We'll still reach him!" the captain shouted back.

"Can you take in any sail and slow down? We'll run right by him."

"We can't slow down without losing control of the *Orion* and being swamped."

The ship was rapidly approaching the old man in the water, who was struggling to stay afloat.

Antonius and the senator leaned out over the railing of the ship, watching intently. One of the sailors in the front threw the float out into the sea toward the man in the water. It fell an arm's length short.

"He'll never reach it; he has no strength left," the senator said.

"Swim!" shouted Antonius. The old man took a weak stroke toward the rope. Antonius felt his heart sink. The front of the ship was now moving past the weakening swimmer. *He is not going to reach it!* Antonius thought. But at the last instant, the old man summoned up some hidden strength, lunged through the water, and was just able to grab the wooden float with his left hand.

"He's got it!" Antonius exclaimed.

The ship began dragging the man through the water as it plowed forward through the waves. The stocky Cretan climbed over the side and down the rope ladder near the waves. The old man had his left arm wrapped around the float and in his right he still clutched the large bundle. As he was pulled through the sea, the force of the water nearly stripped the bundle from his arms, but doggedly he held on. Slowly the old man drew near the side of the ship, where the Cretan awaited him with one arm wrapped around the rope ladder and one arm reaching out to retrieve the man in the water.

Antonius, who was leaning over the side, suddenly exclaimed to the senator, "See the burn scar on that old man's face? I know that man! He is no fisherman. He is Apollinarius, the old scribe of John the apostle. I saw him with John in Ephesus several years ago when my father took me to hear John teach in the Ephesian church, back before the apostle was arrested and exiled."

"You are a Christian then, Antonius? A follower of Jesus the Christ?" the senator asked with surprise.

"Yes, sir. My entire family believes. We are part of the church at Laodicea. And you, sir?"

"Most certainly. That's why I am here—more or less exiled to the provinces."

"Get rid of that bundle, old man!" the Cretan shouted. "And give me your hand."

"No," came the faint answer. "Take my bag." And the old man, still clinging to the float with his left hand, reached up with his right and handed the bundle to the sailor.

"You crazy old man!" the sailor shouted, grabbing the bundle and then flinging it up and over the railing onto the deck of the ship. The bundle bounced onto the deck. It was a large pouch made of goatskin, white with dark spots, wrapped round with the twine of a fisherman's net, and heavy from seawater. Antonius bounded across the deck to retrieve it.

"Wait!" warned the senator.

Before he could say anything else a huge wave crashed over the stern of the *Orion,* and everyone disappeared for a moment beneath the foam. The captain had seen it coming and had braced himself against the wooden guides of the rudder. The senator, however, was knocked down and thrown against the outer railing of the ship. Antonius had just leaned over and picked up the bundle when the wave hit, and he was swept off his feet completely. The water washed him half the length of the ship, tossing him like a wet rag, and finally smashing him up against some water kegs lashed to the right side of the deck.

He lay facedown, stunned and dazed, but still holding the bundle with his left arm. He opened his eyes and stared at the bottom of the wooden water kegs. His head was pounding and he was not quite sure where he was. As he gingerly touched his right cheekbone, he realized that he was also bleeding. Just as he came to his senses he heard footsteps on the deck nearby. Two of the sailors had run across the deck toward him. Antonius lay looking away, listening and trying to focus as they approached him cautiously.

"Be careful," one warned. "I saw him move."

"No, he's out cold," the other sailor said as he stood beside Antonius and nudged him in the back with his foot. "Let's take his sword and throw him overboard."

Suddenly Antonius rolled on to his back, sword drawn. The two sailors stepped back, startled.

"Well?" Antonius shouted angrily. "Have you decided to fight? Or do you only fight people who are unconscious?"

The sailors continued to back away slowly and Antonius scrambled to his feet. His head was spinning and one knee was bruised badly, but he planted his feet firmly and glared at the two would-be assailants.

"Get over there and help haul in the old man," he ordered. The two mariners sheepishly moved across the deck and Antonius picked up the goatskin bag. He placed the bag under his left arm, and with his sword still in his right hand, limped back across the deck to the senator, who was also now on his feet, looking over the ship's rail. As Antonius walked up, the Cretan climbed up over the side and back into the ship.

"You lost him!" the senator said.

"I never had him!" shouted the sailor. "By the wrath of Neptune I swear! That wave plastered me against the planks, and if I hadn't been doubly wrapped into the ladder it would have swept me away. When the wave cleared, I looked . . . and the float was empty. The old man was simply gone. There was nothing I could have done."

Antonius and the senator looked at the sea in despair; trying to find the old man now would be hopeless.

"I told you it was a foolish idea," said the captain behind them. "You two heroes very nearly joined the old fool in his death."

"Watch your mouth, Captain," ordered the senator, rubbing his side and wondering if he had any broken ribs. "Your problems are not over yet."

"What's in the fisherman's bag?" sneered the captain, heedless of the warning. "Fish? Nets? Pretty seashells for his grandchildren? A map to hidden treasure?"

Ignoring the captain, the senator turned to Antonius, whose right cheekbone was starting to turn blue. "Are you certain you recognized that man as John's scribe?"

"His hair was wet and plastered against his face, and it has been several years . . . but, yes, that burn-scarred face is something I remember quite well. It was Apollinarius, the scribe of John the apostle." Antonius looked over the side of the ship at the stormy waves. "I guess we didn't really save anybody, did we? At least no one other than ourselves."

"Well," said the senator, "let's see what's in the goatskin."

Antonius and the senator ducked inside the captain's cabin. As the senator kept an eye on the captain and the sailors, the young man placed the goatskin bag on the small table inside. The senator then drew out his small dagger and methodically, almost ceremonially, cut each of the cords that bound the bag. He carefully opened it, only to discover another bag, this one made of heavy, faded red canvas, probably cut from the old sail of a fishing boat, carefully folded and stitched closed.

"Well, whatever it is, they made it as watertight as possible." He placed his dagger in the seam, sliced carefully through the stitching, and opened the canvas bag. He and Antonius peered in at the contents at the same time.

"It's a scroll!" Antonius said.

"Yes, indeed. And a very big scroll." The senator reached in and pulled out the scroll, a rolled bundle of papyrus, half a cubit in width and extraordinarily long. *This scroll would probably stretch all the way across the width of this ship!* "Very expensive papyrus, too, son. Feel the texture on the back."

"What could it be, sir, that the scribe would risk his life for it? To take a small boat like that out into the open sea . . . all by himself and at his age?"

"The Romans didn't exile John to the isle of Patmos so that he could continue to write about the Christ to other Christians," said the senator. "Perhaps John has written another letter for the church. The scribe must have been trying to smuggle it off the island. Perhaps some new threat or danger of losing it forced him to take such desperate measures."

"A new letter? A longer document? Like his gospel of Jesus?" asked the young man. "That work is revered by all the churches in Asia Minor. We believe it to be as holy as the Jewish Scriptures or the letters of the apostle Paul."

"There is only one way to find out," said the senator. He placed his dagger inside the outer edge of the scroll and moved it up to the wax seal. Antonius held his breath. The senator slowly cut through the soft wax seal and unrolled the scroll slightly, revealing columns of Greek writing. He held the unrolled edge of the scroll firmly against the barrel top, for the wind was still strong and it swirled through the open wooden windows of the cabin.

"Do you read Greek, Antonius?" asked the senator.

"Yes, sir. Don't you?"

"Certainly. But my eyes are not what they once were and I have difficulty in focusing on such small script. Read it to me."

Antonius leaned over the scroll and read the first few lines aloud slowly:

> The Apocalypse of Jesus Christ, which God gave him to show his servants what must soon take place. He made it known by sending his angel to his servant John, who testifies to everything he saw—that is, the word of God and the testimony of Jesus Christ. Blessed is the one who reads the words of this prophecy, and blessed are those who hear it and take to heart what is written in it, because the time is near.

In the far distance lightning flashed, and moments later the accompanying thunder rumbled in over them, growing in intensity to a deafening roar. As the thunder receded, the senator gazed out over the rolling waves of the stormy sea and said softly, "It couldn't have come at a better time."

chapter three

ὅσα εἶδεν. Μακάριος ὁ ἀναγινώσκων καὶ οἱ ἀκούοντες τοὺς

EPHESUS AND JULIA

λόγους τῆς προφητείας καὶ τηροῦντες τὰ ἐν αὐτῇ γεγραμμένα,

The storm had driven the *Orion* well south of the direct route across the Aegean Sea from Athens to Ephesus. When the storm abated, the captain sailed east to the coast of Asia Minor. Then he turned north and laboriously worked his way along the coastal islands toward Ephesus. Sailing at night was dangerous, and as the evening approached the captain took the *Orion* out into deeper waters away from the shore. He took in most of his sails and crept along slowly through the night, watching the dark waters nervously. Halfway through the evening the clouds cleared and the moon illuminated the water for the weary travelers, allowing the captain to put out more sail and make better time.

The night passed slowly for Antonius and Senator Flavius, who dared not sleep. Finally the sun began to peep up over the mountains of Asia Minor in a spectacular sunrise.

The *Orion* continued north throughout the morning, but when the sun was shining directly overhead, Heron turned the ship slightly to the east and headed for the familiar harbor on the bay of the Cayster River that served the busy metropolis of Ephesus.

Antonius and the senator stood together on the deck and gazed out at the green hills that lay behind Ephesus. They had just spent the last hour reading the first half of the scroll and were now taking a break. Neither of them had slept much in the last two days and they were anxious to leave this ship for good.

"Have you ever been to Ephesus before, Senator?" Antonius asked casually.

"No, Antonius, I haven't. I've been all over Italy and Gaul. I even went to Britain once—all on senate business. We spent a summer visiting relatives in Carthage on the North African coast a few years ago and then spent a week in Alexandria. Likewise, I've been often to Greece, but for some reason, never to the province of Asia, even though my family has some estates there, including a villa near your fair town of Laodicea. The villa in Laodicea was actually my brother's. He managed it largely from Rome with stewards; Severus, our cousin in Ephesus, also helped him with the estate. Now, unfortunately, it belongs to me."

"Oh, Laodicea is nothing like Ephesus. I mean, Laodicea is not exactly a rural village. It has its paved streets with bathhouses, temples, and of course, its market area in the agora. But Ephesus! What a city! The last census counted over 250,000 people, just within the city. The theater is gigantic, and there are two huge agoras, thousands of shops with merchandise from everywhere in the world. Athens, of course, is more beautiful, but not nearly the size of Ephesus. Likewise, the Temple of Artemis is twice the size of anything in Athens. And Athens does not have nearly the commercial hustle and bustle of Ephesus. Even Corinth doesn't compare."

"And the Imperial Temple of Domitian?" asked Flavius. "Is it as big and imposing as I hear?"

"It is not as large as the Temple of Artemis, but it is located in the center of the city, while the Temple of Artemis is on the outskirts. Thus its presence and political role is felt more than the old Artemis temple.

"There," Antonius pointed. "You can just make out the top of the theater at the base of Mount Pion. It is huge. That hill to the right is called Koressos. The Temple of Domitian lies to the right of the theater, in the valley between the two hills, at the base of Koressos. It is just out of sight from the harbor. The architecture of the temple is rather overimposing and gaudy—at least that is what people say."

"And the politics of the temple, Antonius? Is it as hostile to Christians as I have heard?"

"Well—were you aware that the high priest of the temple, Caius Titus Munatius, was appointed Imperial high priest for the entire province of Asia?"

"Yes," the senator said sadly. "Domitian made the announcement at the execution of my brother."

"I'm sorry."

"It's all right, Antonius. Continue with the situation in Ephesus."

Antonius gazed out at Ephesus again. He could make out the outline of the harbor facilities, as well as individual temples and public buildings. "After the temple to Domitian was completed, a huge festival was held and all the citizens of Ephesus were required to swear allegiance to Domitian as lord and god. Only the Jews were exempt, due to their special status in the Empire.

"Originally many of the Christians in the Ephesian church were either Jews by birth or were connected to the synagogue as Gentile 'God-fearers.' So for nearly forty years the Roman proconsuls of Asia have considered the Christian church to be a branch of Judaism, and thus covered by the same exemptions. However, with time the church has become overwhelmingly non-Jewish and tensions between the church and the synagogue have grown. A Jewish Christian man from a prominent family in Ephesus married a Greek Christian girl a few years ago and the mixed marriage created a real storm in the Jewish community. My Jewish friend Simeon tells me that the Imperial Priest Caius then approached the synagogue elders in Ephesus to see if they could ally themselves together against the Christians. They came up with a formal plan whereby the Jews could officially expel all Christians from the synagogue. Once the Christians lose their connection to the synagogue, they lose the political cover that exempts them from having to worship Caesar Domitian."

"Clever. What happened? And how did the Jews officially distinguish between Jews and Christians?"

"The Jews have a prayer called The Eighteen Benedictions. Suddenly the recitation of this prayer became a regular part of the synagogue service. The elders would regularly select known Christians to recite the prayer. The twelfth benediction reads, 'May God' . . . uh"— Antonius stumbled on the words—"'destroy the Christians and may He' . . . uh . . . 'blot out their names from the Book of Life.' Thus all of the main Christian leaders have publicly been identified by their refusal to read this curse. Caius and the elders of the synagogue have compiled a list and are pressing to force these people to swear allegiance to Domitian as god. So far, the proconsul Quintus Flavinius has been able to thwart this plan, ruling that it is not the policy of Roman provincial proconsuls to go looking for imperial heretics. He stated that if one showed up in his court that he would gladly have him executed but that he would not stoop to searching through the city looking for heretics on behalf of the Imperial Cult."

"Quintus is a good man," the senator replied. "And a shrewd politician. He fears the growing power of the Imperial Temple priests, and he is probably trying to block any expansion of Imperial Temple power within his jurisdiction. If a reasonable man wore Caesar's crown in Rome, then his strategy would no doubt be successful. No priest of any stripe could normally survive a direct challenge to a Roman proconsul. But High Priest Caius is a clever and conniving snake; I know him well. And with Domitian on the throne . . . I don't know. Domitian is infatuated with the growth of the Imperial Temples. He senses that they will give him unprecedented political power in the provinces. It is a dangerous time, Antonius."

"And the scroll, sir—John's Apocalypse? What do you make of it, based on what we read this morning?"

The senator sighed and gazed out at the blue-green waves.

"John seems to be very much aware of the situation in the province of Asia that you just described. He directly addresses seven of the major churches in the province. I do not know the Jewish Scriptures as well as I should, and there is much of John's symbolism that I do not understand. But much of what he says appears to apply directly to the situation that is developing in Ephesus and across the province. He may be prophesying future events as well. I don't know. There is a lot in that scroll that I do not understand. But I understand enough of it to know that it's a dangerous document for you and me, and that the Imperial priests certainly won't like it. But it speaks words of encouragement to those who are to undergo persecution— and I suspect that in the days to come that will include you and the other believers in your hometown of Laodicea. I suggest that you and I quietly get this scroll copied and then into the hands of trusted church leaders who know more about Scripture and the coming days than you and me."

The *Orion* entered the bay of Ephesus and slowed to a crawl. Dozens of ships were moving in and out of the busy harbor—huge grain ships and small skiffs, one-masted fishing boats and gigantic triremes with hundreds of slaves rowing slowly to the constant beat of drums. The captain had shortened the sail on the *Orion* and she was now creeping forward in the bay against the gentle outflow of the Cayster River. He eased her slowly toward an open dock and was soon close enough for ropes to be used to pull the *Orion* carefully up to the wharf. The sailors quickly pulled in the remaining sail and secured the ship to the wooden dock, crowded with carts, cargo, and workers hustling to load and unload the many ships tied up along the wharf.

Antonius and Flavius each picked up their small bags. The Apocalypse was wrapped securely in the goatskin, and Antonius held it tightly under his arm.

Captain Heron came and stood before them. "Well, Senator? What's to happen, now? Do we drag this unfortunate episode into the courts or do we keep it quiet?"

"You swear to keep quiet about this scroll, and we'll swear to keep quiet about your assassination attempt. Agreed?"

The captain managed a half smile. "Agreed. And we will forget that there was ever a sailor named Marcus?"

"Absolutely," answered the senator. "Antonius?"

"I won't say a word."

As the captain walked away, Antonius looked at the senator, puzzled.

"Excuse me, sir, but are you sure this is the best course of action, to just let those scoundrels go free? If my father had not given me this sword, or if my hand had gotten tangled in my robe, or if they had surprised us, then we would both be at the bottom of the Aegean."

"It is the only option, Antonius, illogical as it might seem. If we report this, there will be an investigation and a trial. This scroll will be confiscated and probably destroyed because of its implied treasonous statements. A Roman judge would not believe that we came across it just by chance. We would be accused of helping John to smuggle the Apocalypse off the isle of Patmos. The sailors would implicate us in a conspiracy. You would be tried for murder. I am a political refugee. I have few friends and numerous enemies. In all probability, because I am from a senatorial family, this case would end up in Rome and Domitian himself would preside. Any or all of us, including you, me, and the sailors, could face execution or sentencing to a slave galley. Domitian is likely to find all of us guilty. It is a losing proposition for all involved, for you and me especially. We must keep it quiet."

Antonius nodded in reluctant agreement as he and Flavius disembarked from the *Orion* and walked down the pier together.

"Well, there is a welcome sight," said Flavius, looking down the wharf. "That tall man in the brown robe at the end of the dock, walking toward us, is my chief steward Demetrius. He must have been waiting, watching all the ships. And look! Here comes my daughter, Julia. What is she doing here at the docks?"

A beautiful young woman rushed through the crowd, ran up to Flavius, and threw her arms around him. "Oh, Father. I am so glad to see you made it. Mother and I have been so worried. In fact, she's absolutely frantic. We heard all sorts of awful rumors about what was happening in Rome. I have been down here every day with Demetrius, watching each boat. Mother was against it, of course, but I insisted and Demetrius agreed. So here we are. But at last, you have arrived, safe and sound. Thank the Lord. But you look awful. Did you sleep in your toga? And you smell like saltwater. Tell me all about your trip."

This was the most beautiful girl Antonius had ever seen. Her hair was arranged up high, exposing her beautiful neck and shoulders. He had never seen such beautiful hair, curled in ringlets with ribbons and flowers in the fashion he had seen among the women of nobility in Athens. Nobody in Laodicea wore their hair like that. Her dark eyes were enchantingly beautiful, and they sparkled as she chattered to her father. She wore a beautiful blue gown that seemed to highlight just the right places. Antonius told himself it was not right to stare and that he should look away or walk away, but neither his feet nor his eyes would obey. Within his head a faint voice of reason was trying to call him back to social reality, warning him that he should remain indifferent to this aristocratic senator's daughter, but his eyes were frozen on her. He became aware that his mouth hung open, and embarrassed, he snapped it shut.

Suddenly Julia released her father and turned to Antonius. She looked him over up and down, smiling playfully at him, waiting for her father's introduction.

"This," the senator finally said, "is Antonius Marius Amulius." Flavius looked around carefully, lowered his voice, and whispered to Julia, "He saved my life on board ship. There was an assassination attempt. He killed a man and scared off five others to save me. He is one of the bravest young men I have met in some time. I owe him my life."

"Really?" she asked with wide eyes. She looked up into Antonius's face. "Thank you so much for saving my father."

She reached up and tenderly touched the bruise on his cheekbone. "Did you get that terrible bruise fighting for Father? You must be very brave . . . and so handsome, too, even with this nasty bruise."

Flavius cleared his throat and frowned at his daughter. Antonius blushed and mumbled something unintelligible. She was even more beautiful up close, and he couldn't help but stare at her. She looked up at him and smiled with those beautiful sparkling eyes. Antonius found himself getting dizzy and he felt his stomach turn slightly. *Look at her hair . . .* He had never seen such beautiful hair. *Look at that face . . . like a goddess from one of the Greek myths.*

"He is turning red, Father." Julia teased. "I believe that he is embarrassed. Can he speak?"

"Uhh . . . hello," Antonius said.

"Oh, he is a regular rhetorician, isn't he, Father." Her eyes danced. "Father? If he truly saved your life, would it be appropriate for me to kiss him on the cheek? In appreciation. With your permission."

Antonius thought he was going to faint. He wondered if Flavius would chide her for such public flirtations, but he saw the senator's frown quickly vanish, and he realized that for all his serious public demeanor Flavius probably spoiled his beautiful daughter and no doubt tolerated her questionable behavior where other fathers perhaps would not.

"A kiss on the cheek might be appropriate for our young hero," Flavius answered. "You are not married, are you, Antonius? Or betrothed? Julia can be quite forward sometimes."

"No, sir, not really," he answered, feeling a twinge of guilt. But it was true. He wasn't *officially* betrothed. Yet his conscience stirred. There was an understanding of sorts that he would marry his childhood friend Monica. The two families were already bonded together closely, and both sets of parents had always assumed that he and Monica would marry when they came of age.

"Good! Don't worry, I'll kiss the cheek that's not cut and bruised," Julia said, and she stood up on her tiptoes and kissed him softly on his left cheek. "Thank you," she whispered in his ear, momentarily brushing up against him. Her perfume smelled heavenly. He had never been this close to anyone wealthy enough to wear perfume. It was intoxicating. His heart was pounding, and he realized that the people around him on the dock had faded into a blur.

"Watch out, Antonius," warned Flavius. "She has a bad habit of breaking hearts. We left several brokenhearted young men in Rome."

Julia looked up at Antonius and smiled again. "Don't believe anything he says about me."

"Furthermore," Flavius explained to Julia, "Antonius lives in Laodicea."

"Wonderful!" Julia exclaimed. "The family villa that Father is dragging us to is near Laodicea. We will be neighbors. You can come and visit us. It will be wonderful to know somebody there. You can show me around."

Demetrius and another servant warmly greeted Flavius and were introduced to Antonius. They took the men's bags—Antonius, however, kept the scroll tightly under his arm—and the group walked down the pier toward shore. Julia stepped between Flavius and Antonius and merrily took each by the arm.

"I can't wait to hear all about the voyage and how you saved Father's life." She held Antonius's arm tightly against her.

"There will be plenty of time for the entire story tonight during supper," Flavius answered. "You are coming to stay with us tonight, aren't you, Antonius? It is too late for you to start home for Laodicea today. Come and stay with us at my cousin Severus's house—he has a sizable villa here in Ephesus and there is plenty of room. Besides, I would like to take another close look at the scroll. After supper we could read it together with Severus. Since becoming a Christian, he has studied the Jewish Scriptures with a rabbi and knows them much better than I do. He can help us. Besides, we read it quickly on board the *Orion*; I couldn't make much sense of it then. But I have been thinking about it constantly and I believe that I am beginning to unravel some of the mystery in the symbolism."

"I'm supposed to take the money from my trip straight to Nathan the banker and then stay the night at his house. Father has arranged it."

"Well, take the money to the banker, but then explain that you simply must come and stay with us. You must meet my wife, Sabina, and my cousin Severus. Tell him I insist. He probably knows Severus and will gladly approve."

"Good!" Julia squeezed Antonius's arm and smiled at him. "It's settled, then?"

"Sure," mumbled Antonius. He wondered if he was dreaming. He had killed a man, saved a senator, recovered a letter in the ocean from the apostle John, and met the most beautiful woman in the world, who had kissed him on the cheek and was now holding tightly to his arm. His whole world was turning upside down.

ὁ γὰρ καιρὸς ἐγγύς. Ἰωάννης ταῖς ἑπτὰ ἐκκλησίαις ταῖς ἐν τῇ

THE IMPERIAL HIGH PRIEST

Ἀσίᾳ· χάρις ὑμῖν καὶ εἰρήνη ἀπὸ ὁ ὢν καὶ ὁ ἦν καὶ ὁ ἐρχόμενος

With Demetrius and the other servant following, Flavius, Julia, and Antonius, still arm in arm, made their way slowly along the crowded wharf, heading for Harbor Street.

The wharf stretched alongside the entire northern shore of the harbor, and it served both as a loading location for the many ships and also as a thoroughfare for people and cargoes moving from the harbor area to the city proper. There were dozens of ships from all over the Roman Empire tied up alongside the wharf, each being either loaded or unloaded by large crews of noisy harbor slaves and sailors, shouting orders and curses in half a dozen different languages, all under the close watch of ship captains, owners, merchants, and harbor storehouse managers.

One of the huge grain ships from Egypt was unloading hundreds of grain sacks. The next ship was unloading baskets of tangerines from Carthage and huge clay pots filled with olive oil from Spain. Some of the cargoes were being stacked on the wharf, and some were being loaded directly into large wooden carts hitched to oxen or smaller wagons hitched to noisy, braying donkeys. Wagon masters grunted and pulled and shouted and whacked their reluctant donkeys and oxen with sticks, trying to move their wagons on and off the busy wharf. Seagulls floated lazily overhead, often adding their voices to the cacophony of sound on the wharf.

Antonius loved the wharf; normally he would have been captivated by the activity of the Ephesian harbor. This time, however, he noticed very little other than Julia. She appeared oblivious to the noise and chaos of the wharf, and she chatted merrily with her father about all that had happened to her and her mother since they had last seen each other. She also held Antonius's arm tightly, and he was extremely conscious of how close she was to him. He carried the large bundle containing the scroll awkwardly in his left hand, and often the three of them had to squeeze together slightly to fit through the stacks of cargo along the main wharf. At such times her shoulder would bump his; indeed, sometimes their shoulders were pressed together quite firmly. Once as they crunched together to squeeze between a stack of grain and baskets of figs piled over their heads, Antonius dared to look down at her and was startled to see her looking up at him, only inches away, smiling coyly and making clear eye contact. He smiled back and nervously glanced at Flavius, who seemed preoccupied—and then back at Demetrius, who frowned, apparently having seen the looks that had been exchanged between the two young people.

Finally they reached the end of the wharf and stepped down onto the paved stones of Harbor Street. "Look how beautiful this street is, Father," Julia said. "For a moment you might think you were back in Rome."

She looked at Antonius, who merely nodded, even though he had never been to Rome. He had been to Corinth and to Athens, however, and he had always believed that the view looking up Harbor Street in Ephesus was as spectacular as anything those famous cities had to offer. The wide street was paved with white stone and lined with hundreds of beautiful marble columns. At the end of the street, dominating the view was the famous Ephesian theater, seating over 25,000 people, carved into the side of the mountain. And beyond the theater, green mountains towered to meet the clear blue sky.

"It is quite impressive," Flavius conceded as they began their walk up the street. He and Antonius were weary from the ordeals of their trip, and they were both thankful for the two servants who carried their bags. Yet in spite of their weariness, the walk through the beautiful colonnaded streets was pleasant and the view of the imposing theater at the end of Harbor Street was spectacular. Besides, Julia's boundless energy was infectious, both to Flavius, her father, and to the starry-eyed Antonius. She had become somewhat familiar with the sights in Ephesus during her three-week stay. Thus, even though Antonius knew the city much better and she identified a few buildings incorrectly, he allowed her to be their guide and to point out to her father the major buildings and temples that they passed along the way. When they reached the end of Harbor Street, they paused for a moment at one of the gates to the theater to allow Flavius to peek inside the spectacular structure. Then they turned right on to another impressive paved road known as Marble Street. Julia continued chattering gaily; Antonius and Flavius simply smiled, both of them happy just to be with her.

Suddenly, Flavius stopped and all evidence of his happy smile vanished instantly as his brow darkened. "Here comes trouble," he commented softly to Julia and Antonius as two men separated from the crowd on the street and walked straight toward them. Julia released the arms of Antonius and her father, and the three of them stood quietly as the two men approached.

Antonius did not recognize either man. The older of the two men was middle-aged, quite thin, and completely bald. He had a small, sloping forehead with narrow slits for eyes and a large beaklike nose that dominated his face. His companion was younger. Antonius supposed that he might be the older man's son, but the younger man's features were remarkably different, for he was exceptionally handsome with thick black hair and sharp, penetrating dark eyes. They were both dressed immaculately in expensive white linen togas with gold trim. Antonius noted that the older man had a haughty scowl on his face and was focused on Flavius, but the younger one was obviously eyeing Julia with approval. As they drew near the young man flashed a smile at her, and she reciprocated with a captivating smile. Antonius looked on helplessly, feeling self-conscious about his workman's clothes and his damp traveling cloak.

"Hail, Senator Flavius Lucius Domitilla!" greeted the older man.

"Hail, Caius Titus Munatius, priest of Caesar and reptile!" answered Flavius.

Julia looked at her father with alarm and dismay, apparently shocked at the rudeness of his greeting to these two men who were obviously from aristocratic families. Antonius, seeing the infamous Caius for the first time, stiffened.

"My dear Flavius," continued Caius. "There is no need to infuse our conversation with insults. Certainly we can interact as civilized, Roman nobles. May I introduce my son, Plautus?" The young man beside him smiled and nodded his head.

Julia nudged her father with an elbow. "Er . . . yes. And let me introduce my daughter, Julia."

"I had no idea that you had such a beautiful daughter, Senator," Plautus said. Then smiling at Julia, "All of the other young women in Ephesus will be overshadowed by your beauty—"

"And this"—interrupted Flavius—"is Antonius Marius Amulius, a wool merchant from Laodicea."

"Most interesting," mused Caius, looking over the young man contemptuously and skipping any type of greeting for the lower-class

Antonius. "How is it that a merchant's son from Laodicea ends up traveling with a Roman senator down the streets of Ephesus, and with the senator's beautiful daughter on his arm? Very curious. Ah, and look at the bruise on his face. Have you have been in a bit of a brawl or did the senator's daughter slap you for being fresh? Marius, you say, is your father's name? That name sounds familiar . . . ah yes, things become clear. Gallus Marius. The mythical hero of Athanel; the so-called 'Bloody Centurion.' He has become a leader in this new heretical sect in Laodicea that refuses to acknowledge Caesar. So you, Flavius, have decided to socialize with these lower-class heretics who share your treasonous religious views. What a pity!"

Antonius was shocked to discover that the principal enemy of Christianity in the province of Asia knew of his father by name. His face betrayed his thoughts. Subconsciously he tightened his grip on the bundle under his arm.

"What is it, young wool merchant?" Caius asked. "Are you frightened to learn that I know of your father? Do you think that your little den of heretics is safe in Laodicea? You haven't heard? We are going to convert an existing temple in Laodicea into an Imperial Temple dedicated to Domitian. Plautus, here, will be the new high priest of that temple. We have been researching the situation in your city to identify where opposition will arise. For some reason your father's name keeps coming up. We will insist that all citizens of Laodicea, including you, young man, and you, beautiful Julia, swear allegiance to Domitian as lord and god."

"But, Father," interrupted Plautus, smiling again at Julia. "Let's put politics aside for a moment. I am sure that something amicable can be worked out with this distinguished family. I, personally, want to welcome the senator and his lovely daughter to Laodicea. When you arrive please notify me; I would be delighted to come visit you. Perhaps, Julia, we can tour the city together in my carriage."

"I'd be most honored—," began Julia, but Flavius cut her off in midsentence.

"Absolutely not," he interrupted sternly. "Imperial high priests who are seeking to destroy the church of Jesus the Christ are not welcome at my house. And neither are snakes."

Antonius was shocked but found it hard to suppress a smile. Julia fumed but kept quiet.

Caius broke the awkward silence. "Keep in mind, Flavius, that you have very few friends anymore . . . either here or in Rome. Your new sect is a threat and a challenge to Rome, and I, the high priest of the Imperial Cult in the province of Asia, am committed to obliterating the movement completely. Caesar is totally behind me. There is no hope for you if you continue in this heresy. The sooner that you and your friends realize the futility of your new religion, the better for all of us. Take care, Flavius, or you will end up as your brother did."

Caius then pronounced a loud, pompous blessing for all around to hear: "May our lord and god, the glorious Domitian, Caesar of the world, bless you in the months to come."

Antonius felt his skin crawl. He looked at the narrow, beady eyes of Caius and thought that the high priest personified evil itself.

Under his breath, audible only to Antonius and Julia, Flavius muttered a blessing in return: "And may you be blessed with the fate of Marcus the sailor."

Plautus smiled at Julia, shrugged, and said goodbye. She smiled in return and watched him walk away into the crowd. When they were out of range she turned to her father. "Why do we have to oppose the most powerful people in the province? You just got here, and already you have been threatened by one of the most powerful men. Mother says that if we can just compromise a little and fit into the society here like normal people, maybe some of this trouble would go away and we could lead a normal life again."

"This is not something we can compromise on," he answered gently.

"But how could you be so rude to them?" she continued. "That is the first young man of noble birth that I have met since we arrived, and you called his father a snake. They offered to welcome us into Laodicean society, and yet you rudely refused. How could you? Are we going to flee proper society completely?" Julia's voice quivered and Antonius thought she might start crying. But she regained her composure and continued: "Father, we left *everything* behind in Rome—the villa, our friends, my future—and you've brought us out to this godforsaken province. Please, Father, give us a chance to live a normal life out here. Just because you and Caius don't get along, why does that mean that we can't be friends with his son, Plautus? He seemed to be extending a hand to us in friendship. Having him as a friend might help us. We are going to need some new friends here, especially important ones like Plautus. He seemed so different from his eerie father. Perhaps we could trust him. Does the son have to be the same as the father?"

Flavius looked at Julia and then at Antonius. "They usually are," he said quietly.

Antonius looked down at the pavement and shuffled his feet. He felt as if he were intruding into a private family squabble. He was puzzled at Julia's inability to spot an evil and dangerous enemy in both Caius and Plautus, even after her father pointed it out to her. He also wondered if her desire to live in the society of nobility was stronger than her desire to follow her new faith.

"This is not politics, my dear Julia," the senator continued. "This is faith . . . and life itself. Those two men are going to attempt to get our family and Antonius's family and all other Christians in the province of Asia to renounce our faith in Christ, to deny all that we are. There is nothing more important. Certainly not our status or position in society."

She remained quiet and appeared to pout. Slowly they turned and continued their walk down Marble Street, with the two silent servants obediently following. Julia still walked between her father and Antonius but she did not take the arm of either. Gone was the gaiety and laughter of their earlier stroll. Each walked in silence.

Soon they came to the side road that led to the agora, the road that Antonius would take to go to the house of Nathan the banker. They stopped for a moment to exchange brief goodbyes. Demetrius handed Antonius his travel bag.

Julia turned to Antonius and mustered an attractive smile. "Well, Antonius. Forgive us for this unpleasant encounter with Caius and his son. When one's father is a senator this kind of thing happens. It used to happen in Rome, too. Anyway, we do not want it to spoil what was otherwise a happy day. I am delighted that I got to meet you and take a walk with you. And I do want to thank you especially for saving Father's life. I will be forever grateful to you."

She stepped close to Antonius, placed her hand on his forearm, and looked right up into his eyes as she spoke, continuing, "I will be looking forward to seeing you tonight at Severus's villa. I have a brand-new yellow silk gown. Perhaps I'll wear it tonight, just for you. Don't be late."

Antonius only nodded. His knees felt weak.

With that she took her father's arm, and off they went down Marble Street toward the house of Severus, leaving Antonius alone and a bit dizzy. Holding the Apocalypse under his left arm, Antonius hoisted his travel bag on his right shoulder and began walking slowly toward the agora and Nathan's house.

As Julia's perfume faded, Antonius's head began to clear and he struggled to put his thoughts in order. An Imperial Temple in Laodicea! Would the Christians in Laodicea likewise lose their protected status as a branch of Judaism? Would they be forced to publicly swear allegiance to Domitian as lord? His father would never do that. He wondered what he himself would do. Were sons usually like their fathers, as Flavius said? Antonius wondered whether he could ever be as strong as his father was. And would he be strong enough to endure real persecution, to stand until the end and "overcome," as the Apocalypse said? He looked down at the Apocalypse under his arm, relieved that Caius had not asked about it. What of the Apocalypse? If it described their time, then they were in for some terrible persecution, a persecution characterized by the death of many martyrs. Would he be one? His father? Flavius?

And Julia? His stomach churned and his conscience bothered him. Why hadn't he just told Flavius and Julia clearly that he was betrothed to a girl in Laodicea? He could have cleared up everything right at the beginning. Yes, his betrothal to Monica was unofficial, but who was he kidding? In truth, he might be married to Monica within a year. She was sixteen already, and most girls in Laodicea married at sixteen, even fifteen, as his mother had pointed out to him a few weeks ago. People were beginning to wonder and to talk.

He realized that his parents (and Monica's) were actually waiting on *him*—to initiate the betrothal process as part of his transition from youth to manhood. He suspected this was part of his father's reason for sending him alone this time to sell their wool in Athens. If he successfully traveled to Athens alone, sold the wool for a good price, carried the money safely back to the banker Nathan, and then returned home, his father would consider him a grown man and a serious partner in the family business. His father would then also expect him to marry Monica, and fairly soon, too. It all went together. He had no business walking through Ephesus with a different woman on his arm—and especially one so beautiful!

He came to the gates of the huge marketplace known as the Square Agora and entered cautiously. He discreetly felt to make sure that his moneybag was still safely secured under his tunic next to his chest. Likewise, he tightened his grip on the bundle that held the Apocalypse. The crowded agora was famous for thieves, and his father had taught him to always pay close attention when walking though the agora with money or anything else valuable. But despite the risks, the agora here in Ephesus was a fascinating place, and Antonius always relished seeing it.

Immediately inside the gate, he entered the livestock area and was greeted with the familiar sounds and smells of farm animals— cows, sheep, goats, even donkeys. To his left, several goats huddled in a pen and bleated pitifully as if they knew the fate that awaited them. On his right, two men were arguing vigorously in Greek over the price of an old donkey that was apparently blind in one eye. Antonius occasionally looked down to ensure that his path was safe, for one had to watch where one stepped in this part of the market. He paused for a moment beside a pen to admire some longhaired sheep—probably from Syria—and was jostled by a man carrying two lambs, one on each shoulder. Antonius held the Apocalypse bundle tightly against his chest. He felt for his father's sword. All was well; he pushed on through the noisy crowd.

Everything was for sale here. He passed through the food section of the market, weaving in and out among the stalls and booths, stepping around the poorer vendors squatting on the paving stones. Food products from all over the Empire were here—oranges, lemons, apples, figs, dates, grain, flour, leeks, cinnamon, peppers, salt. The strong smell of the fruit, followed by the rich odor of the world's spices, reminded him that he was hungry. He wondered what dinner at a rich nobleman's house would be like.

He passed the clothing stalls, noticing the contrast between the rough spun wool that most of the lower classes wore and the linen and silks of the upper class. The contrast reminded him of the social distance between Flavius's family and his. Antonius had heard several sermons from his pastor, Epaphras, proclaiming that in the new Christian faith, there is no social difference, no difference in status or importance, not only between rich and poor, but also between freedmen and slaves.

But the barriers in society seemed fairly well fixed to Antonius, and he knew that they were rarely challenged successfully. Noble patrician families like Flavius's rarely had any association with lower-class plebeian families like his, even if they had Roman citizenship, as his did. He smiled as he tried to envision Monica with her hair up in ringlets and dressed in the beautiful blue gown that Julia had been wearing that afternoon, but he soon found his mind trying to picture instead what Julia would look like tonight in her new yellow gown that she had said she would wear "just for him."

He passed stalls filled with clay pots and lamps, iron knives and plows, and brass candleholders and dishes. The crowd jostled him. He passed the stall of a professional scribe sprawled on the ground, writing a letter in Greek for a short, impatient, red-faced man who had the look of a grain merchant. Antonius wondered who would copy the Apocalypse for them.

At the edge of the agora, just before exiting the great market, he found himself pushing through the crowds in front of the temple-related booths and stalls. These merchants displayed rows and rows of miniature gods and goddesses for sale. Several stalls were devoted entirely to the Imperial Cult; they sold several different sizes of small statues of Caesar Domitian. Antonius stopped for a moment, staring down at the small statuettes, wondering if Domitian really believed he was a god, or if he laughed at the whole cult, playing along solely because of its political usefulness. Was he demented, possessed, or just clever? And what of Caius and Plautus? Were they just power-hungry, or were they inherently evil? And what was the driving force behind their desire to crush the church? Human or supernatural? Antonius shivered and pushed on.

He pondered Caius's threat to destroy the church, which made him think of Julia's reaction, and he found himself once again struck by the sharp contrast between his childhood friend Monica back in Laodicea and Julia here in Ephesus. Was Julia really as frivolous as she seemed? Was her place in society more important to her than being faithful to Christ? Would she—indeed, *could* she—stay faithful to Christ without the strength of her father?

He could not imagine Monica renouncing her faith. She could be extremely mule-headed and obstinate sometimes, and he could imagine her digging in her heels and stubbornly refusing to recant, no matter what Caius or Plautus threatened. He found himself smiling at the thought. That would be a classic matchup—Monica against the might of the Roman Imperial Cult.

And what of Julia? Was she just naive? Or fickle? Had she never had to face anything serious in her life before? Monica definitely had stronger character. But mother of Zeus! Julia was gorgeous! He looked around sheepishly after swearing in his mind, feeling guilty. He knew that as a Christian he was not to swear, and he knew that his mother would throttle him for such an utterance if she knew about it—even if it was only in his head.

Antonius exited the agora into a modest residential area. The streets here were paved with stone, but not colonnaded like the spectacular avenues of Harbor Street and Marble Street. Both sides of these streets were lined with stucco fences and the outside walls of residences, along with the occasional store or home business usually connected to a residence. He found the house of Nathan the banker; he had visited here several times with his father.

Nathan was a bit eccentric at times, but Antonius liked him. Perhaps more important, he *trusted* Nathan. Nathan was a Jew, but he showed no animosity toward the Christians. He seemed to view them as wayward family members. He had handled all of the financial matters for Antonius's family for numerous years, including several substantial loans in the past that allowed Antonius's father, Gallus, to survive some downturns in the wool market.

Antonius knocked at the gate and was received by a tall, thin, elderly but lively servant named Secundus. Antonius knew him fairly well. He fancied himself a deep-thinking philosopher and during earlier visits he would often entertain the young man with riddles and philosophical word games.

"Hail, Antonius Marius Amulius!" the elderly servant exclaimed with exaggerated seriousness and pomp. "Welcome to the humble home of Nathan ben-Yacob. Enter! Be warmed! Be filled! Be refreshed from your long journey!"

Antonius could not help but smile at his reception. "Greetings to you as well, Secundus," he said as he entered into the courtyard. "But I don't know if you are honoring me or mocking me."

Secundus's eyes twinkled. "And are the two different?" he asked, relieving Antonius of his travel bag and the bundle holding the Apocalypse. "Sit here, and I will call the master and then bring you something cool to drink."

Nathan emerged at that very moment from one of the side rooms adjacent to the courtyard. "Ah, Antonius! I thought I heard your voice. Shalom! Welcome!" He embraced Antonius briefly in the Jewish fashion as Secundus disappeared into the house. In contrast to Secundus, Nathan was short and rather stout. There were still traces of brown lingering in his beard, but his hair had turned completely gray. Yet he moved quickly, and his eyes were sharp and focused.

They sat in two plain wooden chairs in the cool shade of a large fig tree in the middle of the courtyard. "It is good to see you! I confess that I was a little worried about you, going to Athens alone with the wool shipment, and then returning alone with the money. Such a trip can be dangerous! But here you are, safe and sound, praise the God of Abraham!"

Soon Nathan asked about the trip, and he listened intently as Antonius shared with him all of the details of his recent adventure—Heron, Flavius, the assassination attempt, Marcus, the Apocalypse, Julia—although he mentioned Julia only briefly and he did not describe her breathtaking beauty.

"What a trip, Antonius! What an adventure!" Then with a twinkle in his eye, Nathan continued, "The God of Israel must still consider you one of his children to watch over you with such protection! Your father will be very proud of you. There are many, many men much older than you who would have failed when faced with such adversity."

Nathan led Antonius into one of the rooms adjacent to the courtyard where he conducted his business. Antonius delivered the bag of silver coins to him, relieved to dispense with some of the dangerous burden he was carrying. Nathan counted the coins carefully, keeping 80 percent and returning 20 percent. He wrote out a receipt and handed it to Antonius, observing, "You did extremely well on this trip. And your family has done very well for the last few years. You now have a substantial balance in your account. Soon you can buy your own ship and expand into the shipping business as well; it's quite lucrative."

"Yes, sir," Antonius answered. "I'll tell Father." Personally, he had no desire to own ships or to enter the world of shipping. He felt as if he had barely escaped from that world. For the time being, he wanted to keep his feet on dry land.

Antonius told Nathan of his plans for the evening. The banker balked at the idea of Antonius spending the night with someone else. "Your father always stays here," he reminded the young man. "Besides, he specifically arranged it when you left for Athens."

But Antonius argued gently with him. After hearing that Antonius would be staying at Severus's house, Nathan relented.

"Severus is a respected man. And a fairly wealthy man as well. You will be safe there. But his position is somewhat precarious at the moment. He has his enemies in this city, and now with his family fleeing Rome, he has lost his political connections. The rumor in the city is that he has been attending the Christian worship services occasionally and has not yet contributed to nor participated in any of the Imperial Cult festivals. He is one of the few leading men of the city to refuse to do so, and no doubt the High Priest Caius is furious. Only the strong will of the proconsul and his commitment to Roman law protects Severus."

Antonius then asked sheepishly if he could borrow some clean clothes.

Nathan and his wife had only one child, a son who had been about Antonius's age and size when he died of fever three years before. Antonius could still see the pain in their eyes when they looked at him, a reminder of their own loss. But they also loved Antonius because of the memories he evoked, and they always treated him much better than the banker-merchant relationship warranted.

Nathan's wife brought out an expensive blue cotton toga, better than anything Antonius himself owned. *Well,* Antonius thought, *I won't look like a shepherd boy fresh from the fields.* He thanked them profusely, entrusted the scroll to their care, and headed for the public baths near the harbor. After a brief time in the hot steam of the bathhouse, followed by an invigorating cold wash and massage, he emerged refreshed and excited about the evening.

He retrieved the scroll from Nathan and walked up Marble Street to Curetes Street. After a short stroll down that avenue, he arrived at Severus's upscale house and courtyard, cut into the side of the mountain. The sun was just setting; the shadows were lengthening and the temperature was dropping slightly. It was going to be a perfect evening.

καὶ ἀπὸ τῶν ἑπτὰ πνευμάτων ἃ ἐνώπιον τοῦ θρόνου αὐτοῦ καὶ

THE BEAST AND HIS MARK

ἀπὸ Ἰησοῦ Χριστοῦ, ὁ μάρτυς, ὁ πιστός, ὁ πρωτότοκος

Demetrius the steward was waiting for Antonius outside the gate to the courtyard.

"You look quite distinguished tonight, sir," he remarked. "And almost as handsome as that fellow we met by the theater today. What was his name? Plautus?"

Antonius looked at him with irritation, but the steward only winked at him. "Would you like some advice, son?" he asked softly.

"Of course," answered Antonius.

"Watch yourself in there. There is no finer man in the Empire than Flavius, and his faith in the Lord is as solid as the rock in this mountain. But Julia is dangerous; you mark my words. I love her as my own child, and I would gladly die for her, but I can see her nature more clearly than her father can. She draws young men like bugs to a lamp at night, and when they get too close they perish like those bugs in the lamp. She likes you and she will flirt with you to amuse herself, but nothing will come of it. Her mother, Sabina, will positively oppose any possibility of a marriage to someone who is not from a patrician family of nobility, and she will probably do all she can to end Julia's relationship with you immediately. So you really have no future at all with Julia, and you would be wise to rebuff her flirtations. Keep that in mind. You are here tonight as a friend of Flavius, not as a suitor of Julia."

Antonius was startled to hear the issue even being discussed. It had never crossed his mind that anyone would consider him a suitor of the senator's daughter. After all, they had met just a few hours ago. Nonetheless, he felt his blood rising as he listened to Demetrius, although he knew that this wise steward probably spoke the truth. "I'll remember your advice."

Demetrius took the bundle containing the Apocalypse from Antonius and then opened the elaborately ornate wooden gate, allowing Antonius to step into the courtyard of the most opulent home he had ever entered. The courtyard, larger than any Antonius had visited before, contained dozens of beautiful, well-manicured trees and hundreds of flowers, punctuated with marble statues and benches. One of the statues was incorporated into a small fountain, and Antonius stared in amazement at the stream of water flowing out of the pitcher that the marble child held in her hand. Four large marble columns dominated one side of the courtyard supporting a red-tiled roof that provided shade and probably collected rainwater, although he wondered if they needed to collect rainwater with a running fountain right in the courtyard.

The courtyard was surrounded on three sides by the rooms of the house, each with exquisite carved wood doors and intricate latticework windows. The ground-level rooms were connected by a long porch, supported by ornate wood columns. Above that porch was a second-floor porch that connected the rooms of the upper floor. This porch was decorated with carved wooden latticework that extended waist high, and carved wooden capitals elaborately connecting the columns to the bright red-tiled roof. Flowers and vines were everywhere, and the sweet, fragrant smell of flowers almost overwhelmed him.

A servant approached them and Demetrius handed him the scroll without saying a word. The servant then vanished into one of the many rooms that lined the long colonnaded porch.

Antonius was escorted by Demetrius across the courtyard and into the main reception room. The young man was stunned by both the size and the exquisite decorations of the room. It was huge! Larger than the entire courtyard at his house. And the entire floor of the room was covered with beautifully colored mosaics depicting rabbits, deer, birds, and flowers of all kinds. The walls were painted with similar scenes, bright with greens and blues and accented by the dark wood of the rafters, doors, and windows, which were likewise covered with ornate carvings of plants and animals.

Many people already reclined on cushions around a large, low table, engaged in several lively conversations. As Antonius and Demetrius approached the table, the conversations stopped as everyone looked up at the new guest.

"Antonius!" Flavius called out warmly. "I'm so glad you could make it. Join us. And let me introduce you to everyone."

Demetrius led Antonius to his place at the table, and he awkwardly reclined there.

"Good friends and relatives," Flavius said, "let me introduce Antonius Marius Amulius. His father is the famous Bloody Centurion from the battle of Athanel. Antonius has inherited his father's valor and I am forever indebted to him for saving my life."

Antonius groped for something appropriate to say in reply. His face turned red. "Thank you, sir," he mumbled.

"And this is my cousin Severus," Flavius continued, motioning toward the pleasant-looking middle-aged man reclining next to him, "his lovely wife, Helena, and their three children, Cleitus, Myron, and Manilius."

"Welcome to our home," Severus said sincerely. One of his young sons whispered something to his brother, who glanced at Antonius and then giggled. Their mother gave them a stern, disapproving look. Antonius pretended not to notice.

"And seated beside you is Polukarpos, pastor of the church in Smyrna," Flavius continued.

"I am honored to meet you," the young pastor said with a warm smile. "I am anxious to hear all about your exploits with the senator. And I am particularly interested in the scroll you rescued. You brought it with you, I hope? Severus, with such an interesting guest and a new scroll from the apostle John, we might be up all night talking."

"It wouldn't be the first time," Helena interjected.

Everyone laughed pleasantly.

"Polukarpos is here in Ephesus on church business," Severus said. "And to survey the situation regarding the Imperial Temple. It is fortuitous that he is here, because he studied personally with the apostle John several years ago before John was arrested and exiled."

Antonius liked Polukarpos immediately. He found himself drawn to the pastor's engaging personality and affirming smile.

"And this," Flavius continued, "is my dear wife, Sabina." Flavius's wife was still very attractive at middle age. Antonius could see where Julia's beauty originated.

"I am honored to meet you," he said as graciously as he could, but she only frowned.

The awkwardness was broken by Julia's grand entrance into the room. She glided in, dressed in the new yellow gown as promised, even more stunning than Antonius had anticipated.

"Antonius!" she exclaimed, rushing over to him. "I thought you'd never get here." He rose awkwardly to meet her, unsure what action would be proper. She took him by the hand, turned to her mother, Sabina, and announced, "Mother, this is the man who saved Father's life."

Then Julia stood back and eyed the nervous Antonius up and down. "Amazing! He left us as a farmer and he has returned as a refined nobleman. Look at this beautiful toga. And I believe that he's been to the public baths and even shaved!"

"Julia!" scolded her father. "You will embarrass the young man."

"Oh, he likes it. Don't you, Antonius?"

At that moment one of Severus's servants entered and announced that supper was ready to be served, thus sparing Antonius an answer.

"Come, hero of the *Orion*," she said, still holding his hand. "You can sit next to me." With that she led him to the other side of the table from where he had been seated by Demetrius. He followed obediently, not knowing what else to do.

Supper was both wonderful and awkward for Antonius. Flavius was warm and friendly. He told the story of the assassination attempt on the *Orion,* stressing the heroic actions of Antonius. Julia listened with wide eyes and looked at Antonius admiringly. Severus and Polukarpos were likewise impressed. Antonius told the story of the scroll, likewise pointing to Flavius as the hero who insisted that they rescue the occupant of the boat. For the rest of the meal the conversation was generally pleasant. Severus and his wife were polite and cordial, as was the guest Polukarpos. Sabina, however, was coldly polite, barely able to conceal her disdain for Antonius and her disapproval of the evening. He felt very uncomfortable around her. But Julia continued to captivate him. She chattered away—flirting, teasing, and always smiling at him with that smile that melted his resolve and good judgment. She seemed oblivious to her mother's disapproval.

Toward the end of supper the conversation turned to the Apocalypse.

"In my judgment, John the apostle wrote this scroll to encourage Christians in the province of Asia to stand firm against the Imperial Cult," said Flavius. "And since Christians all across the province are being excluded from the synagogue, I expect that all Christians in Asia will soon be required to swear allegiance to Domitian as lord and god or face serious consequences." Flavius then looked at Severus. "What are your thoughts, Cousin?"

"I fear that evil days are indeed coming soon," answered Severus. "Only by the intervention of Quintus the proconsul has Caius been prevented from demanding this of us already. And, as you may have heard, Quintus has been recalled to Rome."

"I personally don't see the problem as unavoidable," interjected Sabina. "Everyone else in the entire Empire is swearing allegiance to Domitian, even though they worship other gods. Everyone knows that Domitian is not divine. The oath is merely a political necessity, a formality. We know in our hearts that we worship Christ as the Lord; what we say to Caius in the Temple of Domitian does not affect that. We can simply mumble that Domitian is lord and god—knowing full well that he is basically an idiot—and then go on about our business. We do not have to fight them over this."

"Surely we can be loyal Romans and faithful Christians, too," chimed in Julia. "What do you think, Antonius? What will your family do?"

"I suspect that in a life-or-death decision, one doesn't really know what one will do until the time comes," answered Antonius seriously. "But one thing I did understand from the Apocalypse is that John tells us to stand firm to the end. I think that means to resist the Imperial Cult and to never swear allegiance to anyone as lord and god except Christ. I hope that I and my family find the strength to endure whatever comes."

"Well, beloved family and honored guests," interrupted Severus before Julia or Sabina could respond, "we are all about finished with supper. Let's move to the garden and take a look at that mysterious scroll that you two fished out of the water."

Severus suggested that Julia lead everyone out to the garden, where the servants had placed tables, chairs, and lamps. Antonius, however, he requested to remain behind for a moment while one of Severus's servants retrieved the scroll. Polukarpos stayed behind with

Antonius, anxious to see this new scroll from the apostle John as soon as possible, while the rest of the dinner party followed Julia out a side door toward the garden.

Soon a servant approached Antonius and Polukarpos with the goatskin bundle that contained the Apocalypse. Antonius carefully removed the scroll from the goatskin pouch and handed it reverently to Polukarpos, who gazed at it with excitement.

"Antonius," the young pastor said without unrolling the scroll, "I hope you realize what an honor it is for me just to hold this scroll. Imagine! A new revelation from God, written down by the venerable apostle John. And here it is! The original, right in my hands! All of the churches in the province of Asia will want a copy. And somehow we must get copies to Antioch, Alexandria, and Rome."

Antonius watched as Polukarpos carefully unrolled the outer edge of the scroll and read out loud the opening words: "'The Apocalypse of Jesus Christ, which God gave to show his servants what must soon take place.'" The young pastor let out a low whistle. "This is incredible, Antonius! This scroll will, no doubt, play a very important role in building up and strengthening the church. I suspect that it will help us tremendously to face the difficult days ahead of us." Gingerly he rolled the scroll back up and handed it to Antonius. "Come—let's take it out to the others and read it. I am extremely anxious to hear what it says."

Polukarpos led the way out through the same side door from which the others had exited just a few moments ago. Antonius followed along behind Polukarpos, gawking at the house decorations— beautiful mosaic floors, spectacular paintings on the walls, ornately carved wooden chairs inlaid with ivory, fancy dark wooden doors comprised of intricate latticework and incredible patterns carved into the heavy wood. They passed through two elegantly decorated rooms before emerging into a garden.

Antonius had thought at first that the "garden" Severus mentioned probably meant the courtyard where he had first entered. As Polukarpos led him out of the house, and as his eyes adjusted to the dim light of the evening, he was stunned to see that they were not in the front courtyard but were now to the side of the house in a very large garden thick with trees, shrubs, and flowers. Through the trees they could just barely make out the lights on the far side of the garden where the others had gathered. There were several paved pathways leading from the house into the garden, and the two young men hesitated for a moment.

"Hmm . . .," Polukarpos mused. "Let's try this one." And he led the way into the darkness of the garden. The path seemed to wander aimlessly through the garden, and after a few moments Antonius wondered how embarrassing it would be if they got lost in this private garden. They could still see the lights through the trees however, and they stumbled in that direction.

Suddenly Polukarpos stopped. Antonius stopped just short of colliding into the pastor's back. He could hear voices just to their left—Sabina and Flavius. They appeared to be having a disagreement, but they were speaking in hushed tones, apparently trying to remain private.

He heard Flavius say, "He is *not* a farmer's son. He is the son of a wool merchant, and more importantly, the son of the Bloody Centurion, one of the most famous and respected soldiers in the entire Roman army. They sing marching songs in honor of his father."

"But a mere centurion? Can't you at least find a low-level general like my nephew? Someone from a noble family?"

"No one in the army sings marching songs about your nephew. And you must remember, my dear Sabina, that *we* may no longer be considered in the noble class by many. And the apostle Paul has told us that in Christ there is no longer any difference. For Christians there are no longer class distinctions."

Polukarpos then continued quickly and quietly on his way toward the lights. Antonius followed, embarrassed to have overheard the private conversation and particularly embarrassed because they had been talking about him.

A few moments later, they emerged into the well-lit opening where the others had gathered. Numerous lampstands had been placed around a table. Several servants stood around the perimeter of the opening holding torches. Antonius noticed that several additional servants, including Demetrius, were there, apparently also anxious to hear the Apocalypse read and discussed. Antonius looked at Severus with respect, realizing that the presence of servants at such an after-dinner discussion was probably a serious breach of normal social etiquette. Here was a man who apparently took his faith seriously.

"Ah, there you are!" exclaimed Julia. "We thought that perhaps you got lost in the garden. Now if we can just find Mother and Father."

At that moment Flavius and Sabina walked in out of the darkness, neither of them smiling.

"Excellent," said Severus dramatically. "Now that everyone is here, I invite our illustrious visiting guest, Antonius Marius Amulius, to show us this mysterious scroll from the apostle John."

Antonius nervously laid the scroll on the table, unrolled part of it, and then looked up, uncertain what to do next. Severus placed a large lamp on the table next to the scroll and then took a seat beside the table. Everyone except Antonius sat down in chairs around the table, leaving the young man, who was still standing, feeling rather awkward.

"Well, son," Flavius stated, "as I said before, you have the best eyes. Read it aloud to us."

"I would be honored," answered Antonius, and he began reading: "'The Apocalypse of Jesus Christ . . .'" The young man read slowly and clearly, pausing occasionally for everyone to ponder the meaning. He moved on through the opening lines, "to the seven churches in the province of Asia . . . I am the Alpha and the Omega . . . who is and was and is to come . . . I, John, your brother and companion in the suffering and the kingdom . . . saw one like the son of man . . . standing among the seven golden lampstands . . . holding the seven stars in his right hand . . . "

"Wait, Antonius," interrupted Flavius, "did you say that the Son of Man held seven stars in his hand?"

"Yes, sir," answered Antonius, looking up from the scroll. "That's what it says. Do you know what it means?"

"Perhaps. Domitian, as you know, has not only proclaimed his own deity but also the deity of many of his relatives. Several years ago, when his baby boy died, Domitian also proclaimed the infant to be a god, and to honor this proclamation, he issued a coin—over the objections of the senate, I might add. The picture on the coin was that of the infant seated on a globe with his hands extended into a field of seven stars."

"I remember the coin," added Severus. "But what does it mean? As I understand the Jewish Scriptures, the Son of Man is identified by the prophet Daniel as the Messiah."

"Hmm," said Flavius, deep in thought. "John is probably rebuking or even perhaps ridiculing the Roman Imperial claim of sovereignty over the world. John seems to be stating that Jesus Christ is the one who rules with sovereignty, not a dead infant of Caesar Domitian." Flavius let out a low whistle and looked at Severus and Polukarpos.

"Nobody in Rome is going to like this," commented the young pastor solemnly. "You need to have copies made of this scroll as soon as possible. And, in the meantime, this original would probably be safer in Laodicea than in Ephesus. And it is probably safer with

Antonius than with you, Senator Flavius. Caius will keep a close watch on you."

"Agreed," stated Flavius. "Antonius, read on."

Antonius continued. "John next addresses the seven churches in our province." Antonius read through John's admonition to each church—Ephesus first; then Smyrna, where Polukarpos pastored; followed by Pergamum, Thyatira, Sardis, Philadelphia, and finally, Laodicea. Antonius paused after reading about Laodicea and asked for a drink of water. A servant quickly poured him a glass. Antonius took a few quick sips, then picked up where he had left off. He read of a throne in heaven surrounded by seven spirits and by twenty-four other thrones with elders sitting on them. He read of a sealed scroll and of a slain Lamb standing on the throne, and of the elders singing that the Lamb is worthy to open the seals on the scroll. Next, thousands of angels sang of the Lamb's worthiness and then every creature in heaven and on earth joined in the chorus, "To him who sits on the throne and to the Lamb be praise and honor and glory and power, for ever and ever!"

"Whew." Antonius looked up. "I need another drink of water."

"What do you make of that scene, Pastor?" queried Severus.

"I don't know," answered Polukarpos. "Certainly this scroll is different from anything John has written before, but obviously he is describing the crucified Christ upon his throne and all of creation worshiping him."

"What I find interesting," interjected Flavius, "as a senator familiar with the Imperial court in Rome, is the way John describes this scene using symbols and terms that have specific points of reference within the Imperial court."

"Do you think the scroll mentioned in that last scene refers to Caesar's judicial decisions?" asked Severus.

"I think anyone involved in the Imperial court or the senate would tend to understand it that way," answered the senator. "But it is a parody or a polemic. John is *ridiculing* Rome, showing how much greater Christ is than Rome. Thus he uses typical portrayals of Imperial regalia, presents the court in a series of concentric circles, and shows attendant servants. Then John also appears to pick up on the astrological aspects of Roman government and Roman superstition as well—the seven planetary signs, the doubling of the twelve signs of the zodiac into twenty-four, and so on. I think that John has taken the symbols of authority used in Rome and transferred them to Jesus Christ. At least that's how a Roman senator would read it."

"This scroll is even more dangerous than I thought," muttered Severus.

Julia let out a big yawn. "Oh my. It is getting late. I've heard as much about strange symbols as I can handle in one night. Figure it all out for us, Father, and tell me in the morning. I'm turning in."

"I think I'll join her," added Sabina. "And, Julia, I want to talk to you for a moment before you turn in."

Julia flashed a smile at Antonius and then left the group, accompanied by her mother and a servant with a torch.

"Anyone else too sleepy to stay up with us?" asked Severus. There were no takers. Antonius looked around at the servants, realizing that they were probably all Christians and both enthralled and frightened by what they had heard so far.

Antonius read on into the night, stopping occasionally for the group to discuss the meaning of what he had read. After a while, Severus shook his head from side to side and declared with exasperation, "This scroll is impossible! Seven seal judgments, seven trumpet judgments, and seven bowl judgments. Then two mysterious witnesses in Jerusalem and heavenly war between Satan the dragon and Michael the archangel."

Antonius took another drink of water. "It is an incredibly severe judgment on the world. But what does it mean? Who is the judgment on? When does it come?"

"It may refer to some great future cosmic end of the world," suggested Flavius. "But I tend to think that John is primarily addressing us now. Thus, this judgment will fall on Caesar and those who worship him, especially those who persecute Christ's faithful followers for refusing to worship Caesar."

"And what of the beast from the sea and the mark of the beast?" asked Polukarpos.

"I am not at all certain," responded Flavius. "And I would like to see what the elders in the church think. But I suspect that the beast from the sea perhaps refers to the huge statue of Domitian that is being completed even now in Rome and will soon be brought by ship here to Ephesus to be placed in the Imperial Temple. And the mark of the beast? I have a hunch that John is referring to the certificate that Caius and his Imperial Priests are issuing to those who swear allegiance and worship Domitian. That's why my dear Sabina is so mistaken in her assessment of the situation. We are wrong if we think we can say with our mouth that we worship Domitian, but say in our hearts that we are faithful to Christ and still everything will be all right. If we acknowledge Domitian as lord we will receive this certificate from Caius's priests, and indeed, life may seem to be easier for us, at least for a short while. But if I'm correct, John declares this to be the mark of the beast, and a sign that we are not truly one of Christ's but one of Satan's."

Antonius let out an audible breath. He was about to say, "Mother of Zeus!" but he caught himself just in time. He heard one of the Galatian servants behind him mutter something in the Galatian dialect; Antonius suspected that it was a comparable statement.

"What about the reference to the harlot sitting on seven hills?" asked Severus. "Isn't that an obvious reference to Rome?"

"Most certainly," said the senator. He took out a small silver coin from a leather pouch that he wore. "Look at this coin, a sestertius. What can you read on the coin, Antonius?"

The young man took the coin and squinted to read the fine engraving. "It says '*Dea Roma* seated on the seven hills.'"

"When Caesar Vespasian minted that coin," explained Flavius, "he was stating that his power derived from the goddess Dea Roma. And Rome is famous for its seven hills."

"So the great harlot John calls Babylon is actually Rome itself ... or a combination of all that is involved in the Roman Imperial worship system?" asked Antonius.

"Absolutely," answered Flavius. "That's the way it looks to me. But it will be good for others to read this scroll as well. I would be interested to know how the elders and pastors of the many churches in Asia understand it. What are your thoughts so far, Pastor Polukarpos?"

"Honestly, I am quite bewildered by much of it, and I would like more time to study it. There are many clear references to Rome, as you have noted. But there are also many, many connections back to the Hebrew prophets Ezekiel and Daniel, and I suspect many connections back to Genesis, the first book of Moses. I would like to go home and reread those scrolls as well."

When Antonius finally reached the end of the Apocalypse, it was late at night. Flavius had left his seat and was pacing back and forth across the clearing, apparently deep in thought. The younger man rolled up the scroll with care and remarked sorrowfully, "I wish we had been able to save Apollinarius. It would have been wonderful to have him here to lead us in this discussion. No doubt he would have had some insight into what John's vision really meant."

"I fear that the faithful old scribe has gone on ahead of us to prepare for the many Christians from the province of Asia that will soon join him," said Polukarpos.

"Antonius," said Severus, "I would greatly appreciate it if you would leave early in the morning and take this scroll with you. It is too dangerous to have in this house, especially when the senator is here."

"Certainly, sir. I will leave at dawn, which is not far away."

"Well, son, try to get some sleep," advised Flavius. "We'll see you off in the morning. If it is acceptable with you I would like Demetrius to accompany you to Laodicea. He will need to make some preparations at our villa before we arrive. And two are often safer than one."

"I would be honored to have one as wise and trusted as Demetrius to accompany me on the road."

Demetrius nodded and turned to go. The others rose as well and Severus led the weary Antonius through the garden and to a bed in one of the guest rooms. The young man placed the scroll carefully beside him and was soon fast asleep. However, Antonius had a fitful night filled with bizarre dreams—beautiful Julia danced on the deck of the *Orion* by moonlight as Marcus lay dying. Monica and Antonius's mother stood on the dock and called him to leave her and to come ashore to them. Then suddenly a giant harlot dressed in red flew over the city and swooped down toward him. As she drew near, he saw that it was really a ferocious dragon coming to devour him. He turned to run to his mother and to Monica, but could not run. Julia was smiling at him. As the dragon descended on him and latched its giant claws around him, he woke with a start. He sat up and noticed the first gray streaks of dawn creeping into the house.

τῶν νεκρῶν καὶ ὁ ἄρχων τῶν βασιλέων τῆς γῆς. Τῷ ἀγαπῶντι

FAMILY, FRIENDS, AND FAITHFULNESS

ἡμᾶς καὶ λύσαντι ἡμᾶς ἐκ τῶν ἁμαρτιῶν ἡμῶν ἐν τῷ αἵματι αὐτοῦ,

From Ephesus, Antonius and Demetrius took the main road south, walking up and over the mountains. They didn't talk much on the first day. The climb over the mountains kept them breathing hard, especially the middle-aged Demetrius, and it was difficult to talk. Antonius still carried the Apocalypse under one arm and hauled his travel bag up on his other shoulder. Demetrius carried a light bag as well, and although he offered to carry the scroll for Antonius, the younger man insisted on carrying it himself, for which Demetrius was thankful.

Early on the morning of the second day, however, they descended into the Maeander River valley, approaching the city of Magnesia. From there the road followed the river eastward past the town of Tralles to Laodicea. The Roman road was excellent, and once in the river valley the traveling was not difficult, but the road was still long.

The day was beautiful. The sun was just beginning to creep up over the mountains, and rivulets of light streamed through the trees lining the road. The river paralleled the road, often no more than thirty or forty paces away, and the pleasant sound of the flowing river complemented the noisy birds celebrating the new day.

"Tell me, Demetrius," the younger man asked as they walked, "how does one get to be the chief steward of Flavius the senator?"

"My parents are from Gaul, captured by the Roman legions and sold as slaves in Rome. Sabina's father, Lucius, bought them and trained them as household slaves. I was born five years before Sabina was and I grew up in her family's house. As a young man I was trained by their chief steward. He taught me how to read and write, how to manage accounts, how to invest money, how to assess the winds of political change in Rome, and how to interpret the constant stream of political rumors that always swept through the city. When Sabina married Flavius, I accompanied her as part of her dowry. After a few years, Flavius put me in charge of his entire household and all of his financial affairs. A few years later, after Flavius became a Christian, he gave freedman status to all of his household slaves. I became a freedman, but continued to work as the senator's chief steward."

"Did you become a Christian then, too?"

"Well, when the master of the house embraces a new religion, the entire household usually follows along. That is to be expected. So, certainly, I was baptized not long after Flavius was."

"So what did you think about the Apocalypse? And what will you do if the Imperial Cult really tries to stamp out all Christianity in the province of Asia?"

"I am but a household steward. And not a great thinker like my master, Flavius. So who am I to interpret the scroll or the times?"

"But what do you think?" Antonius asked insistently. "You are not just a household steward. You are Senator Flavius's chief steward. You know about the political situation. What do you think will happen?"

Demetrius looked at Antonius and frowned. "The house of Flavius Lucius Domitilla is in an extremely dangerous situation and I am very worried. I do not know how much pressure will be brought against Christian families like yours, Antonius. In your case, it will depend on how the Wool Guild in Laodicea responds to Caius. But I don't think that Caius and his Imperial Cult will tolerate a Christian senatorial family, especially one headed by someone as outspoken as Flavius."

"But what about you, Demetrius? Where will you stand?"

Demetrius shrugged in response. "As the chief steward I will of course support the family and do whatever my master asks of me. Hopefully I can help us find a way out of this dilemma. I am resolutely committed to the survival and well-being of this family."

"Do you think that Sabina and Julia are right? That quiet compromise is the proper course of action? Even after reading what the Apocalypse says?"

"I am not as thrilled by this new scroll as you and the young Polukarpos seem to be. And perhaps the years and experiences of my life have made me more pragmatic and less idealistic. My master Flavius is totally committed to following his new religion, and for the sake of his new Lord he is willing to follow his brother to the grave if that is required. I respect him for that, and I, as his steward, will comply with all of his requests and support him in all of his decisions. But I also serve Sabina and her daughter, Julia . . . and I don't know how deeply committed they are to the new faith. I think that they are more pragmatic and less idealistic about religious things in general.

"Also, Sabina is extremely distraught over their change in fortunes and is nearly frantic with worry about their very survival and about Julia's future. Their fall from the upper echelons of Roman society has been almost more than Sabina can handle. And Julia? Julia adores her father, and she is trying to stay optimistic, but she is slowly realizing that the happy carefree life she expected to live is slipping away and she senses a tragedy on the horizon. I don't know how they will stand up under the coming pressure. And what will happen to them if Flavius is arrested or—heaven forbid—executed as his brother was? Sabina sees the reality of that possibility and the devastating consequences that such events would have on the family. From her point of view, compromising a little in order to save the family seems a wise and prudent thing. From my point of view . . . well, my future is tied to theirs."

Antonius and Demetrius talked of many things that day and the next. Antonius wanted to know all about Rome, and he listened intently as Demetrius described the city, its social life, and its politics. The steward also explained many of the details relating to the arrest and execution of Flavius's brother.

On his part, Demetrius asked much about Laodicea. Who were the powerful people there? How were the trade guilds organized? How much power did they exert? Which gods were worshiped there and how powerful were the temples? He also asked about the wool business of Antonius's family and about sheep and wool in general. He was also curious to know about Antonius's famous father and how the Bloody Centurion went from being the hero of the Battle of Athanel to being a wool merchant in Laodicea. Antonius found the older man to be extremely perceptive and quick to absorb and digest new information.

The two had many lively conversations as they followed the Maeander Valley toward Antonius's home city. Finally, late in the afternoon of their third day of traveling, the two dusty, weary men saw the imposing stone walls of Laodicea stretching out across a small hilltop in the distance. Drawing nearer, they crossed the stone bridge that spanned the Asopus River, a small tributary that fed the Lycus. Just beyond the bridge stood the huge three-arched Ephesian gate, flanked on both sides by massive stone towers.

"So these are the walls that held back Labienus and the Parthians during the time of Mark Antony," said Demetrius.

"You know your history well. The citizens of Laodicea are all proud of that. But this particular gate has been rebuilt since then, completed only a few years ago. It is dedicated to Domitian."

They entered through the gate into a wide, colonnaded street paved with white stone. The street was crowded with farmers and their families returning to their farms after a day at the market. Despite the crowd, the two men could see at the end of the street the beautiful fountains for which Laodicea was famous.

"What a beautiful city, here in the middle of nowhere!" Demetrius declared.

"Not nearly as big as Ephesus," Antonius replied. "But it has its charm. Look, there to the left. You can just make out the top of the theater. And in the distance to the right, you can see the stadium."

Antonius was elated to be back in Laodicea. As he walked through the streets of his hometown he felt as if he had been gone for years rather than weeks. But his joy at being home was intermixed with a certain foreboding about the future. He felt much older than when he had left, and he sensed that he now carried a new, heavy burden. He was worried about what would happen here in Laodicea to Flavius and his family. He was likewise concerned about the future of all Christians in Laodicea, including his own family and Monica's. And he was also worried about his own immediate future—was it time to talk to his father about marrying Monica?

Flavius had given Demetrius money to hire a professional scribe to make copies of the Apocalypse. Just inside the city gates, Antonius gave the steward directions to the house of Creon the scribe, reputed to be the best scribe in the city. He also gave Demetrius directions to his own house, and likewise to the big villa just on the other side of the city that now belonged to Flavius. They parted ways and Antonius headed home.

As he passed the agora, a familiar voice called out, "Hail, Antonius Marius Amulius! Sea traveler and world explorer! Famous wool merchant!"

Antonius turned to see two of his best friends walking toward him. "Simeon! Isaeus! How glad I am to see you."

The two young men approached and each embraced Antonius. The oldest of the two, Isaeus, was tall and thin. Although he was only six years older than Antonius, his dark brown hair had already begun to thin, giving him the appearance of one much older. He was a servant in Antonius's household—technically, a slave. Antonius's father had purchased him ten years before on a trip to Cappadocia after learning that he was a new believer but owned by a very unpleasant Scythian magistrate who refused to allow any of his slaves to worship any other than the local deities. Gallus had offered Isaeus his freedom several times through the years, but Isaeus always refused. He had become part of Gallus's extended family, and was, in fact, like a brother to Antonius. He had tutored Antonius, but he also kept the accounts for their wool export business. He had been married for several years and had two small children.

The other young man was Simeon, a Jewish Christian from a family that, like Antonius's family, dealt in Laodicean black wool. Simeon was slightly shorter than Antonius, with a thick stock of black hair and a full beard that hid much of his face. His father, Ephraim, was a respected rabbi in the synagogue. Ephraim had not embraced Christianity, but he tolerated it, viewing it as one of the many minor aberrations of Judaism that had emerged through the years. He disagreed with his son Simeon's conviction that Jesus of Nazareth was the Messiah, but he still considered his son to be a Jew. Simeon, out of respect for his father, continued to follow as many of the Jewish customs and traditions as he could.

"Antonius!" Simeon said, laughing and slapping him on the back, creating a small cloud of dust. "Look at how dusty you are. You didn't *walk* here from Ephesus, did you? We thought you might arrive in a chariot." Antonius could tell from the smirk on their faces that they knew some great secret.

"A chariot? Why is that?" he asked.

"Well, we heard that you have moved up in the world socially, and that you dine with senators and kiss the fair daughters of Roman nobility. " Isaeus laughed. "Please remember us lowly wool merchants when you become proconsul of Asia."

"How did you hear all this? I can't believe that everything I did in Ephesus is already known in Laodicea even before I arrive home!" exclaimed Antonius in exasperation.

"That's the weakness of being a freedman," declared Isaeus. "You have no network of communications between cities, no grapevine of rumor and slander. We slaves, on the other hand, see all and know all."

"But how?"

"Simple, really," continued Isaeus. "Your distinguished host Severus has a servant who is the cousin of my friend Apollos who works for the old one-eyed olive oil merchant in Colosse. Apollos was in Ephesus on business and heard all the news, much of which had to do with you. Since he is in the lucrative olive oil business and not in the lowly wool business, he also has a horse, so he beat you back by a day and a half."

"Agghh!" said Antonius. "Does everyone in Laodicea know this?"

"Apollos is my friend. But he also has several relatives in this city, one or two who are known to be fairly free and indiscriminate with their information, although they exaggerate only mildly. So I would say yes, most of the servants that I know are aware of your contact with Flavius and his outrageously beautiful daughter, Julia. I doubt that the masters know."

"And Monica?" demanded Antonius.

"Well, I certainly didn't tell her," said Isaeus. "But she did get wind of it and cornered my wife yesterday, insisting that she tell her all of the rumor."

"Oh, this is great."

"It's true, then?" asked Simeon. "You came off the ship in Ephesus arm in arm with a Roman senator and then kissed, right on the dock, his daughter, Julia, a vivacious young woman known back in Rome as the most beautiful of all the nobles' daughters? You, my humble and not-very-eloquent friend Antonius, *you* did this? It's true?"

"Not exactly," Antonius tried to explain. "It's rather complicated. And I certainly did not kiss Julia—that is a false rumor. She kissed me."

Simeon and Isaeus hooted and howled. "She kissed you?" Simeon repeated, incredulously. "The daughter of a Roman senator, the most beautiful and most desired of all nobles' daughters in Rome, kissed *you?* That's even better. Does she have any friends? Can I go with you on your next trip?"

"First the girl kissed you, and then the father invited you to eat supper with them and stay the night?" asked Isaeus. "Are you crazy? Didn't you tell them you were betrothed to Monica? How can you even look at another girl when you have someone like Monica waiting anxiously for you to return? Rich or not, beautiful or not, how can she compare to Monica?"

"Everything happened very quickly; it was difficult to think clearly," said Antonius. "Besides, I am not officially betrothed to Monica. And you haven't seen Julia."

"You're not really serious about this rich girl, are you?" responded Isaeus suspiciously. "There is a gigantic social gap between wool merchants and senators, regardless of whatever ideals the apostle Paul may have given us. Furthermore, she is in Ephesus and you are in Laodicea."

"For heaven's sake, Isaeus, I am not serious about her. The whole episode with Julia was a lark. However, Senator Flavius and his family are moving to Laodicea. They should arrive within two or three weeks. He has inherited the villa just beyond the springs on the Iconium road. They have already invited me out for a visit."

"Really?" Simeon said. "That's news to us. Isaeus's sources have failed us, or else they are holding back. Antonius, you are about to get yourself into a very complicated situation."

"And you don't even know the whole story yet," said Antonius.

"But, Antonius," probed Isaeus, "*why* did the girl kiss you?"

Simeon answered before Antonius could. "Obviously his good looks overwhelmed her. All the guys in Rome are short and skinny."

"Would you shut up for a moment?" snapped Antonius. "This may look funny to you two but it isn't. On board ship, some sailors tried to assassinate Senator Flavius. I was able to help stop the attempt. She kissed me in appreciation for saving her father's life."

Simeon whistled. "This story gets better all the time."

They started walking toward Antonius's house. Simeon took Antonius's bag and Isaeus took the scroll.

"What's in the goatskin?" Simeon asked.

"I'm not sure I want to tell you two, after all the fuss you made over Julia and the senator," said Antonius. "But this bundle is the most important feature of my whole incredible trip."

"Perhaps you should tell us everything—all the details—from the beginning," suggested Isaeus.

So the three friends strolled through the streets of their beloved city toward the northwest corner of town where the members of the wool guild all lived. Antonius told them the entire story—the storm, the death of Marcus, Heron the captain, the rescue of the scroll and the death of Apollinarius, Julia on the dock, Caius and Plautus, and Flavius's interpretation of the scroll. He had meant to tell all, but he found himself omitting a few details—the sparkle in Julia's eyes, his weak knees and tumbling stomach, the yellow gown just for him, his jealousy at Plautus's flirtation.

As they approached Antonius's house, Isaeus shouted out the announcement, "Cassandra! Gallus! Your prodigal son returns!"

From inside the courtyard of Antonius's house a dog started barking happily.

"It sounds as if Caligula at least is glad you're home," said Simeon.

Suddenly Antonius's mother, Cassandra, flew through the gate and rushed out to Antonius, giving him a warm embrace. She was considerably shorter than her son, and slightly plump, but with a happy, cheerful face. The black hair of her youth was now streaked with gray, betraying the onset of middle age. Her eyes—she had the same eyes as Antonius—likewise had the beginnings of wrinkles at the edges, but at the moment they were beaming with joy at the sight of her son. She was followed by a large, shorthaired, light brown dog, barking and wagging his tail furiously. Cassandra fussed over how dusty her son was and how thin he had become, kissing him on the forehead and cheeks as if he were still ten years old. She saw the cut and the slight discoloration still showing on his right cheekbone.

"What happened to you?" she asked, examining his bruise carefully.

"It's nothing, Mother. I fell down on the ship. I'll tell you all about it later."

"We were so worried about you! And then we began hearing the wildest rumors about you! But now you're home safe. Come in and I'll get you something to eat."

Antonius's father, Gallus, also emerged from the house. He was slightly taller than Antonius, with broad powerful shoulders. He had deep-set penetrating eyes and short dark brown hair, just beginning to show traces of gray. He likewise embraced his son. "The business in Athens went well?"

"Yes, sir. We were able to get a very good price. Even Nathan was impressed. Here is our percentage for expenses." Proudly he handed the bag of money to his father, who in turn gave it to Isaeus.

"We have a lot to talk about, Antonius. You've been a busy young man."

"Yes, sir. It was an eventful trip, to say the least."

"Let's go in and hear about it."

Gallus, Isaeus, and Simeon walked briskly through the gate into the courtyard of the house. Cassandra, still in the street, had taken Antonius by the arm, refusing to let go of her boy just yet. They turned and walked toward the gate together. Just as they reached the gate, Antonius heard the voice he feared to hear.

"Antonius!" From across the street Monica exploded out of the gate to her house and raced toward Antonius. She looked as if she would throw herself into his arms for an embrace—which would have been normal for them after a long absence—but she stopped just short and they stood a few feet apart, looking at each other awkwardly.

His mother broke the silence. "I think I'll go on inside and get started on your supper, Antonius." She led Caligula into the court-yard and closed the gate, leaving the two of them alone on the street.

Antonius looked down at Monica and tried to smile. She was quite attractive, but definitely different than Julia, that was certain. Her straight black hair was long and plain. Her complexion was much darker than Julia's, reflecting her father's Berber ancestry and the long hours spent in the sun. She wore a rough woolen robe that was a bit too short, revealing her dirty bare feet; obviously, she had been working in the house and had rushed over without sandals. Her eyes were dark brown, without the bright sparkle that Julia's radiated. But they revealed her strong character, one that could be persistent, even stubborn. It was a trait that Antonius had always admired in her. But at the present moment, he thought he detected some hurt in those eyes as well.

And she is definitely growing up, he thought as he looked at her. *She is sixteen already, and even the rough robe can't hide her womanly shape.* In his mind the two of them were always still children— ten and twelve years old—throwing rocks at birds, climbing trees, playing with the baby lambs that occasionally lived in their courtyards. She had always been like a sister to him as well as his best friend. But both of them had changed in the last two years, and he knew that they both were feeling different things than they used to about each other. It had made their relationship somewhat awkward, as if they were no longer sure how to act toward each other. And now here she was—a very attractive young woman. He realized that he had really missed her and that he was glad to see her. He wanted to tell her everything about his incredible trip. He wanted her to be proud of him. But at the same time he dreaded this initial encounter. Who knew what she had heard already?

"You've hurt your face," she said with concern. "Are you all right?"

"A wave knocked me down on the deck of the ship. It's nothing."

Awkward silence again.

"You were in a storm then? I didn't hear about a storm. Was it serious? Were you in danger of being shipwrecked? Was anyone hurt?"

Antonius let out a weary sigh. "It's a long story, Monica. Come in and listen while I tell Father and Mother all about it."

He turned toward the gate, but Monica made no move to follow. Awkward silence again.

"Antonius, did you really kiss her?" she finally blurted.

"No, it was not like that. Some men tried to assassinate her father and I helped to stop them. One of them was killed. Julia wanted to say thank you, and she kissed me . . . on the cheek."

"Oh . . . I'm glad you're all right." She stood there quietly, looking down, twisting the belt from her robe round and round one of her fingers nervously. Finally she looked up and asked, "Is she as beautiful as everyone says?"

"Monica, listen . . ."

But tears had begun to well up in her eyes, and she suddenly turned, ran across the street, and vanished through the gate, leaving Antonius standing alone with a sudden pang in his heart, feeling like a traitor. He had known that she would be angry about Julia and he had prepared himself for that. What he saw in Monica, however, was not anger, but pain, for which he was not prepared. He stood in the street just staring at the closed gate, regretfully acknowledging that he had hurt her. He realized that it was important to him that Monica be proud of him. Everyone was proclaiming him to be a hero, but he wanted *her* to think he was a hero. He now realized that all the rumors flying around Laodicea about him and the beautiful Julia had embarrassed Monica—and probably her family as well—since everyone knew that they were practically betrothed.

Why did I get myself into this mess? When Flavius asked about my status, why didn't I tell him immediately that I was betrothed? Where was my sense of right and wrong? How could I bravely fight Marcus the sailor on one day and then crumble completely before Julia on the next? And Julia is just a rich, spoiled flirt. I am nothing special to her. Monica is the one I care about, and now I've hurt her and embarrassed her.

Slowly Antonius trudged over to the gate of his house and entered the courtyard.

"Come on, Antonius!" Isaeus called. "We are all gathered around in rapt excitement to hear the tale of your odyssey. Don't keep us waiting. Tell us all, especially, about kissing the senator's daughter."

Simeon and Isaeus laughed, but Antonius noticed that his father was frowning. As he took his seat, he also saw his mother looking at him with a creased forehead, obviously concerned.

"Well," began Antonius, "I left Father in Ephesus, and I sailed for Athens with a shipload of wool." Antonius told them the entire story, sharing all of the details. He tried to downplay how gorgeous Julia was, but his two friends pressed him on that issue, and it was difficult for Antonius to hide the fact that he had been overwhelmed by her striking beauty. Even his mother, who clearly disapproved of Julia, was curious about what Julia and Sabina were wearing and about how they wore their hair.

Finally, to Antonius's relief, he was able to turn the conversation to John's Apocalypse. He unrolled the scroll and read the first column to them. Then he summarized the basic content as well as he could remember, pointing out the connections Flavius and Severus had observed between the themes in the Apocalypse and the pressure that the rapidly rising Imperial Cult would exert on the Christians in the province of Asia.

Cassandra pulled away reluctantly to prepare supper. A short time later Gallus gathered them all—his family, Isaeus's family, and Simeon—around the table and gave thanks to God for the food and for the safe return of his son. Throughout the meal and even after, the scroll and the growing threat of the Imperial Cult dominated the conversation. At last, sensing his son's exhaustion, Gallus announced that it was time to retire. Simeon headed toward home, and Antonius, feeling as weary as he had ever been, collapsed into bed and immediately fell asleep.

καὶ ἐποίησεν ἡμᾶς βασιλείαν, ἱερεῖς τῷ θεῷ καὶ πατρὶ αὐτοῦ,

A WALK WITH FRIENDS

αὐτῷ ἡ δόξα καὶ τὸ κράτος εἰς τοὺς αἰῶνας τῶν αἰώνων· ἀμήν.

Antonius was awakened early the next day by the familiar sounds and smells of morning. The obnoxious rooster from the wine merchant's house next door carried out his daily job of ensuring that everyone in the neighborhood was awake. Antonius could also hear the braying of a donkey in the distance, the chatter of birds, and the occasional bark of a dog. The smell of wood smoke from the fires being kindled all over the city crept into his room as persistently as the crowing of the rooster. He could also hear his mother puttering around in the courtyard preparing the morning meal, talking softly with Isaeus's wife, Caecelia. The familiar sounds and smells were pleasant—even comforting—to Antonius, and lying in bed half awake, he reflected on how wonderful it was to be home.

Breakfast, enjoyed in the cool morning air of the courtyard, was a noisy, happy affair, involving both Gallus's family and Isaeus's, not to mention the ever-present Caligula, who circled the table excitedly throughout the meal, looking at each member in eager expectation, hoping for a morsel of food. Usually one of Isaeus's two small children succumbed to the pleading look of Caligula and smuggled a piece of bread to the grateful dog, often drawing a frown from their father, but rarely a reprimand.

Just as they were finishing breakfast, Caligula ran to the gate barking, announcing that a visitor had arrived.

As Antonius opened the gate, he was greeted tersely by a man Antonius knew only by reputation—Creon the scribe. Antonius was surprised to see him so soon, but he knew that the copies of the Apocalypse should be made as soon as possible, and he realized that the efficient Demetrius had acted quickly to employ the scribe and thus fulfill an important charge that his master had given him. Antonius was fairly certain that Creon was a Greek and from a long line of professional scribes. He was not a Christian but he had a reputation as an honest and discreet man and the best scribe in the region. He was thin and gray-haired with a long, narrow beard. He stooped slightly when he stood and he walked with a shuffle. He was a rather taciturn, almost surly, man.

After exchanging very brief morning greetings with Antonius and Gallus, Creon got right down to business, explaining that Demetrius had employed him to make three copies of a long scroll written in Greek.

"I must examine the scroll, before I give my final price to this fellow Demetrius."

Antonius brought the scroll; Creon unrolled it on the table and looked at it closely.

"Ah . . . yes," he mumbled to himself. "This is the work of a good scribe and on good papyrus, too. Yes . . . very good."

"It is extremely important that you make the copies exactly like this one, with no errors," Antonius stressed.

"What?" said Creon, startling Antonius and the rest of the family. Caligula rose to his feet and emitted a low growl. "I did not come here to listen to insults! All of my work is exact, completely accurate and completely error free. If you mention such a thing again, you will have to hire another scribe!"

Antonius apologized, noting the amused look on his father's face.

Creon continued: "I will work here, in this courtyard, where the light is good? Yes?"

Antonius looked at his father, who nodded.

"And I will eat the midday meal with you each day?"

Father and son looked at Cassandra, who shrugged and nodded.

"Agreed," Gallus answered. "One other thing. The contents of this scroll are strictly private. No one else is to know what the scroll contains."

Creon once again bristled indignantly. "Do I not write letters and make copies of the most private affairs of people throughout this city? And have you ever heard of me mentioning one iota of what I wrote to anyone? Never!" He glared at Gallus. "I will finalize the price with Demetrius and start tomorrow morning. Good day." The scribe turned and left, walking quickly out through the gate and into the street.

"Well, it should be fun having him here every day," quipped Cassandra as Antonius closed the gate.

Gallus shrugged apologetically, "What can we do? He is the best scribe in Laodicea. And this is an important task."

Antonius carefully rolled up the scroll and returned it to the goatskin bag, which he placed in the storeroom where Gallus kept all the important documents regarding their wool business.

"Well, son," his father said as Antonius returned to the courtyard. "Your adventurous trip is over, and it's time to get back to work. Isaeus has been picking up most of your tasks while you've been gone, so he is delighted to see you back and ready to work."

Gallus, Antonius, and Isaeus said farewell to their families and headed out into the street, where they soon separated. Gallus needed to visit a sheep owner to the south of town who had not been giving them the quality of wool that they required. Isaeus was going to the agora to keep track of the sheep being bought and sold; often the contracts for wool followed sheep from owner to owner. Antonius went to the guild storehouse, where the family collected and stored its wool until they were ready to ship it to market.

That night, after the day's work was finished, Monica's father, Juba, invited Antonius and his family over to share supper with them so that Antonius could share the adventures of his trip with them.

Monica was polite but distant. He could tell that she was listening carefully, but for most of the evening she would not look at him, and she did not ask any questions. As the young man related the story of the assassination attempt and of his fight with the sailors, he caught her looking intently at him, and he thought he saw—or at least he hoped he saw—admiration in her eyes, along with concern over the danger he had been in. And certainly her father, Juba, was proud of Antonius and his heroic action. He complimented Gallus profusely on the bravery of his son. But Monica looked away, still troubled. Both sets of parents sensed the tension between the two, and they looked at each other in puzzlement, uncertain what to do about it.

Antonius accompanied his parents back to their house without having had any direct conversation with Monica other than polite greeting. He knew that he needed to talk with her and try to straighten things out. *Perhaps tomorrow*, he thought.

However, on the next day Antonius was busy with work throughout the day, and in the evening there was no opportunity to talk with Monica. Days slipped by, and Antonius continued to procrastinate. The days stretched into a week, and still he delayed. In addition, as he settled back into the daily routine of a hardworking wool merchant, his encounter with the sailors on the *Orion* and the smell of Julia's perfume seemed more and more to him like something he had merely dreamed. The reality of his adventure started to fade into mere memory. He knew that he needed to have a serious talk with Monica and apologize to her. Hopefully that would help to patch things up.

Antonius also made time each night to pray about this matter. After praying for several nights, he felt that he needed to talk with his father seriously about marrying Monica. An official betrothal should be announced and dates set. That announcement would stifle some of the ridiculous rumors that continued to circulate throughout the city about Julia and him. He also suspected that it might be wise for him to make this decision and publicly announce his commitment to Monica before Julia arrived in town, thus eliminating the possibility of any more confusing encounters with the flirtatious beauty.

Yet several more days slipped by and Antonius remained silent, upset with himself for his timidity and his procrastination. Each night he went to bed resolving that on the next day he would talk to Monica and then with his father. Finally, one night he swore to himself that he would talk to Monica the next day, no matter what. It would be Saturday, the Jewish Sabbath, and the day would afford him several opportunities to talk with both Monica and his father.

On Saturdays, Antonius's and Monica's families typically met in front of their houses for the short walk to the synagogue. The Christians in Laodicea held their own worship service on Sundays, meeting late at night so that those who were required to work could still attend. Most of the Christians, however, also attended the Jewish synagogue on Saturday, the Jewish Sabbath. Although tensions between the groups occasionally flared, normally the Jews and Christians in Laodicea coexisted under an uneasy truce. The non-Jewish people who attended the synagogue, such as Gallus and Juba and their families, were called God-fearers, and had been accepted into the synagogue for over a hundred years, although they had to sit at the back. In fact, most of the construction cost of the synagogue in

Laodicea had been borne by Gentile God-fearers over eighty years before and the Jewish community had not forgotten that.

As the two families exchanged morning Sabbath greetings in the street, Antonius went to stand beside Monica, who turned slightly away from him, looking down. Gallus stepped closer, looking at the couple disapprovingly, one eyebrow cocked. "Are you two still not talking?" he asked.

"We're talking, Father. It's all right," answered Antonius. "You go on ahead. We'll follow behind together as usual." Monica looked away, but stayed to walk with Antonius. Juba and Gallus headed down the street, discussing the faults of sheep from Galatia. Cassandra and Monica's mother, Vivia, followed, along with Monica's twin brothers, age ten. As they turned to follow the parents, Marcellus, the most daring of the twins, caught Antonius's attention and made a big puckered kiss with his mouth. Antonius took a step forward and the boy ran down the street to catch up with the fathers. Antonius made a mental note that the next time he took the boys fishing he would dunk Marcellus thoroughly in the cold stream. He and Monica waited in silence for a moment and then started down the street together, behind their families.

"Our fathers are worried about more than sheep, aren't they, Antonius?" asked Monica after a short while. "They are bothered by events in Ephesus and by the strange things in your scroll, aren't they?"

He looked at her and smiled. It was a start. At least she was talking.

"Yes," he answered. "And me, too. Plautus, the new Imperial high priest for Laodicea, has been talking to the Wool Merchants' Guild this week. He warned that if they don't support the new Imperial Temple and help to finance the festivals, their taxes could double or even triple. And who knows what they might charge us in Ephesus, he pointed out. The guild in Colosse has already pledged support for their temple. Plautus may have enough clout to shift the entire Laodicean wool operation to Colosse, if the guild here resists. It is not an idle threat. If Laodicea as a whole balks at supporting the Imperial Temple and its festivals wholeheartedly, Caius could respond with serious economic restrictions. A lot of people in this city could lose a lot of money."

"Isaeus says that we will soon be asked to publicly swear allegiance to Caesar Domitian as lord. Can they do that, Antonius?"

"If the synagogue evicts us, then we will no longer be exempt from taking that pledge. There are thousands of Christians in the province of Asia, Monica, and this will create a real uproar. The Proconsul Quintus will try to prevent it and to maintain peace. But I don't think he can stand against Caius."

"Father is not sure that taking the pledge would be all that wrong." She looked up at him and smiled weakly. "He is worried about Mother and the boys. I think that he may be worried about me as well. Anyway, I think that the talk in the guild has scared him. He is trying to convince himself that we can stay faithful to Christ in our hearts, and that God will understand the pressure to pledge allegiance to the Caesar. I think that Mother disagrees with him."

"I know," Antonius said gently. "Isaeus told me. All of the Christians here are asking themselves that question. What about you, Monica? What will you do?"

She stopped him in the middle of the road and looked up into his eyes intently. "I will never renounce Christ or worship any Caesar. Never. I thought you knew that."

They stood there in the street for several moments, just looking at each other and thinking the same thoughts: *Will we marry each other? Will we raise children together? Will we face the awful days ahead together?* Finally Antonius touched her arm and said, "We'd better go, Monica. We'll be late." She smiled at him and they turned to continue their stroll toward the synagogue.

When they arrived, they could tell something was wrong. Many of the people still stood outside the building, talking in nervous, huddled groups. As Antonius and Monica walked up, Simeon hurried over to meet them. "I've got lots of important news to tell you!" he said excitedly. "First of all, Quintus has been dismissed as proconsul of Asia and exiled to Spain. Domitian has announced that Sulla will be the new proconsul of Asia."

"Sulla!" exclaimed Antonius. "What possible worst choice could there be? Sulla hates my father and he hates Christians. He is corrupt to the core. He'll give Caius everything he wants. How can this be? Why does God let this happen?" He looked up to see his father and Juba talking animatedly with Ephraim the rabbi, Simeon's father. All of them seemed distraught.

"Furthermore," Simeon continued, "one centurion and twenty-five soldiers from the praetorian guard have arrived, assigned to the new Imperial Temple here in Laodicea."

"But there is no Imperial Temple here yet," protested Antonius.

"Perhaps they are here to ensure that opposition to the idea is minimal," suggested Simeon.

"What other news do you have?" asked Monica.

Simeon looked at the two of them for a moment, appearing uncertain. He let out a sigh. "Flavius and his family arrived yesterday, a week ahead of schedule, apparently due to the situation in Ephesus."

"Simeon!" Antonius scolded. "Did you have to bring that up now? Here in front of Monica?"

"I'm sorry, Antonius, but the senator and his family may show up here at the synagogue any minute. I thought that the two of you might want a few moments to talk about it first."

"Thank you, Simeon," said Monica curtly. "This will give me some time to gather rocks. This one looks good." And she bent down and picked up a rock the size of a small orange. Antonius looked at her with alarm. On several occasions when they were younger, he had seen her hit the vultures behind the butcher's shop with rocks. In fact, he remembered being hit once or twice himself by stones she had thrown at him. He noticed Monica's mother, Vivia, looking at her daughter with the rock in her hand and frowning.

"Monica," said Antonius softly. "I hope you're jesting with the rock."

Just then, a pretty young woman in Jewish dress stopped before them. "Well, Monica, are you going to throw that at Antonius? I hear that he deserves it. But don't bring it into the synagogue; I think that hauling rocks on the Sabbath is prohibited by the Torah—not that you Gentiles care that much about keeping the Torah."

"Miriam," protested Simeon, "please behave yourself. These are my friends, remember, even if you don't like them."

Antonius looked back and forth from Simeon to Miriam. Ironically, Simeon probably had more problems relating to his own marriage situation than Antonius did. Miriam's father, Jonathan, now standing on the steps to the synagogue and arguing animatedly with another Jew, was the most influential elder in the synagogue, and also a wealthy man. As Simeon had explained to Antonius, Jonathan and Simeon's father had been friends for years, and had recently been discussing a marriage between their two children. However, Simeon's acceptance of Christianity had complicated things. He now would prefer a Jewish Christian wife, he had told Antonius, although he did like Miriam quite a bit and thought she was very attractive. Miriam and her family, however, insisted on a Jewish husband, and they had their doubts whether Simeon qualified. Antonius knew that things were tense between the two families.

At that moment, everyone's conversation was interrupted as all turned to watch a beautiful carriage drawn by two magnificent black horses approach the synagogue and stop in front. Flavius, Sabina, Demetrius, and Julia all climbed down. Antonius was struck by the wealth that the carriage represented. No one else at the synagogue had come by carriage. No one else in the synagogue, he realized, not even Miriam's family, even owned a carriage. Several people had horses, and a few had ox-drawn carts that they used for work, but no one owned an expensive carriage like this.

Antonius suddenly felt sick. Flavius waved at him, but Julia bounded over to see him—as vivacious as ever, dressed in a stunning rose-colored gown with her hair done up high in gold braid and flowers. As she drew close, her perfume was fragrant, but not overpowering.

"Antonius, how good to see you again!" she exclaimed brightly. "I thought it would be forever before we came here to see you. We just got in yesterday—what a wretched trip through the mountains! We must be in the middle of nowhere here! Do you feel that way or is it just me? Anyway, please forgive me for not contacting you sooner. We are trying to settle into the new villa. But we must have you over for dinner soon."

Then turning to look at Monica, she asked, "Are these your friends, Antonius? Demetrius told me that you had a special friend here."

"Uhh, yes, Julia," stammered Antonius. "This is Miriam. Her father is an elder in the synagogue. And Simeon, his father is Ephraim the rabbi. And this is Monica. Her father, Juba, fought with my father in Gaul. We grew up together."

"How wonderful to meet all of you—especially you, Monica. Monica is an unusual name. Is it a local name from this region?"

"No," replied Monica, remarkably civil. "It comes from the province of Africa."

"Really? A Carthaginian name?"

"No again. It is a Berber name. My father is a Berber from the inland plains of North Africa. Monica was his mother's name."

"How fascinating! Nice rock you have in your hand there. Are you going to throw it at me or at Antonius? Oops! Mother is signaling me to come. Better run! See you after the service. Nice to meet you, too, Simeon. You are as handsome as Antonius is . . . almost." She smiled cheerfully at Antonius and winked at Simeon, and then glided away to her mother, Sabina.

Simeon stood with his mouth open. "Yes, indeed, Antonius, I understand everything now. I think I could kill a whole boatload of murderous assassins if that girl promised *me* a kiss." Instantly Simeon regretted his comment. Miriam poked him in the side with her elbow and Monica dropped her rock on his sandaled foot.

"Ouch!" He hopped on one foot while trying to rub the injured one. Miriam stomped away, making sure that she bumped Simeon as she went by, just enough to knock him off his one-footed balance.

Ephraim the rabbi was trying to get everyone into the synagogue. Jonathan the elder had exchanged greetings with Flavius and was escorting him and his family, as honored guests, into the building. Flavius could only pause for a moment as he passed Antonius.

"Greetings, Antonius. You heard about Sulla?"

Antonius nodded.

"I need to talk to you alone for a few minutes right after the service. It is quite important. I would like to meet your famous father, too, if I could."

chapter Eight

Ἰδοὺ ἔρχεται μετὰ τῶν νεφελῶν, καὶ ὄψεται αὐτὸν πᾶς

THE SYNAGOGUE

ὀφθαλμὸς καὶ οἵτινες αὐτὸν ἐξεκέντησαν, καὶ κόψονται

Everyone filed into the synagogue and took their seats. The Jewish men sat in the front, with their women and children sitting in the following rows. The God-fearers—the non-Jewish participants—sat in the back by families. Gallus's family sat on the same row as Juba's family, but Monica sat by her mother instead of next to Antonius. Flavius and his family were seated several rows up. Julia turned around briefly to locate Antonius, smiling brightly at him. Antonius smiled back and turned to see if Monica was watching. She glared at him.

Gallus nudged Antonius slightly with his elbow and muttered, "We are entering a very dangerous time, son. Please keep your feet on the ground and don't forget who you are."

The service began in typical fashion. Ephraim read from the Torah and expounded briefly on the meaning of the text. The congregation recited some blessings and sang a few songs. Antonius found it impossible to concentrate. The news about Sulla troubled him, his problem with Monica and Julia troubled him, and he wondered what Flavius wanted to talk about that was so urgent. Monica wouldn't look at him through the whole service; Julia turned several times and sought him with bright eyes.

Toward the end of the service, there was a stir down at the front of the synagogue. Several elders crowded together, apparently discussing something. A few of them became quite animated and appeared to be angry. Finally they sat, and Miriam's father, Jonathan, stood to address the congregation.

"Men of Israel," he began. "Rabbi Phinehas from the synagogue at Ephesus has suggested that we add a new feature to our worship: a reading of the Eighteen Benedictions at the end of each service. I have discussed this with the other elders and we agree that this would be a beneficial addition to our service and to the added glory of the God of Abraham."

Audible groans and sighs could be heard from the back where the God-fearing Christians sat, but most of the Jewish men in the front gave approving nods.

"This could be our last trip to the synagogue," whispered Gallus to Antonius. "I'll be the first one called." Antonius glanced at Monica, who was now looking intently at him. *If I get up and leave,* he thought, *she would go with me.*

However, before Gallus or Antonius could make any decisions, Rabbi Ephraim rose to his feet and addressed the crowd.

"Friends," he began. "Let's not rush into something that we may later regret. We have allowed Gentile God-fearers to worship with us in Laodicea for over one hundred years. We have worshiped together in harmony since the time of my father's father. True, many of the God-fearers have now been drawn to follow Jesus of Nazareth as well—who was also a Jew, I might remind you—but I do not see this as a reason for them to be expelled from this synagogue. We have always tolerated minor theological differences within Judaism. My own son has joined these Christians, but to me he is still a Jew. Why should we force him out of the very synagogue he grew up in?"

Several men nodded their heads in agreement, but Jonathan stood for a rebuttal.

"Our wise rabbi has given us good advice that served us well in the past. But the present is different. Things are changing in our city. New powers and forces are arriving. If we as a Jewish community are to thrive, we must adjust and react to these changes. The Christians have been identified as a threat to Rome. If we are seen to be harboring them and giving them protection, Rome will turn on us as well."

Jonathan then nodded at the rabbi with satisfaction as if his speech had settled everything, but the old man stood again.

"Hmm . . .," the rabbi began. "A moment ago we were to say the Eighteen Benedictions for the glory of the God of Abraham. Now the reasons are changing, are they not? And perhaps now the real reasons are surfacing. Now you say that the reason for expelling the Christians is so that we will remain in favor with Rome. Friends, this is a very different reason indeed! But let us drop the rhetoric for a moment and deal with the real issues. The high priests of the Roman Imperial Temple are trying to forge an alliance with the Jews of Asia in order to evict the Christians from the synagogue so that the Christians can be forced to worship Domitian. The Romans hold before us the carrot of economic benefits, and they also wave a threatening stick, the removal of economic benefits. So for *financial* reasons we are to force these Christians to exchange their worship of the God of Israel for the worship of the man Domitian? Would we not be as guilty as they?"

"Ephraim," Jonathan spoke sternly, "sit down. The elders have decided. It is not for you to challenge."

"Quite to the contrary," countered the feisty old man. "I am the rabbi of this synagogue, and we will not do this terrible thing while I am part of it. This service is now over. Everyone go to your homes and think through this matter very carefully. Let us discuss it throughout the week and then see how the entire congregation feels about it next Sabbath."

He then pointed to the cantor and said, "Sing, my son!" The cantor began singing the closing song. Furious, Jonathan was forced to sit down. Soon the cantor finished and everyone filed out of the synagogue.

Flavius sent Sabina, Julia, and Demetrius home in the carriage, then asked Antonius if he and his father would walk with him. Cassandra went home with Vivia and Juba, and Monica followed them reluctantly, glancing back accusingly at Antonius as she walked away.

Antonius introduced Flavius to his father, Gallus, and they began walking down one of the paved colonnaded streets near the synagogue. After a brief exchange of pleasantries, Flavius got right to the point: "There is something that I wish to discuss with you, Gallus, and with you, Antonius." Flavius let out a deep sigh, as if choosing his words carefully. "As you may know, Sulla the new proconsul is a sworn enemy of mine. Likewise, Caius has singled me out as one of the major obstacles to his Imperial Temple in Laodicea. I will probably be one of the first Christians in Laodicea forced to choose between Domitian and imprisonment, perhaps even death."

"Unfortunately," said Gallus, "what you say is probably true. However, I suspect that I, also, am high on their list. I think that Sulla still hates me for embarrassing him at Athanel."

"That's true, Gallus," the senator agreed. "However, keep in mind that Sulla and his high officers have consistently told everyone that your valiant escape through the heart of the enemy army never happened. The official report denies it. If Sulla has you arrested, everyone will know that the Battle of Athanel was true and Sulla will be shamed. Ironically, your disfavor with Sulla may be the very thing that protects you. In my opinion, your real danger comes from Caius, who might think that he could weaken Sulla and thus strengthen himself by arresting you, making it look like Sulla's revenge."

Gallus pondered this. "I hadn't considered this. Political schemes can become too complicated for soldiers like me to predict."

"I don't think that Caius will come after you for a while," continued Flavius. "And even if he does, I don't think that the attack would spill over on to Antonius, especially if he were married and set up in his own separate household."

Antonius almost choked. He looked at Flavius and then at his father.

"What is your point, Senator?" Gallus asked.

"Gallus, this is quite awkward for me. I had hoped that over time I could visit with you and your family and earn your friendship. But I am afraid that there is no longer much time, and that the events described in the Apocalypse may come quickly to you and me. Thus I am forced to be forward and impolite. Forgive me."

"What is it that you seek, Senator?"

"I am worried about Julia and Sabina. Neither of them is strong enough to survive the coming trials if I am gone. If I am arrested or executed, their status, even their safety and welfare, will be uncertain. What if the Imperial Cult confiscates the villa? They could lose everything, and unless Julia is safely married into a good family, they could find themselves all alone—with nothing."

Antonius felt his throat going dry.

"How does this concern us?" Gallus asked.

"I would like to arrange a marriage between Julia and Antonius, and fairly soon."

Antonius turned with a start. He hesitated in his breathing, swallowed wrong, choked, and began to cough. Despite the seriousness of the situation, both older men smiled at Antonius, bent over coughing and trying to get his breath back.

Flavius continued when Antonius had recovered. "As a dowry I would purchase a small villa and farm for them a day's walk or so from Laodicea. I think that if we set them up as a separate household away from the city then the storm might pass them by, regardless of what happens to me or to you."

"What are your thoughts on this proposal, Antonius?" asked Gallus.

"Well, sir . . . I, uh . . . well . . . Julia is . . . well . . . she is . . . but Monica is . . . you know . . . and I . . . well . . . I don't know what to say. I've had so much come at me today that my head is spinning."

His father rescued him. "Perhaps, Senator, you could give us some time to discuss this and to think about it. Things are very confusing for us at the moment. I had always planned on Antonius marrying the daughter of my friend and former comrade Juba. And a marriage as you propose, between a senatorial family like yours and a plebian family like ours, would be most unusual, even scandalous in some circles."

"Certainly," Flavius agreed. "I am aware, believe me, of the difficulties involved. Yet I have committed the matter to the Lord; indeed, I have pledged to Him that I will do everything I can to marry Julia into a Christian family. I have also read the words of the apostle Paul, who proclaims that in Christ there is no difference between you and me, or between your family and mine. And I want Julia to marry someone who is strong and who can protect her. Furthermore, she seems to like Antonius. And was it mere coincidence that Antonius was on the same ship that I was and that he was the one to save my life? Was this not the hand of God working? I had been praying earnestly about finding a husband for Julia out here in the provinces, and then suddenly Antonius appears, sword in hand, fighting my enemies, saving my life. When I discovered that he was also a Christian . . . well, to me it sounded as if perhaps the Lord was speaking."

Flavius looked at Antonius, who was still dizzy and unable to speak. His heart was racing and he struggled to focus.

"Gallus," the senator continued. "I have been made aware of the unofficial betrothal between Antonius and the daughter of Juba, your good friend and honored former legionnaire. I apologize for intruding into the relationship between your two families. Yet his daughter seems to be an attractive young woman, and surely there are other honorable young Christian men in this city who would be interested in her and acceptable to him. My own situation is deteriorating rapidly, and recent events force me to take desperate measures. I apologize for springing this on you so quickly and unannounced. Discuss the matter. I will be waiting for your reply."

"Excuse me, sir," Antonius blurted as the senator turned to go. "Does Julia know about this proposal?"

"Yes. But Sabina does not. Good day, gentlemen."

Gallus and his son stood in the middle of the street, watching the senator from Rome walk away. Antonius noticed how weary he looked. Gallus and Antonius then turned and trudged slowly in the other direction, toward their home. They walked several streets in silence, both of them deep in thought, although Antonius's head was still spinning and he was having trouble thinking coherently. After a long period of silence, the retired soldier put his arm around his son and said with an ironic smile, "For ones who live in a little city in the middle of nowhere, our lives have certainly become rather complicated, haven't they?"

ἐπ᾿ αὐτὸν πᾶσαι αἱ φυλαὶ τῆς γῆς. ναί, ἀμήν. ᾿Εγώ εἰμι τὸ ἄλφα

HORSEMEN IN
THE NIGHT

καὶ τὸ ὦ, λέγει κύριος ὁ θεός, ὁ ὢν καὶ ὁ ἦν καὶ ὁ ἐρχόμενος,

Creon the scribe normally worked on the Sabbath, not recognizing it as anything other than a regular workday. So when Antonius and Gallus arrived back at their house after hearing the startling proposal by Flavius, Creon was already hard at work. He sat cross-legged on the ground in the center of the courtyard where the light was good. He was usually oblivious to everyone else in the courtyard when he was working, so Gallus's family could generally go about their normal business while he was there and not distract him.

Caligula, however, was a different matter. At first the dog had snarled and barked at Creon. After a while, however, Caligula had given up trying to run off the intruder and had tried a new, more effective tactic—friendship. Caligula lay down right beside Creon and slowly moved closer and closer until he snuggled right against the scribe. In exasperation, Creon had declared that he could stand it no more. Either they would remove the dog from the courtyard or he would refuse to work on this project. Caligula was thereafter exiled across the street to Juba's courtyard anytime that Creon was working.

On this particular Sabbath day, Cassandra quietly prepared the midday meal and Creon, as was his practice, took a short break to eat the meal with Gallus's family. Conversation was brief; Creon cared nothing for small talk, and the intrusion of a non-Christian stranger at the table stifled all serious discussion of the morning's events, even though the family was facing momentous decisions.

After the meal, as Gallus took Cassandra aside to relate to her Flavius's proposal, Antonius went for a long walk to think and pray. Taking Caligula, he meandered out through the Eastern Gate and up the wooded mountain that lay behind the city. He walked for several hours, trying in vain to apply rational thought to a decision that was inextricably intertwined with deep emotion.

After a while, he found himself at his favorite lookout spot, a ledge cut into the face of a granite cliff on the side of the mountain, not far from the top. Actually, as he reminded himself, it was Monica's favorite lookout spot, too, and through the years the two of them had often come here to sit and talk. From here they could see most of the valley on the east side of Laodicea, including the main road that came from Galatia. As children he and Monica had watched many travelers come and go on the road below.

Monica had enjoyed concocting wild make-believe stories about each traveler. *Look, Antonius, the one in the oxcart is really a Parthian spy, come to spy out Laodicea. Perhaps the Parthian army is massed just beyond that hill and will attack us in the morning.*

Hidden along the ledge behind some hardy bushes was a small narrow cave. He had once explored the small cave—which really was no bigger than a small room—on a dare from Monica. Holding a small lamp he had brought for that purpose, he had ventured in with Monica close behind. Once inside, she had blown out the lamp, and then stepped back into the darkness, making monster noises in an attempt to scare him. Even though he had never admitted— especially to her—that he had been the least bit scared, he did not like dark caves, although he was a lot more worried about finding snakes in them than he was about finding noisy monsters.

Antonius sat on the same rock on which he and Monica always sat when they visited this place. He recalled the happy hours they had spent here throughout their childhood. *And not all limited to our childhood,* he reminded himself with a smile. He had kissed Monica for the first (and only) time on this very rock less than a year ago. She had looked quite startled. For a moment he had thought that she was going to slap him. But she had just stared at him and said nothing. As children they had always been best friends, almost like brother and sister. Now that they were becoming adults, the relationship had started to change. He had concluded at the time that perhaps she was not quite ready to make that change. He had not pursued another kiss since then.

He now realized that from here he also had a very good view of Flavius's villa. He could see the entrance gate on the main road, and he could just make out the main house and courtyard through the many trees on the estate. He wondered what Julia was doing. Was she out in the courtyard with her mother? Or strolling alone in their beautiful, large garden? Was she thinking about him? Was she worried about her father? About her future?

The quiet of the woods and the serenity of the view were comforting and calming. He recalled a statement that Epaphras had made last week in their worship gathering: "God is above nature and not in nature; nevertheless, I can usually hear God better in the woods than in the city." *I suppose that is true,* Antonius mused. But what was God trying to say in all of this? He wondered about the many "coincidences" in his life recently. *What if my father had made the trip to Athens instead of me? Or what if I had simply booked passage on a ship other than the* Orion*? Flavius would be dead, and the Apocalypse lost. Julia would probably have stayed in Ephesus and I would never have met her.*

But it is no use dreaming of what might have happened, he reminded himself. *I was on the* Orion *and I did kill Marcus and I can't change that fact. I did meet Julia, she is beautiful, and she did kiss me. And I must make some decisions soon.*

He returned to the house shortly after the sun had set. Creon had already finished for the day. Undoubtedly the scribe had, as he did at the end of each day, given both the original and the partially completed copy to Isaeus, who would have secreted the copy in a hiding place and then delivered the original to Shabako, one of the Christian elders, who had asked to use it to prepare a message for the next day's worship.

A small lamp was burning in the courtyard, and Antonius flopped down in a chair beside it and kicked off his sandals. Cassandra brought him a large drink of cold water, frowned at his sandals lying in the yard—a bad habit Antonius had developed in his childhood years—and then returned to the house, leaving him to his thoughts.

After a few minutes, his quietude was interrupted by the barking of Caligula, followed by the voice of Simeon calling from the other side of the gate.

"Antonius! Cassandra! Isaeus! Anybody home besides that terror of hounds, Caligula? Creon, perhaps? Hello? Can someone in this house please unlock the gate and let this poor vagabond in?"

Antonius chuckled as he rose. His friend Simeon always lifted his spirits. He unlocked the gate and his friend followed him back into the courtyard. Simeon took a chair beside Antonius, and then promptly finished off the rest of Antonius's water. Caligula sniffed Simeon for a short while to see where he had been recently and then lay down at Simeon's feet and went to sleep.

"Quite a ruckus in the synagogue today," Simeon commented as he finished the water.

"Father and I thought for a moment that it might be our *last* day in the synagogue. And it would have been, too, if not for the strength and wisdom of your father."

"Mother and I were very proud of him. That clever Jonathan thought he could just brush Father aside and impose his will on the entire synagogue. I guess Father showed him. I wonder if they can still be friends after that public showdown.

"Anyway," Simeon continued, "I wanted to chat with you and Monica about all this after the service, but I noticed that Flavius whisked you and Gallus away for some private talk." Simeon looked at Antonius with inquisitive eyes, waiting for him to share the details of that conversation.

Antonius answered cautiously, "He and Father have concluded that they—especially Flavius—will probably be the first Christians to be singled out as examples and forced to decide between Domitian and . . . well, no one is exactly sure what the alternative will be. Perhaps merely economic ruin and banishment beyond the frontier. Perhaps worse."

"They didn't need you for that conversation. What else did they talk about?"

"I can't say."

"Come on, Antonius, we don't keep secrets from each other. Did you discuss Julia?"

"Simeon, I can't say. Not now. I'll let you know some day what we discussed."

"All right, suit yourself. But let me give you some advice, my friend. The Imperial Temple and Domitian are not your main problem. Your main problem, Antonius, is that you have *two* women in your life. No man can handle such a situation for long. But never fear, for I, Simeon, can help you out. I will be more than happy to take either Monica or Julia—especially Julia—off your hands and make your life easier . . . for *your* sake, of course. As a friend."

"Of course. What are friends for?"

"Precisely."

"But, Simeon," Antonius said, laughing, "you already have a woman in your life and a very pretty one, too. Your family wants you to marry Miriam, and admit it, you like her. And besides, she is the most attractive eligible daughter in the synagogue, aside from Monica."

"And Julia," Simeon corrected.

"And Julia."

"My problem is that Miriam and her father have told me quite bluntly that there will be no marriage unless I quit attending the Christian worship services. Father is talking to them and trying to work things out, but we are at something of an impasse, and after this morning . . . well, I don't know what will happen."

Gallus entered the courtyard from the house and greeted Simeon. "I wanted to let you know how proud we were of the courage your father showed today, and how thankful we are to him."

"Thank you, sir," Simeon said. Looking puzzled, he asked, "Excuse me, Gallus, but didn't you have a special Wool Merchants' Guild meeting tonight?"

"No, I heard nothing about a meeting tonight. Not from Juba— nor from Isaeus, and he knows everything that happens in this city. Besides, Archelaus, the president of the guild, is in Ephesus; there can be no meeting if he is out of town."

"That is strange," said Simeon. "At sundown, as the Sabbath ended, my father received a message from a servant we didn't know, announcing a very important meeting of the Wool Merchants' Guild to be held at the third hour after sundown."

"But—there is no meeting," Gallus said with alarm. "I fear foul play. Has Ephraim left yet?"

"He was at home when I left, preparing to go. He is probably on his way to the Guild Hall now."

"Alone?" Gallus demanded.

"Of course."

"Antonius!" commanded Gallus, suddenly transformed once again into a centurion. "Get my sword from the house. Quickly! And take the small dagger for yourself. Hurry! There is no time to lose. Simeon, run across the street and get Juba. Tell him to bring his sword and come immediately."

Antonius raced into the storeroom to get his father's sword and the dagger. From the storeroom he heard Gallus shout, "Cassandra! Cassandra!" Antonius rushed out of the storeroom with the two weapons as his mother scurried out of the house. "Please take Isaeus's family over to Juba's," Gallus told her, "and stay there with Vivia and Monica until we return. Don't open the gate for anyone."

"How can I be of service, sir?" Isaeus asked as he entered the courtyard, pulling on his robe, a dagger tucked inside the belt of his tunic.

"Isaeus, run to the West city gate and wake the magistrate on duty. Ask for as many guards as he can give you and rush to the Wool Merchants' Guild Hall. Then backtrack to Rabbi Ephraim's house. Maybe it is nothing, but I fear an attempt on his life."

"Do you think the guards will help? Is Rome not against us in this?" Isaeus asked.

"For now, we must continue to trust Roman law. Go. Quickly!"

Isaeus left in a flash. A worried Cassandra hustled out Caecelia and their two small children. Juba and Simeon arrived, along with Monica, Vivia, and the twins. Caligula sensed that something was about to happen, and he nervously circled the people.

"We suspect they may be trying to assassinate Ephraim the rabbi," Gallus explained quickly to the wives, and with that the four men rushed into the darkness of the street. Caligula slipped out with them. Antonius made no attempt to stop him; perhaps the dog could help.

They ran silently through the dark city. Simeon took the lead, followed closely by Antonius. Caligula ran beside Antonius. The two former legionnaires, well into middle age, brought up the rear, keeping up with the younger men, but just barely. There was no moon and many of the streets lay in total darkness, the high walls of the courtyards blocking the faint starlight. The men stumbled more than once.

Soon they arrived at Simeon's house. Simeon pounded furiously on the gate until the startled family servant finally opened it.

"Has Father left already?" Simeon demanded.

"Yes, a short time ago," answered the servant. "Is something wrong, Simeon?"

Without answering, the four men bolted down the street, heading in the direction of the Wool Merchants' Guild Hall. With each block Antonius grew more alarmed. As he and the other men ran, they encountered a few other people on the street, and each time Antonius saw someone walking alone in the dark his hopes rose that perhaps it would be the old rabbi. But he passed each one with disappointment.

At last, as they turned a corner, Antonius saw a familiar form several hundred paces ahead of them, walking slowly, carrying a small oil lamp.

"Father!" Simeon shouted.

The form turned around to look. It was Ephraim! Antonius felt a surge of relief, but he and the others kept running toward the rabbi.

Suddenly, several men wearing long hooded cloaks sprang out of the shadows just in front of Ephraim, and a few more emerged quickly from the darkness behind him.

"What do you want?" the old rabbi demanded.

"Leave the rabbi alone or you will die!" shouted Juba to the assailants in the distance, his sword now drawn and in his hand, as was Gallus's. All four men sprinted toward Ephraim.

"Run, Father!" Simeon shouted, but one of the assailants grabbed the rabbi from behind, knocking the lamp from his hand. It crashed to the ground near the wall, spilling the oil and instantly igniting. The flames hugged the ground, following the oil and curling around the paving stones, illuminating the assailants in faint, flickering yellow light.

The hooded captor held a sword to Ephraim's throat and shouted down the street as he moved away from the flames, "That's far enough. Come no further or I'll kill him."

Simeon, Antonius, Juba, and Gallus stopped and stood, breathing hard. They were only about fifty paces away. Antonius could see five men, one holding Ephraim and four others, two on each side.

"They have infantry swords and not daggers," Juba observed softly. "And they certainly don't look like ordinary thugs or bandits. And look at the size of that one on the far right. He must be a full head taller than the others."

Antonius heard the one who held the rabbi say to his comrades, "I count four—two with swords and one with a dagger."

Unobserved by all was Caligula, who had not stopped when Antonius stopped but had continued running toward the assailants in the dark. Suddenly Caligula snarled and attacked from behind the men, biting the tall assassin viciously in the calf of his leg.

"Aggh!" he cried out. "Son of Jupiter! There is a cursed devil of a dog here." The man struck wildly at Caligula with his sword, but by that time the wily dog had withdrawn into the darkness, where he barked and growled at them menacingly.

"Kill that dog, Maximus," commanded the leader. However, the flames from the spilled oil suddenly grew faint, glowed blue for a moment, and then went out. Antonius could hear the men stomping around in the dark, cursing as they tried unsuccessfully to kill Caligula, who continued to bark at them in the darkness. Another dog in a courtyard nearby also began barking, then another just up the street. Someone nearby cried out from the other side of the wall, "What's going on?"

"We could take these four," their leader muttered, "and the cursed mutt, too, but others may come if we delay for a fight. Speed and secrecy is better than bravery. Let's get to the horses."

He released Ephraim, who fell to the ground immediately. The five hooded men turned and ran up the street, with Caligula barking and nipping at their heels.

"Father!" cried Simeon in a panic. The four of them flew up the street toward the crumpled form on the ground.

Juba reached the rabbi first and rolled him over, struggling to see in the darkness. He stood up suddenly and turned away, exclaiming, "Mother of Zeus, Gallus, they cut his throat."

Simeon fell on his father, sobbing. Antonius and Gallus hesitated a moment and then raced down the street after the assailants, with Juba close behind. They sprinted around a corner and down a small side street, led by the incessant barking of Caligula.

At the end of the street, an open window on the second floor of a house emitted enough faint lamplight for Antonius to see that the five assassins had reached their horses, held for them by a sixth man. They were trying to mount quickly and flee, but Caligula was making that difficult by terrifying their steeds, running in and out among them, yapping and nipping at their legs. The men struggled to hold their skittish horses still enough to mount, and eventually all of them except the biggest man were able to mount and bring their horses under control. Maximus was still on his feet, holding his horse's bridle in one hand, and with the other, flailing unsuccessfully at the dog with his sword.

"Forget the cursed dog, Maximus!" commanded the leader. "Mount up and let's go!"

As the last man climbed on to his horse, Antonius came racing down the street. The six men turned their horses to face him. He stopped twenty paces away; his father and Juba soon caught up and stood beside him. Caligula ceased barking and ran to Antonius's side.

The leader of the assassins had drawn his sword. He pointed it at Antonius. "I don't know who you are, but you are woefully outnumbered. The wise thing to do, stranger, is to run, not pursue."

"Come down off that horse and fight, you murdering coward!" Antonius shouted back in rage. "Or can you fight only against unarmed old rabbis?"

The assassin spurred his horse forward several feet. Caligula growled. Gallus whispered quietly, "Control your rage, Antonius. If they charge, fall back behind us immediately and protect our rear. Stay clear of our swords and finish off anyone we dismount. Juba, I have the lead rider; you the second."

"You have an impertinent mouth, young man," the assassin said, "and I would take great pleasure in killing you and your friends, but alas, there is no time, and we must be off."

Several of the hooded men in the back had turned their horses to leave, but Antonius ran forward a few feet and hurled his dagger at the leader, who was still facing him. It hit the startled rider in the chest. But it bounced off his chest with a metallic *clink* and fell with a clatter on to the paving stones of the street.

"Ha!" exclaimed the killer. Quickly he turned his horse and vanished into the darkness. Caligula gave chase, following them to the end of the street, where he stopped and barked for a few moments. Then he returned to his master.

"What happened?" asked Antonius, searching in the street for his dagger.

"The man was wearing a breastplate under his cloak," said Juba.

"But even legionnaires in this province don't normally wear breastplates, do they?" Antonius said. "Who, then, would be wearing one?"

Gallus stood staring down the street after the fleeing horsemen. "Centurions of the praetorian guard wear breastplates."

Slowly they walked back to Simeon, who sat on the cold stones of the street with his slain father in his arms, still sobbing in the darkness.

chapter ten

ὁ παντοκράτωρ. Ἐγὼ Ἰωάννης, ὁ ἀδελφὸς ὑμῶν καὶ

THE FOLLOWERS OF BALAAM

συγκοινωνὸς ἐν τῇ θλίψει καὶ βασιλείᾳ καὶ ὑπομονῇ ἐν Ἰησοῦ,

Antonius spent most of the next day trying to be of some comfort to Simeon and Simeon's mother. Miriam and her father, Jonathan, also came over to visit Simeon and to console the family of their slain rabbi. Antonius scowled at Jonathan, wondering if he was in any way part of the murderous plot. It seemed inconceivable, and yet . . . everything was changing so rapidly and once-unthinkable things were now possibilities. Antonius was convinced that neither Jonathan nor Miriam was to be trusted.

Simeon, however, clearly seemed to brighten when Miriam arrived. She immediately took charge of the household and began organizing the many friends and acquaintances pouring into the courtyard. Many of the women were wailing; some were singing laments in Aramaic. The entire Jewish community showed up, and soon Simeon was surrounded by fellow Jews. Miriam hovered nearby, pampering and mothering him, never moving far away. Antonius, the only Gentile in the courtyard, began to feel out of place. Simeon no longer seemed to need him. Seated alone in the back corner of the courtyard, Antonius yawned and looked down at his feet. He noticed bloodstains on his sandals. He stood up and silently slipped out through the gate.

Antonius did not feel much like attending the regular Sunday evening worship service of the Christians that night. His father, however, encouraged him to go, because the service might be an important one—and because it was precisely during times of sorrow and anger that they needed to gather with other believers and worship Christ together. They walked to the meeting hall with Juba's family, as usual. Monica and Antonius walked and sat together, but talked little.

The Christians were quiet and solemn as they filled the rented Guild Hall that they used for worship. Flavius and his family sat near the front, as honored guests and newcomers. Julia tried to get Antonius's attention. He managed to ignore her.

After they had sung several songs of praise, Shabako stood to speak. He was an Ethiopian from the city of Meroe, located on the banks of the Nile far south of the Egyptian border. Like Juba, he had been part of an auxiliary unit in the Roman army. Part of a renowned Egyptian unit of archers, Shabako had spent most of his Roman military career fighting the Parthians. Upon retirement, he had purchased a beautiful young Persian slave, married her, and settled just outside of Laodicea, where he grew olive trees.

Not as sophisticated as the pastor—it was hard for a veteran Roman soldier to completely transform back into a civilian— Shabako was nonetheless a good speaker. Antonius actually preferred him to the main pastor. Shabako was fiery and he preached with excitement. Antonius thought that Epaphras, their regular pastor, tended to be a little boring at times. Shabako's skin was black as coal and he spoke with a delightfully different accent. *I wonder what he thinks of the Apocalypse and what he will say about it.*

"Brothers and sisters," Shabako began, walking back and forth in front of the congregation. "As you may have heard, Senator Flavius and our own brother Antonius, by the grace of God, were given possession of a new scroll from our beloved apostle John, who to this day still languishes on the forsaken island of Patmos.

"This scroll, called the Apocalypse, contains visions from God that the apostle saw there on the isle of Patmos. John also addresses seven key churches here in the province of Asia; we, the Laodiceans, are one of those churches.

"What is it that John says to us? The scribe who smuggled this scroll off the isle of Patmos for John died trying to deliver it to us. Only by the grace of God were Flavius and Antonius able to rescue the scroll from the raging sea. So the message in this scroll is important . . . and it is timely. John knows the situation here in our province. God has given him a vision to deliver to us, to encourage us, and to challenge us to stand firm and strong."

Or to confuse us, to scare us? wondered Antonius.

"And what does he tell us?" the Ethiopian continued. "He calls our province the 'throne of Satan.' This is because worship of the man Domitian is sweeping across the province. Imperial Temples have been built in dozens of our cities, including Ephesus. All people in the province are being forced to acknowledge Domitian as both lord and god, which is clearly blasphemy of the worst kind.

"Moreover, John labels our Jewish synagogues as 'the synagogues of Satan.' All across the province synagogues are evicting Jewish Christians and Gentile Christian God-fearers so that the Imperial guards can identify them and force them to worship in the Imperial Temple. It has happened in Ephesus, Colosse, Miletus . . . dozens of other cities.

"Here in Laodicea, one holy rabbi stood alone for truth and righteousness. One Jewish rabbi stood alone before the might of the Roman Imperial Cult, and you know the outcome. He did not compromise, and he paid the ultimate price. Can you and I do otherwise?

"Some of you are suggesting that we compromise with Caesar. Some are saying that it is all right to worship Domitian in public, before the people, so long as we worship only Jesus secretly in our hearts.

"But, brothers and sisters!" Shabako shouted. "Hear me! Hear me! The apostle John condemns those who teach these things! He calls them followers of Jezebel, the most wicked and deceitful of queens in the Jewish Scriptures. He calls them followers of the wicked magician Balaam, who was unable to defeat Israel by his magic, so he *deceived* them into worshiping Baal, and thus led thousands to destruction.

"We cannot compromise! We must not even consider it! We cannot say Lord or God to anyone save our Lord Jesus Christ. We cannot worship Rome *and* our Lord Jesus. God requires us to choose whom we will worship. To acknowledge Domitian publicly as Lord and God is to deny Jesus. How can we do such a thing? I, for one, will not deny our Lord. I, for one, will never follow Balaam and worship Domitian or any other mere mortal. I, for one, will stand firm to the end. What will *you* choose?"

After the service, the Christians brought out food and ate a simple meal together, seated by families in the meeting hall. Antonius was relieved to see that Pastor Epaphras and the elder Shabako had commandeered Flavius and his family, seating them down at the front with the pastor's wife and Shabako's wife. Antonius tried not to look; he was afraid that if he made eye contact, Flavius would motion to him to join them. He sat instead next to Monica, along with his parents and with Juba's family.

As the meal ended, the Christians began leaving the building, greeting and talking with one another as they went out. Monica walked next to Antonius. Flavius kept Julia close beside him. She caught Antonius's attention once and smiled. He nodded. She looked as beautiful as ever. Perhaps a little more somber, thought Antonius. She even showed a trace of weariness, something he had never seen in her before. *I guess the tension is starting to show on all of us.*

Flavius led his family to the carriage without stopping to talk to Antonius or his family. The young man was thankful. However, he had not totally escaped. As he and his family entered the street, he was stopped by Demetrius.

"Could I have a private word with you?" he asked.

Monica watched Antonius walk away with Senator Flavius's servant, feeling worry tighten and stretch the skin of her face. Her parents were talking with some other Christians about the murder of Ephraim and they had not noticed Antonius's departure. Isaeus and Caecelia, however, were standing beside her.

"Monica, it will be all right," Isaeus offered.

"Tell me something, Isaeus," she demanded quietly, "and I want a straight answer and an honest one."

"I'll do my best."

"I heard a rumor that Flavius has proposed a marriage between Antonius and Julia. Is that true?"

Isaeus stood in silence, looking at the ground.

"Isaeus, answer me! Is it true?"

"Yes, Monica, it's true," he said. "But so far neither Gallus nor Antonius has given an answer."

The young woman fought for composure. Isaeus and Caecelia stood beside her in helpless, awkward silence. Monica looked down the street at Antonius and Demetrius walking together, talking seriously.

"Mother," she said, stepping over and taking her mother's arm and pulling her away from her group of friends. "I don't feel well. Can we go home?"

"Certainly, dear. Is something the matter?"

Monica merely shook her head.

"Look, Antonius, I will be completely frank with you," Demetrius said as the two men walked along. "Things are moving much quicker than I had anticipated. With Sulla as the new proconsul, Caius can now go after Flavius with impunity as soon as he wishes. Indeed, any day now the senator could be forced to swear allegiance to Domitian, with prison or even death as a consequence for refusing. And as you know, Flavius is adamantly against any action that might be construed as a compromise with the Imperial Temple. So the house of Flavius is in an extremely dangerous predicament. As I told you on our trip from Ephesus, my fortunes are tied to his fortunes. And if anything happens to him, then my fortunes are tied to Julia's and Sabina's. This is where you come in."

"Go on," said Antonius uneasily.

"Flavius thinks that he can marry Julia to you and then whisk the two of you out into the countryside and out of danger. Personally, I don't think that will happen. There is a good chance Caius will also go after your father, and there is a strong chance that you yourself will likewise be forced to publicly acknowledge Domitian. Moving out of town will not protect you. Too many people know you and too many know of Julia. As a matter of fact, I have heard from several servants that Caius's son Plautus has taken an interest in Julia, as you saw yourself in Ephesus. Flavius and Sabina have received several invitations from him to bring Julia and come to his house for dinner. Of course, Flavius has refused all of these requests, to the ire of Sabina—and Julia, I might add."

Antonius stopped and stared back down the street at his parents, wishing his father had come with him for this talk.

"My point is this, Antonius. If you intend to be as unwilling to compromise as Flavius is; that is, if you are going to rebuke the Imperial Cult and refuse to publicly acknowledge Domitian as Lord, then do me a favor and please do not marry Julia. Your family will also come under close scrutiny. If you refuse to acknowledge Domitian, then you will be ruined, and we—Julia, Sabina, and me—will be ruined along with you. Don't you see, Antonius? This decision does not affect only you. If you marry Julia, you carry the responsibility for Julia, Sabina, and me, as well as the other servants. If you anger the Imperial Cult, they will destroy you, and us along with you. I can't allow that to happen. Julia's beauty is becoming well known throughout the province. With a little time, Sabina and I can find her a husband who won't destroy us all."

Antonius realized what a formidable alliance Demetrius and Sabina formed. He wondered whether Flavius had any idea of their scheming. For all of Demetrius's profession of loyalty to Flavius, here he was, plotting against the will of his master.

"If, on the other hand," Demetrius continued, "you show some reason and comply with Caius and Plautus . . . Antonius, you don't have to actually worship Domitian, you know that. Just acknowledge the decrees of the Imperial Temple. Show them some respect in public. You can worship Jesus all you want at home. Then you can marry the beautiful Julia with my blessings and live happily ever after. Raise a houseful of children. I will ensure that you get a beautiful villa and profitable farmlands. I am a good manager. I am a shrewd investor, and Flavius actually has more money than he thinks he does, and I can keep it safe for you, Julia, and Sabina. You can have a happy life married to the most beautiful woman in the province, living in a nice villa with a good income and lots of servants. From such a position, you may also be able to protect your parents—at least your mother. I've heard from reliable sources that the Wool Merchants' Guild will expel Gallus and Juba by the end of the month at the latest. What will your family do for income? You can provide for them if you marry

Julia and say some mumbo jumbo toward Domitian. Think about it, Antonius; it's the biggest decision you will make in your life."

With that, the chief steward of Senator Flavius said farewell to Antonius and departed. The young man trudged back up the street to his waiting parents. As they walked home together, he shared with them what Demetrius had said. When they reached their house, as Gallus opened the gate, Cassandra put her arm around Antonius and said reassuringly, "It will be all right. God has always looked after us, and He will continue to do so. You know how much I love Monica, and you already know that I would prefer that you marry her. However, I can see that Julia is a beautiful and captivating young woman. If you decide to marry Julia, you will have our blessings. But don't marry her out of concern for me, thinking that your marriage to her will provide for me. I will gladly place my future in the hands of God. He has cared for us in the past and He will care for us during the difficult times ahead."

chapter eleven

THE BEAST ARRIVES

Gallus and his family rose early on Monday, as was their custom. In spite of the brewing crisis, there was work to do. Life went on. Even on the eve of a serious persecution, and even with the important decision regarding Antonius's marriage before them, the mundane details of life still needed attention. Gallus and Isaeus hoped to locate a certain farmer who lived several hours' walk north of the city. This farmer owned a prosperous fig orchard. He had recently used some of his profits to purchase a small flock of black Laodicean sheep. Gallus wanted to negotiate a contract with him in advance to purchase the farmer's wool when shearing time came.

After breakfast, Gallus and Isaeus packed some bread and figs, kissed their wives, and departed for the countryside. Creon arrived and was greeted noisily by Caligula. Caecelia asked her oldest child to take Caligula across the street to Juba's house. Creon then took his usual place in the courtyard and began to work. Cassandra and Caecelia cleaned up after breakfast, then took Caecelia's two children and crossed the street to rendezvous with Vivia, Monica, and the twins. They all headed for the agora to do the day's market buying.

Antonius also left early. His job on Mondays was to visit the storehouse that the Wool Merchants' Guild owned and check on his family's wool stored there. He usually made this trip with Simeon, but Antonius suspected that Simeon might not want to make the routine inspection today. Besides, Antonius could check Simeon's wool for him.

At the storehouse, Antonius began his inspection. It had not rained recently, so there was little dampness in the storehouse, usually one of his major concerns. He also checked for any insect damage. Everything looked fine; their wool was in good shape.

He walked across the storehouse to inspect Simeon's wool. The guild guard knew Antonius and knew that he and Simeon were friends, so he permitted Antonius to probe into the murdered rabbi's wool stockpile without question.

As he was finishing up, Archelaus, the president of the guild, approached him. "Greetings, Antonius!" Archelaus said.

"And greetings to you, President Archelaus," Antonius answered.

"I see that you are checking on the deceased rabbi's wool for Simeon."

"Yes," the young man answered. "Usually on Mondays Simeon and I come together to inspect the wool. I thought that today he might be . . . preoccupied."

"Yes, certainly. And what a tragedy, this senseless murder of Ephraim. And an outrage! Right in the streets of Laodicea. The streets are becoming unsafe these days, what with all the thieves and bandits."

"I don't think they were thieves or bandits."

"You saw them up close?"

"Close enough to know that they weren't bandits."

"Well, whoever they were," continued Archelaus, "we are certainly entering into a dangerous and difficult time, especially for the families of those who defy the Imperial Temple. Your father, Gallus, puts the guild in an awkward position, Antonius."

"My father is an honest and hardworking man who has been more than loyal to Rome. He is not the one who puts you in an awkward position."

"True, true," admitted the president, "but nonetheless, we all have to come to grips with the reality of the situation. Despite whatever gallant accomplishments Gallus may have achieved for Rome, he simply cannot defy Caius and the Imperial Cult without serious repercussions. While we here in the guild admire him and respect him, we cannot back him if he takes such an unwise position. It would ruin all of us in the guild. Look at what is happening in Ephesus."

"Has something new developed in Ephesus?"

"You haven't heard? Perhaps not. I only returned yesterday. I have notified several guild members, but I haven't contacted Gallus or Juba yet."

"Go on."

"Well, Sulla arrived in Ephesus a few days ago and met immediately with Caius. It appears that the new Roman proconsul, unlike the last one, will cooperate closely with the high priest of the Imperial Cult. On the same day, the new gigantic statue of Domitian arrived in port, creating quite a stir. Everyone there is buzzing about the new political power of the Imperial Temple. Twenty or so of your Christian friends in Ephesus were arrested and taken to the Imperial Temple to see if they were going to comply or defy the new order; many others fled. New laws and economic decrees are coming from the high priest and the proconsul every day. Those who pledge allegiance to Domitian are issued certificates that allow them to carry out business in a favored status with special benefits like low gate tariffs, priority shipping arrangements, and so forth."

"The mark of the beast," Antonius muttered.

"What's that?" asked Archelaus.

"Something in a new scroll called the Apocalypse from our apostle John. He says that those who comply with the beast and worship him receive the *mark of the beast*. Some Christians have suggested that this certificate is that mark."

"Call it whatever you like," said Archelaus, "but without it you won't do business in the Roman province of Asia. Without the certificate you will face all kinds of impossible economic barriers—outrageous tariffs, inflated transportation costs, restricted access to harbor facilities and guild storage facilities, and so forth. Within a few weeks at most, and maybe sooner, Antonius, it will be impossible to be a wool merchant in Laodicea without this certificate. We all respect your father, Gallus, both as a legendary legionnaire and as a fellow guild member, but we simply cannot support him in this. Business is business. We have our futures and our families to think of. We will do whatever is required to receive this certificate—call it the mark of the beast if you want to—and if that requires expelling Gallus and Juba, too, if they insist, unfortunately, that is what we will do. This is not a threat, Antonius, just the plain facts. You need to know these things."

Antonius was silent. Demetrius had warned him of all this, but he had not expected it to come so soon.

"There is a possible solution to this problem, Antonius," the guild president continued. "It may be possible for *you* to become a full guild member even if your father is expelled. Of course it would mean giving this silly pledge to Domitian. But you are old enough to make your own decisions, Antonius. Your father is on a disastrous course. There is no need for you to follow him."

"He has been in difficult situations before, and as you know, he came through," answered Antonius defiantly.

"I fear that he may find Caius and the Imperial Temple more cunning and much more dangerous than the barbarian hordes in the forests of Gaul."

be next year before we officially dedicated a temple in Laodicea to Domitian. But things have moved much more quickly than even I had dreamed. Our lord and god Caesar Domitian has approved the transformation of the old Phrygian Temple of Kybele here in Laodicea into a new Imperial Temple, dedicated to himself. Furthermore, Domitian's birthday is in two weeks, and he wants the dedication to take place then."

Archelaus whistled. Antonius felt stunned.

"I know, I know," Plautus said to Archelaus. "Two weeks is nearly impossible. The preparations for the associated festival will be quite extensive. So I have come here first, to the most prominent guild in the city, to the guild with the wealthiest and most prominent citizens of the city, in order to ask you to pledge your utmost and complete support for the new temple. Also, to enlist you to throw your considerable resources into our urgent—and somewhat frantic—effort to prepare for the festival in honor of our lord, Caesar Domitian."

"We would be most honored to help, and we will pledge our total support to this endeavor," promised the guild president.

"Will all your members participate?" asked Plautus, looking at Antonius.

"Most assuredly! Anyone who does not give their total, wholehearted support will no longer be a member of the guild."

"I thank you, Archelaus," Plautus said as he bowed respectfully. "I knew that the leading guild in Laodicea would want to be the first to commit to this new era of prosperity for our fine city. Can you attend a meeting today in the old temple? We have so much to plan. There is a statue of Domitian on its way. No, not the huge one. That one is slated for Ephesus. But a significant statue of Domitian was carved in Corinth last month. It had originally been commissioned for a plaza in Rome, but Caesar has graciously allowed for it to be diverted here to Laodicea and erected here in our new temple. And

Their discussion was interrupted by the loud echoing clatter of horse hooves on the paving stones just outside the entrance of the storehouse.

"It appears we have some guests," observed Archelaus.

The two of them walked to the entrance of the storehouse and emerged into the bright sunlight of the small courtyard. Five men had just dismounted under the shade of a large fig tree. One of them held the reins of the five horses, while the others walked across the courtyard toward Archelaus and Antonius.

"It's Plautus," warned Archelaus under his breath, "accompanied by his new praetorian guards from Rome."

The three soldiers with Plautus were indeed dressed in the flashy red tunics and bright-feathered helmets of the praetorian guards. One of the guards towered over the others; he was more than a head taller than Antonius himself.

Antonius also observed that the tall soldier walked with a slight limp. He felt his temper rising. He knew it was a foolish thought, but he wished he had brought his father's sword.

"Hail, Archelaus, president of the Wool Merchants' Guild!" called Plautus.

"Hail, Plautus, high priest of the Imperial Temple!" answered Archelaus.

"Ah, and the son of Gallus is here also, I see," said the young high priest. "The one who is friends with the beautiful daughter of Flavius . . . um . . . what is your name again?"

"Antonius."

Plautus smiled and continued, "Oh yes. Antonius. The valiant man who saved the honorable Senator Flavius from assassination. Rumors about you are flying all over Laodicea. You may develop into a mythical legend like your father. Rumor has it that you killed a man at sea, yet there was no report of it made in Ephesus when you arrived.

How can that be? Are you and the senator in the habit of ignoring Roman law?"

Antonius walked to the three praetorian guards standing behind Plautus. He held the small measuring stick he had been using to measure his wool. He pointed it at the soldiers and answered, "It seems that others have ignored Roman law as well recently." The guards stared back at Antonius with surprise, for they recognized his voice.

Plautus ignored him and continued, "I also heard that you kissed the voluptuous Julia in public, right on the dock in Ephesus. It's an outrageous rumor, I admit, one that is even more unbelievable than your murder of the sailor at sea. But I am intrigued by this rumor; there must be some kernel of truth to it. How is it that a wool merchant's son can draw the social notice of a senator and his daughter? What exactly is your relationship with the beautiful Julia? And what else have you been up to lately?"

"Well, lately I have been out with my dog chasing cowards who murder old men in the dark," answered Antonius, still standing beside the praetorian guards, who bristled at his obvious accusation.

"But unfortunately, you did not catch the bandits who did it, did you?" sneered the tall guard.

"No, I didn't. But my dog did. How is your leg?" Antonius smacked the praetorian guard on the back of the leg, right on the wound. He winced with pain. "You kill helpless old men, but run from dogs and boys with sticks, don't you?" accused Antonius.

"I'll cut that smart-mouthed tongue right out of your head!" the guard cried with fury, reaching suddenly for his sword.

Antonius reacted with lightning speed, grabbing the soldier's right hand and blocking it from reaching the sword. He then jerked the guard's arm upward and kicked him on the outside of his knee— just above the dog bite—sending him to the ground. Antonius

grabbed the man's sword and drew it out, then stepped back to face the other two guards, who had also drawn their swords and were advancing slowly.

"Gentlemen! Gentlemen!" intervened Archelaus, stepping between them. "There is no reason to shed blood here in the Wool Merchants' courtyard. I'm certain that this is just a misunderstanding. There are courts and magistrates for accusations and arrests. We are still under Roman law here in Laodicea." Archelaus looked sternly at the guards, then at Antonius.

The guards gradually lowered their swords. Antonius backed up several steps, increasing the distance between himself and the guards, but he did not lower his sword. The tall guard scrambled back to his feet, seething, but Plautus gave him a look, and the guard could do nothing but glare at Antonius.

After a moment Plautus spoke, "Thank you, Archelaus, for pouring water on the fire of tempers here. You men, go back to the horses and wait for me there. Antonius, drop the sword; I came here to honor the Wool Merchants' Guild, not to fight with it."

Reluctantly, the three soldiers walked back across the courtyard to the horses. The tall guard was limping more noticeably, Antonius observed with satisfaction. He tossed the borrowed sword to the ground. Plautus casually picked it up.

"Let's step inside," suggested Archelaus, as if nothing had happened. "What was it, honorable Plautus, that you wanted to see me about?"

They began moving toward the shade of the storehouse. "Antonius," Plautus said, "join us. You might be interested in what I have to say."

The three men entered the storehouse.

"I have an announcement that will bring great joy to all of Laodicea," began the high priest. "We originally thought that it would

not only do we have to plan immediate renovations for the temple, but also we must have feasts, parades, games, and also a large circus in the stadium with gladiators and wild animals. There is much to do. Your help will be greatly appreciated, Archelaus."

Plautus and Archelaus exchanged polite farewells, and then the high priest and his four praetorian guards rode off. Antonius had said nothing. He and Archelaus stood in the courtyard watching the horsemen disappear.

Archelaus muttered an old Phrygian insult: "He is truly the son of the blackest rat ever born at midnight."

Antonius looked at him in surprise. "Well, you were incredibly nice to him—for the son of a black rat."

"What a man does and what a man thinks are often not the same, young man. You need to learn this. I will support that cutthroat and his Imperial Temple because I must if I am to prosper in this town. It doesn't mean that I like him. They all but admitted that they murdered Ephraim, although confronting them like that was foolish of you." The president looked at Antonius and chuckled. "Did your dog really bite that big oaf in the leg?"

"He did indeed, sir," answered Antonius. "But I fear that Caligula's bite may be the extent of any justice that will occur in this city for the time being. At any rate, thank you for being frank with me. I should be going. I'll inform my father of your position, although I doubt it will change anything."

"I have one other piece of advice for you, Antonius," added Archelaus. "Tell your father that I recommend that you sell all of your raw wool and all of your wool cloth immediately, while you can. You may need the money, and before long there may not be any buyers of your wool."

Antonius nodded and left. He trudged up the street toward his home feeling as if a gigantic burden had been placed on his shoulders.

Is the situation completely hopeless? Why doesn't God do something to help us? He tried to order his thoughts, but he found himself utterly unable to focus. *Hopefully,* he thought, *Father will know what to do.*

Across the city, Plautus and the four praetorian guards arrived back at the new Imperial Temple courtyard. Renovations were already under way and the courtyard was a buzz of activity. Several carts loaded with stone and lumber were being unloaded at the base of the columns that lined the right side of the courtyard. Directly across the courtyard, dozens of workmen scurried around the main temple building like ants, raising scaffolding and carrying building materials inside.

A servant ran to Plautus and took the reins of his horse as he dismounted. The four praetorian guards likewise dismounted, and they too gave the reins of their horses to the servant. He led the horses across the courtyard to the left, where new temporary stables had just been added. Plautus led the four guards away from the activity of the courtyard to an isolated area near the wall, well out of the hearing of any workmen.

"You swore that no one saw you kill the rabbi!" he exclaimed. "Now I find that Gallus's son saw you and even recognizes you! And none of you mentioned a dog biting you! And Gallus's dog! You idiots! How incompetent can one be? The famous praetorian guards from Rome! Protectors of Caesar! Can you not kill a simple dog? Furthermore, let me point out for you, since you fail to see anything by yourselves, that we cannot publicly spit in the face of Roman law. You practically admitted you were guilty back there. Right in front of the president of the most influential guild in the city! Morons and idiots! Why did Father send me idiots?" Plautus's eyes flared and his face grew red.

Maximus smarted under the rebuke. "Just turn us loose. And we will kill that loudmouthed boy and his dog. We will do it quietly, and no one will know."

Plautus sneered at him. "Well, you certainly did a fine job of illus-
trating your competence today. That loudmouthed *boy* disarmed you
and threw you to the ground. I cannot afford for you to make this
mess any bigger than you already have. You will do nothing until I
instruct you. Understood?"

Maximus and the other guards nodded.

"Incompetent idiots!" Plautus muttered and marched away shaking his head.

"We'll see who is incompetent," Maximus said to his comrades
when Plautus was out of hearing range. "I swear by all the gods of
Rome that soon I will kill both that son of Gallus and his wretched
dog. No one gets the best of Maximus and lives to tell of it. No one."

Late that evening Gallus and Isaeus, weary from a long day's
traveling, returned home. Cassandra and Caecelia had a light meal
waiting for them in the courtyard, and the two tired men gratefully
sat to eat. Antonius lit an additional lamp, placed it on the table, and
then took a seat near his father. Cassandra and Caecelia likewise sat
to listen. Caecelia's two children were asleep already, and the courtyard was quiet and still. Caligula curled in a ball under the table and
dozed off.

"Well," Gallus began, between bites, "the day was not very successful. The farmer we went to see had been informed by a relative
in the city that he would soon be forbidden to sell his wool to anyone without an Imperial Temple certificate. So, although the farmer
had not heard anything official, he was reluctant to commit his future
wool in any way, especially to someone without a certificate. There are
aspects of this coming persecution that I had not anticipated." He
shook his head. "What about you, Antonius? How was your day? How
are things at the guild storehouse?" He took a bite.

Antonius recounted his conversation with Archelaus and his
encounter with Plautus and the guards. He told of the upcoming

festival for Domitian and of the certificates issued in Ephesus, without which no one could carry out any business. When he finished, everyone sat in silence for a moment.

After a moment Gallus spoke, "We knew this was coming. We just didn't expect it to come quite this fast. May the Lord give us strength and wisdom to endure the days ahead, and, as the Apocalypse says, may we overcome the evil one and the adversity he brings upon us."

ἐν τῇ κυριακῇ ἡμέρᾳ καὶ ἤκουσα ὀπίσω μου φωνὴν μεγάλην ὡς

THE PARTING
OF THE WAYS

σάλπιγγος λεγούσης, ὃ βλέπεις γράψον εἰς βιβλίον καὶ πέμψον

On the following day at midmorning, Antonius and Monica went together to Simeon's house to visit their grieving friend. They chatted as they walked, and Antonius was glad that she was talking to him again, although he sensed that things were still tense. Neither was relaxed, and the conversation was often forced. She frequently stared at him when she thought he wasn't looking, as if trying to peer deep down into his soul. When he caught her at it, she would simply look away quickly. *Does she know about Flavius's proposed marriage between Julia and me? Probably—everybody else in this city seems to know everything there is to know about me. No wonder she is acting odd.* He knew that he needed to talk to her about it, but he could not bring himself to broach the subject, not until he had decided what to do.

She was telling him some silly story about a new water pot that one of the twins had broken yesterday and how upset Vivia had been. Monica was definitely blossoming into a beautiful woman; he acknowledged that once again as he gazed at her. Perhaps not as beautiful as Julia, but nonetheless attractive. He liked listening to her tell stories of her household life. Was it love he felt for her? Or just the deep friendship of a shared childhood? Now she caught him staring. They smiled at each other and she blushed.

At Simeon's house, they called out from the gate. They could tell from the gentle murmur of voices coming from the courtyard that many other people were visiting the family. This was normal; they had expected to find several friends and relatives still at the house. Ephraim had been buried quickly on Sunday, the day after his murder. It was now two days later, but Jewish families tended to maintain a formal mourning period of at least a week.

The gate was opened by Jonathan, the synagogue elder. He greeted them politely but did not invite them in. His daughter Miriam appeared beside him and also greeted them, but she did not invite them in either. It was becoming awkward.

"We would like to see Simeon, if we could," suggested Monica, hoping to break the impasse.

"Simeon is in mourning," Jonathan answered.

"That's why we have come," responded Monica. "To mourn with him."

"We are mourning the death of our rabbi," explained Miriam. "Thus we are mourning here as Jews. Outsiders, *goyyim*, Gentiles like yourselves . . . are . . . well, they are not invited."

"I am hardly an outsider," Antonius said. "I have visited in this house and played in this courtyard all my life. Simeon is my best friend. Don't call me an outsider. Now let us in, please."

Antonius realized that he had raised his voice more than he had intended. The courtyard grew very quiet. Simeon himself suddenly appeared at the gate.

"Greetings, Antonius, Monica," he said in a subdued voice. They returned his greeting and waited again to be invited in, but Simeon just stood, looking at them.

"We've come to visit you, Simeon, to see how you're doing," tried Monica.

"I'm doing fine, as you can see. But it might be better if you didn't come in."

Antonius could feel his heart sinking. "Simeon, my friend, we have come to mourn with you. We loved your father too. We share your grief. You told me three days ago that there were to be no secrets between us. Remember?"

Miriam answered for him. "As you know, things in the synagogue are changing. Christians will no longer be part of the synagogue. Simeon, likewise, will be severing ties with all Christians."

"Simeon, forgive me for intruding in your hour of grief. But to be thrown out of the synagogue is one thing; to be thrown out of the life of my best friend is another."

Simeon stepped through the gate into the street. He turned back to Miriam and said softly, "Excuse us for a moment please, Miriam." He then gently closed the gate. "I'm sorry, Antonius. This has not been easy for me. We have been good friends, and I will always treasure your friendship. But things are changing. It is time for both of us to grow up. I was trying to be both Jewish and Christian. I had assumed that I would be able to live as both, with friends in both groups. Even my father defended my freedom to do this. But I understand now that such notions were too idealistic and not grounded in practical reality. Miriam and Jonathan tried to point this out to me earlier, but I was unable to see it until now. Father was murdered for trying to defend the right of Gentile Christians to stay in the synagogue. But his effort was futile. Neither the Jews nor the Imperial powers want Christians in the synagogue, and the times are becoming extremely dangerous. If Christianity remains identified with Judaism, then the very survival of Judaism may be at stake. Father's murder made it clear to me that I cannot be both Jewish and Christian. The two faiths are going to be ripped from each other, and no one will be able to stay in both groups. I have had to decide where my allegiance lies— with my family and my Jewish heritage, or with my Christian friends. Where does my future lie? With you? Fighting against the Imperial

Cult, expelled from the synagogue? What future is there for me in that? On the other hand, I can return to the synagogue, marry Miriam, and be a Jew. I can have a future within a community and with a family. Antonius, it was not an easy decision. I fear that you feel I have abandoned you or rejected you. But in the end, I must grow up and do what I must. And I must choose family and my Jewish faith."

"Simeon, I saw no Jewish synagogue elders in the street with us as we ran to save your father's life. The elders of this synagogue are in league with the Imperial Temple high priests, the very people who killed your father. They are the harlot of Babylon that John writes about in the Apocalypse, and they are in bed with the Romans! We are your friends and your family, not them."

The gate flew open and Miriam rushed out, bristling with anger. "How dare you speak like this!" she snarled. "Rabbi Ephraim was killed because he was trying to protect you Christians, you who shouldn't have been in the synagogue anyway. If not for you, he would still be alive. *You* are the ones responsible for his death. *You* are the ones who have prostituted the Jewish faith, turning it into paganism by worshiping three gods, thus blaspheming the God of Israel. How dare you try to blame his death on us! *You* killed him! Not us. Now get out! Go away! Leave us alone. Leave Simeon alone. We don't care what the Romans may do to you." She grabbed Simeon by the arm and began leading him back into the courtyard.

Simeon stopped at the gate and turned to look back at Antonius. "I'm sorry, Antonius." Miriam tugged on his arm, and Simeon turned away from his friend and entered the courtyard with her. Jonathan stepped into the doorway behind her to block Antonius's entry into the yard.

Antonius couldn't believe what was happening. Monica turned to go and even pulled lightly at his sleeve, but Antonius stood still, refusing to admit in his heart what his head had just heard.

"Simeon!" he called after him in desperation, but received no answer.

Jonathan the synagogue elder closed the gate firmly and latched it. Antonius stood motionless in front of the closed gate in utter disbelief. Monica waited for him in the middle of the street.

After a few moments, reluctantly and sorrowfully, he turned away, head down. "Not Simeon," he said, wiping his eyes with his sleeve. "I never thought Simeon would do this. How can he turn his back on Christ? And on us?"

Monica took him by the arm and turned him in the right direction.

"It will be all right. Trust in the Lord; we will get through this."

Back at their homes, the two young Christians told their parents of their encounter at Simeon's gate.

"Well," consoled Cassandra, "perhaps all this foolishness will die down in a couple of months and everyone will return to reason. Don't judge him; perhaps he will come to you and ask forgiveness in a few months and you will be friends again. Perhaps this whole thing will blow over like a storm. We just need to stay calm and focus our eyes on the Lord. Can I fix you something to eat?"

Gallus quickly put Antonius to work to get his mind off Simeon. In accordance with Archelaus's advice, Gallus had decided to sell all of their wool while they still could. He sent Antonius to the storehouse again to take a final inventory, a tedious and time-consuming task. There were several different grades of raw wool and of wool cloth; Antonius had to classify the wool and count each by category while inside the stuffy storehouse.

At dusk he returned home. Caligula met him at the gate, and as he entered he heard his father, Gallus, in the courtyard talking with Shabako the Ethiopian. Antonius was not surprised; he had seen Shabako at their house often lately, usually to discuss the Apocalypse or to borrow and read it overnight. Often Gallus had insisted that the Ethiopian stay with them for the evening meal. As Antonius entered the courtyard, he heard the two former soldiers laughing and sharing humorous memories of the mistakes and misconceptions of new army recruits. They stopped their reminiscing to greet Antonius, inviting him to sit with them and talk.

"When will Creon finish making his copies of the scroll?" the elder asked Gallus as Antonius took a seat near him. Caligula lay down at Antonius's feet.

"As a matter of fact," Gallus answered, "he completed the third and final copy today. Take that copy with you tonight and keep it permanently as the Laodicean church's copy. Now you won't have to come here every night to borrow one—although we have enjoyed your visits to our house."

"I will miss my visits here as well. And thank you, Gallus, for permitting me to borrow the scroll. We must certainly thank Flavius as well for paying for these copies. I know it must have been quite expensive. Creon does not work cheaply and the papyrus he has used is of the finest quality."

Antonius, too, had spent a considerable amount of time in the evenings reading and contemplating the Apocalypse. Many, many things in the book confused him. His father was not much help in elucidating the meaning for him. Gallus understood the broad strokes of meaning in the Apocalypse—stand firm and don't compromise with the Imperial Cult—but he did not understand, nor did he care about, the many symbols and subtleties of the book. Antonius, on the other hand, was fascinated by all of it, and he often pondered the mysterious things in the book.

"Shabako?" he ventured.

"Yes, Antonius."

"How do you interpret all of the terrible judgments in the Apocalypse? There are seven seals and seven trumpets and seven bowls—

all referring to severe judgments by God upon the earth. These judgments are very frightening. Are these things in the far future or are
they coming soon? Are they symbolic? Or literal?"

"It is interesting that you should ask about the judgments, Antonius, for this is the very topic that I wanted to read and study tonight.
Pastor Epaphras and I have been arguing, in friendship of course,
over the meaning of the judgments. For tomorrow's discussion, we
have decided to focus our attention on the seven seal judgments. We
each want to reread that section of the scroll and then discuss—and
argue about—it some more. My own inclination at the moment—
and Epaphras disagrees with me—is to believe that some of these
judgments have already taken place."

"Already taken place? How can that be?"

"Well, first of all, remember that the prophets in the Jewish Scriptures, men like Jeremiah, often blended together past, present, and
future events. Thus one sentence may refer to the future, the next to
the past, and the next to the present. Who knows? John may be doing
the same thing. This is what complicates our understanding."

Antonius nodded. "Go on."

"I think that there is a good possibility that some of the seal
judgments describe the Roman invasion of Palestine and the destruction of Jerusalem twenty-five years ago."

"Why do you think so?"

"First of all, the language that John uses is similar to that used
by Jesus in the gospel according to Matthew and in the gospel
according to Mark when Jesus talks of the coming judgment. When
Jesus gives his speech on the Mount of Olives, he speaks of coming
judgment and of the destruction of the Jewish temple in Jerusalem."
Shabako paused and glanced at Gallus.

Antonius did not remember much about the speech on the
Mount of Olives, but he nodded in thoughtful agreement. "Is there
more?"

"You may not know this, Antonius," Shabako said, again glancing at Gallus, "but I was there at the siege and destruction—or should I say massacre—of Jerusalem."

"I didn't know that. I thought that you spent your career fighting the Parthians."

"Most of my many years in the Roman army were spent on the Parthian frontier, that is true. However, when I was a youngster like yourself, and a raw recruit in the Egyptian Auxiliary Archers unit, we were assigned to Syria, to the army of Titus. The Jews in Palestine had just revolted against Rome. I was part of the army that put the revolt down."

Shabako hesitated, again looking at Gallus.

"Tell him," said Gallus. "Tell him the whole truth."

"Rome could not tolerate a rebellion in a place like Palestine, right in the heart of the Empire. We descended on the Jews with a vengeance. By our own estimates, which are probably not exaggerated, we killed—massacred really—over a million Jews. I have many Jewish friends in this city, so I rarely speak of this.

"Anyway, the siege of Jerusalem and the horrific events that took place right after its fall always come to my mind as I read through the seal judgments in the Apocalypse. The entire campaign was a nightmare for me, even though we were victorious. Our siege produced famine and starvation in Jerusalem; many died before we even entered the city. When we did finally breech the walls and pour into the city, we slaughtered hundreds of thousands of men, women, and children—everyone. I also had friends in the army who said that they saw strange cosmic events in the sky—indeed, several said they saw a new constellation of stars resembling a sword standing over Jerusalem just before it fell. There was also an earthquake just before the end; we took it as an omen of victory. I think that the defenders of the city likewise saw it as an omen—of their doom. It was bizarre

and terrible, and I have tried to forget it, but now as I read the Apocalypse, it all comes back. The similarities are great."

Shabako paused for a moment. Antonius tried to visualize the
siege and the terrible slaughter. The night was very still. Antonius
could smell the lingering wood smoke from his mother's cooking fire.
He could hear the sounds of insects in the trees. The faint voices of
people talking as they passed by on the street beyond their courtyard
fence floated into the courtyard in an indistinguishable muffled mur-
muring. In the distance, a dog barked, barely audible to Antonius's
ears. Caligula rose, sniffed the air, and then returned to lie down at
Antonius's feet.

"There were some Christians then," Shabako continued, "and
there are some now, who think that the terrible destruction of
Jerusalem came upon the Jews because they rejected and killed Jesus
their Messiah. In the Jewish Scriptures, in the book of the prophet
Jeremiah, it was due to Israel's unbelief in the prophet's word and to
their rebellion against God that the ancient Babylonians destroyed
Jerusalem. Some believe that the Roman destruction was similar.
Even the Jewish historian Josephus—although I would call him a
traitorous scoundrel—wrote that our invasion was really God's
judgment on Jerusalem."

"And the other judgments? The bowls? The trumpets? Are they
on the Jews as well?"

"I don't know. But I suspect that the worst of the divine judgments are reserved for Rome herself: 'the great whore who drinks
the blood of the Christian martyrs,' as the Apocalypse says. Perhaps,
as Epaphras argues, the judgments will fall on all those who persecute the Lord's church at some time in the future. But as I read this
book here and now, having seen the fall of Jerusalem, and now seeing the arrival of the Domitian Imperial Cult and hearing the threats
and ominous warnings, I see *us* in this book. And, of course, for us

the meaning is clear. John is calling on us to stand firm—no matter what."

"But in the scroll the Christians win in the end, don't we?" asked Antonius hopefully.

"God and his church ultimately triumph and God establishes his reign. This is true. But the victory only comes through the death of many, many martyrs, and at the moment, *we* look to be the most likely candidates."

He and Gallus exchanged glances.

"But, Shabako," Antonius said, "don't you think that most of the Imperial Temple persecution coming to Laodicea will be economic? Don't you think that it will be limited to expelling Christians from the guilds and forcing them to pay higher tariffs . . . things like that?"

"The pressure will certainly start out as economic, and I hope it stays that way. But I suspect that it will not stop there. Keep in mind that Rabbi Ephraim has already been murdered. John wrote this scroll to encourage us to stay strong in spite of the worst persecution. He seems to expect a persecution that involves martyrdom. He wants the Christians in the province of Asia—and throughout the Empire and even beyond the frontier—to stay faithful even though many of us are killed. We must be prepared for this."

Cassandra entered the courtyard just in time to overhear the final, ominous words of Shabako. Her voice was nearly a whisper: "Let us hope and pray that it will not come to that."

chapter thirteen

LUKEWARM
LAODICEA

Late Friday afternoon, Gallus and Antonius walked home after a day spent at the guild storehouse. The streets were crowded with people and carts, the large ones pulled by oxen and the smaller ones by donkeys. Father and son walked briskly in spite of the crowd, weaving in and out, until finally they turned on to the street that led to their house. When they arrived, Gallus opened the gate and stood aside for Antonius to enter. Antonius hesitated, looking across the street toward Monica's house just in time to see Monica emerge from the gate with her market bag in her hand, apparently on her way to the agora.

"Hello, Monica," Antonius called with a warm smile.

"Hello, Antonius," she said brightly, between the many people passing by on the street. "And hello, Gallus," she added politely. He returned her greeting, then entered quickly through the gate, leaving the couple together in the street. Antonius walked closer to Monica, who was still standing next to the gate of her house.

"He has some good news for my mother," Antonius explained. "He seems anxious to share it with her."

"And what news is that?" Monica asked, smiling, taking a step closer.

"We were able to sell our remaining wool for a good price. A Greek friend of ours from Pontus named Liollio, a fellow member of the guild, bought it for perhaps not as much as we would have received in Athens, but given the unsettled circumstances, the price looked good to us."

"I suppose that it is wise—to sell your wool now . . . while you can."

"What about your father? Has he sold his wool?" Antonius asked. "Liollio would probably buy his wool as well."

Monica looked around nervously and then stepped even closer. "Oh, Antonius. I am worried about my father. He is not even trying to sell his wool. He seems to be hoping that he can compromise ever so slightly and thus escape any coming pressure from the Imperial Cult. He expects to stay in the guild. Mother disagrees and they have argued over it. It's terrible."

She was very close to him now and she stared up into his eyes without looking away. He was again reminded how pretty she had become. He had a strong urge to put his arms around her, but he knew that would be improper out here in public.

"Where are you going?" he asked, changing the subject.

"To the agora to buy a few things for the evening meal. I need to hurry. Many of the vendors will be closing their stalls soon."

"Can I walk you to the end of the street?"

"I would be delighted." She smiled and her eyes sparkled. They turned and walked slowly down the street together toward the agora. The street was still crowded and they were frequently jostled by busy people. The couple walked close together, with their shoulders touching occasionally. Antonius was enjoying the moment.

"What will your father do with the money from the wool? If you can't invest in more wool, what good does the money do you?"

Antonius had always been impressed with Monica's quick grasp of household money matters. He knew of other girls who seemed so frivolous about their father's business affairs, even oblivious to critical issues of the family's livelihood. Monica, on the other hand, had always seemed to be able to discuss important aspects of the family business.

"Father will keep a small amount hidden at the house. But the majority of the money he will send with Isaeus to Nathan the banker in Ephesus. In fact, Isaeus will probably leave tomorrow. Father also wants him to find out what is happening to the Christians in Ephesus and he wants him to take one of the copies of the Apocalypse to the church at Ephesus, so that they can study it . . . and for safekeeping, too."

"Do you think the scrolls are in danger?"

"Sooner or later, Caius or Sulla will find out that John has written another scroll, one openly critical of Rome and that encourages all Christians to stand against the Imperial Cult—indeed, to stand against Rome itself. Yes, there is a good chance they will try to destroy it."

"Will the scroll be safer in Ephesus?"

"I don't know that Ephesus is any safer for Christians than Laodicea these days. But just spreading the three copies of the scroll around makes it harder for Caius or anyone else to confiscate all of them. And once we get a copy to Ephesus, they can make additional copies as well. When several copies have been scattered across the province of Asia, it's bound to continue to spread."

When they reached the end of the street, Antonius reluctantly said goodbye. Monica walked on toward the agora. Antonius stood watching her walk away. Finally he lost her among the many people in the crowded street and turned back toward his house.

The next day was the Sabbath, and for the first time in years no one from the house of Gallus or from the house of Juba attended the synagogue. Instead, near midday, Juba and his family came to Gallus's house for the noon meal and a short time of prayer together.

After the prayer, the house and the courtyard became the center of considerable activity. Cassandra, Vivia, and Monica chatted as they cleared away the meal, while Gallus and Caecelia helped Isaeus prepare for his trip to Ephesus. Juba sat in the shade of a tree, trying to doze. Antonius was helping Monica's twin brothers, Marcellus and Mardonius, try to teach Caligula a new trick, but Isaeus's two smaller children were also running around the courtyard, chasing each other and shouting, distracting the dog and keeping Juba from actually sleeping.

Suddenly Caligula barked and ran to the gate. A voice from the street cried out, "Hail, house of Gallus. Is Isaeus present?" Juba looked up. Cassandra went into the house to get Isaeus while Antonius opened the gate. In stepped Nicias, a distant cousin of Isaeus, servant to one of the Jewish elders in the synagogue. He was slightly older than Antonius, married and with several children. Antonius did not know him well.

"Greetings, Antonius!"

"Greetings, Nicias!"

"Ah, Nicias!" Isaeus called out as he rushed across the courtyard to greet his cousin. They embraced warmly.

"Come in. Sit down. Let us get you something to eat and drink. What brings you here?"

"I can't stay but a moment." He greeted Gallus and Juba and their families. He hugged the two children of Isaeus and tickled them briefly as they laughed and squirmed. "I am on my way home after the Sabbath service at the synagogue. I decided to take a slightly longer route home so that I could stop and tell you what happened at the synagogue this morning. I thought you might want to know."

By now everyone else had gathered around Nicias.

"Thank you for coming," Isaeus said. "Please tell us what happened."

"It was a very strange Sabbath service," Nicias began. "For the first time in years, no non-Jews or God-fearers attended, except for a few Gentile servants like myself, seated in the back among rows of empty benches. There was also a stranger sitting in the back with us. Demosthenes, the brassmaker's servant, was sitting with me, and he recognized the man as one of the praetorian guards from the Imperial Temple. He was dressed in a plain toga rather than his soldier's uniform, and he sat quietly at the back, simply observing. The Sabbath day service was carried out normally, but at the end of the service today, five elders stood and each in turn read the Eighteen Benedictions.

"I think that several of the synagogue members are angry at the turn of events, especially concerning the expulsion of you Christians, many of whom are their friends. They understand that since you no longer have the protection of membership in the synagogue, you will be forced to pledge allegiance to Domitian or face persecution. Most of the members, however, apparently think it to be the prudent course of action. The elder Jonathan and his daughter Miriam, for example, who know that I am related to you, smiled a cunning and revengeful smile at me as they walked by scanning the empty rows at the back of the synagogue."

Nicias paused for a moment and looked around at the anxious faces that had gathered around him. He then continued, "I think that some of the Jewish elders in the synagogue are in league with the Imperial Cult to eliminate Christianity completely from Laodicea. Gallus, Isaeus, I fear for your safety."

Isaeus nodded. "Thank you, Nicias, for your concern and for coming to give us this news."

"And now, I must be off. They will be expecting me back at the house soon. Take care, Isaeus. Farewell, Gallus, Juba, Antonius. Take care." He embraced Isaeus again and then quickly disappeared through the gate.

Gallus put his hand on Isaeus's shoulder. "The sooner you leave for Ephesus the better. Let's finish packing and get you on the road."

Juba and his family said farewell to Isaeus and wished him well on his trip. Thanking Gallus and Cassandra for the meal, they departed for their house. Monica gave Antonius a warm smile just before she slipped through the gate to join her parents.

Soon Isaeus was ready to go. He carried a large traveler's bag that contained the copy of the Apocalypse. The money from the sale of the wool he carried in a belt inside his tunic next to his body. He also carried some miscellaneous papyri letters, several dealing with business between Gallus and Nathan the banker, and one from the church elders in Laodicea introducing him to the church at Ephesus.

Isaeus kissed his wife and children goodbye and had just opened the gate, when a well-dressed servant approached the gate from the street and introduced himself.

"Greetings, sir," he called out, bowing formally. "I have a message for the young man Antonius."

Isaeus looked back at Antonius, who stepped around him to face the messenger.

"I'm Antonius."

"It is my privilege to announce, good sir," the servant proclaimed dramatically, "that the presence of Antonius Marius Amulius is requested tonight for the evening meal at the villa of Flavius Lucius Domitilla, Roman Senator."

The servant then stood still, awaiting an answer. Antonius looked back at his parents, unsure of what to do. He had just concluded that the right choice for him would be to marry Monica—after all, he really did love her—and he feared that an evening with Julia might weaken his resolve. Yet it would be considered a serious insult to refuse such an invitation. That would jeopardize the friendship between the household of Flavius and the household of Gallus. He looked at his father for help.

Gallus shrugged and said, "I suppose that you are obligated to go."

"I . . . ah . . . I accept," Antonius said.

"Very good!" the servant announced. "I will inform the senator. We will send a horse for you at dusk." With that he wheeled around and quickly marched away.

Antonius spent an anxious afternoon wondering what the evening would bring. His mother, Cassandra, gave him worried looks as she helped him to get ready. At last the sun began to disappear behind the mountains. The servant returned, this time with an extra horse. Antonius wore his best clothes. However, even though his mother assured him that he looked quite handsome, he still did not feel properly dressed for the evening. He stepped out into the street quietly and mounted the extra horse—a beautiful white Arabian mare—just as the gate to Juba's house opened. He turned to see Monica standing motionless at the gate, just watching him. The young man and the messenger rode by slowly, not saying a word. Antonius wanted to speak to her, to say something, but he could not think of anything appropriate to say. He and Monica just stared helplessly at each other as he rode by in silence.

The evening at Flavius's villa went much as he had expected . . . and feared. Flavius was a magnanimous host, warm and friendly. Sabina was distant, nearly hostile. Julia, on the other hand, was even more beautiful and charming than he remembered. She teased and laughed and told humorous stories. Her eyes sparkled and her gorgeous smile melted his heart. Her gown was stunning. She flirted with him incessantly. Against his will, he found himself contemplating how wonderful life would be if he were married to such a delightful creature.

The food was outstanding as well. After the meal, Julia took him outside for a walk in their spectacular garden. The entire villa was more lavish than he had expected, and much more extravagant than Severus's estate in Ephesus. Julia walked so close to him that their shoulders touched. He could smell her wonderful perfume. He was struggling with an incredibly strong urge—one that almost overpowered him—to take her in his arms and kiss her. As they reached the middle of the beautiful lamp-lit garden, she stopped and smiled up at him. With a coy look, she said, "Antonius, you know that if you marry me, all of this will be ours. We will live here and enjoy this garden. We can come walking here together every night if we want to."

She stood up on her tiptoes and kissed him softly on the mouth. Then she backed away, smiled, and said, "That's just something for you to remember as you think about me and try to make your decision."

"Julia," he said, when he finally got his breath back and the landscape quit rotating, "don't you ever worry about the events transpiring around us? The whole world is turning upside down. A serious persecution is about to fall on all Christians in the province of Asia. All of us will be affected by this—your father, my father, me, even you. It is difficult to make a decision about marriage when I don't even know what will happen next week. My family may have to flee the province. Yours, too. As pleasant as your vision of our future is, it is unlikely that we will be walking peacefully together in *this* garden."

"You sound just like my father," Julia said, pouting a little to show her displeasure at the change in mood. "You and Father worry too much. Everything will be all right. You'll see. It always works out. Father takes care of everything and it always works out all right. He was worried when we lived in Rome and he thought we would all be killed—but here we are! Safe in Laodicea! Alone in the garden! Just you and me." She tilted her head to one side mischievously, flashing that beautiful smile that destroyed all his attempts at rational thought.

"Julia," Antonius began again, now struggling with himself to stay on the subject. "This is important. The Imperial Temple praetorian guards will soon try to force us to swear allegiance to Domitian as lord. We will all be forced to make some critical decisions about our faith . . . about who we are. Don't you ever think about this?"

"No," she said. "I don't. I try not to think about unpleasant things. And this Domitian thing seems ridiculous to me. Mother thinks so, too. She thinks that Father should just acknowledge Domitian publicly like everyone else in the Empire. To call him 'lord' or 'god' when you know in your heart that he is not . . . well, it just does not seem to me to be a gigantic sin. Everyone is making this into a huge problem and I don't see that it has to be. And Mother and Father have had some very unpleasant arguments about it. I do hate to see them argue.

"We won't argue about things when we're married, will we, Antonius?" she asked sweetly, replacing the frown with her best smile again. She then leaned over to smell one of the white flowers that lined the path. "We'll be happy together here, won't we? We won't ever fight or argue, will we? I won't if you won't. I promise. We'll just be happy together forever."

Antonius was rescued by Flavius and Sabina, who now also strolled out into the garden and called to the younger couple.

"This is a beautiful garden, sir," Antonius stated when they drew near.

"Yes, it is," Flavius said. "I just hope that we all get to enjoy it in the future."

After some small talk with Flavius and Sabina, Antonius paid his respects and returned home, accompanied by the same servant. Neither of them talked on the way. Antonius's head was spinning. He still told himself that he should marry Monica, but . . . Julia was *so* gorgeous. She took his breath away. Only an idiot would turn down a life with her in that villa.

His parents met him at the gate.

"Do you want to talk?" his father asked.

"Not now."

"Tomorrow, then?"

"Tomorrow would be better."

As he turned to walk away, his mother stopped him and hugged him. Then she pulled away, frowned, and said, "Antonius Marius Amulius!"

"Yes, Mother?"

"You smell of perfume."

"Good night, Mother." He walked into the courtyard, leaving them by the gate.

He kept to himself for most of the next day. Dark clouds rolled in, threatening rain. When late afternoon arrived, the two families met as usual for their walk to the Christian worship service. Gallus and Juba discussed the weather, concluding that the rain might hold off until later in the evening. Monica ignored Antonius and walked with her brothers. At the meeting hall she sat with her family, never even glancing at him.

When the senator's family entered the building, however, Antonius noticed that Monica stared at Julia. Julia ignored her and smiled sweetly at Antonius. As Julia glided down the aisle to her seat beside Flavius the Roman beauty drew admiring glances from just about every man in the building. Everyone seemed to be watching her. After being seated she turned around to smile again at Antonius. He looked at Monica, who quickly looked away. She was biting her lip and he thought she seemed to be fighting back tears.

The mood at the Christian worship service was somber. They tried to sing some uplifting songs, but the task was formidable. After a short time of emotionless singing, Pastor Epaphras stood up to speak.

"As you know by now, the apostle John addressed his Apocalypse to the seven churches of Asia. We, the Laodicean church, are the last one addressed. When this scroll first arrived here in our city, I read to you the apostle's words to us, the Laodicean church. Since then, the events predicted in the Apocalypse have been unfolding right before our eyes. Today, as we each ponder the coming difficult decisions to be made, let me once again remind you of what John says specifically about us here in Laodicea."

He unrolled the scroll containing the Apocalypse and began reading in a loud voice. "'To the angel of the church at Laodicea write: These are the words of the Amen, the faithful and true witness, the ruler of God's creation. I know your deeds, that you are neither cold nor hot. I wish you were one or the other! So, because you are luke-warm—neither hot nor cold—I am about to spit you out of my mouth! . . . I counsel you to buy from me gold refined in the fire . . . Those whom I love I rebuke and discipline. So be earnest and repent. Here I am! I stand at the door and knock . . . .'"

Epaphras paused for a moment, staring intently at all those in the audience.

"Do you realize, brothers and sisters, how serious is this indict-ment against us? The Lord accuses us of being lukewarm, that is, of compromising with Rome. We are proud of our wealth here in Laodicea, not realizing that true wealth comes only from God, and only from our obedience to him. To continue to have the worldly wealth we are accustomed to having, we must sell ourselves to Cae-sar! Become his puppets! Compromise! But if we yield to Caesar we will force Christ away. And yet our Lord says here that he stands outside and calls us to repent, open our doors, and let him in to fellowship with us.

"Do you not realize that we are in danger, at this very hour, of being expelled, not from the lowly synagogue built by men, but from the very kingdom of Christ? We must repent of our lukewarmness and pledge total faithfulness to Jesus alone as Christ, and never, never to Caesar."

At that moment the doors of the meeting hall flew open and ten praetorian guards marched in. Antonius could see another twenty or so in the courtyard outside. The ten who entered the hall marched to the front and then spun around to face the audience. Antonius recognized the tall one named Maximus; the soldier still limped slightly.

Antonius fidgeted in his seat. He felt his blood starting to boil. His father leaned over and quietly advised, "Be calm. Don't do anything rash."

Another member of the praetorian guard then walked casually into the building. He wore a centurion's rank and his shiny helmet and breastplate glistened brightly in the candlelight.

Juba leaned over and whispered to Gallus, "These pretty uniforms are much more appropriate in the Imperial Court than on the battlefield. I wonder if these pretty boys can really fight, too, or if they just excel at looking impressive."

The centurion of the praetorian guard walked to the front of the meeting hall without comment and snatched the Apocalypse from the hands of Pastor Epaphras. The congregation gasped. The centurion then rolled it up and placed it under his arm.

He addressed the audience in a loud voice: "This scroll contains seditious material against Caesar; it has been confiscated by the Imperial Temple and it will be burned immediately in the courtyard. All copies of this scroll are likewise declared to be illegal and seditious. All citizens of Laodicea are required to report the location of all existing copies of this scroll or face appropriate punishment."

"He is the leader of the assassins, the man on the horse that spoke to you, isn't he?" whispered Gallus to Antonius.

"Yes, he is," answered Antonius, still fidgeting in his seat.

Juba had apparently come to the same conclusion, and he looked over at Gallus for confirmation. Gallus nodded.

"Furthermore," continued the centurion, "until you have written approval from the Imperial Temple to engage in renting meeting halls in this city, you are forbidden to rent any facility of any type for any purpose. Thus, any gathering for religious purposes without the written authorization of the Imperial Temple is forbidden."

He then marched out of the meeting hall, followed by the other praetorian guards. The Christians timidly crowded around the door and looked out. The other soldiers in the detail had built a small fire in the corner of the courtyard. The centurion marched dramatically to the fire and with great ceremony threw the Apocalypse into the flames. At the same instant, a blinding streak of lightning flashed across the sky, followed immediately by a deafening roar of thunder. All of the praetorian guards jumped and looked up uneasily. Their gaze into the heavens was met by an instant downpour of rain, which immediately soaked them—and the fire. The rain fell by the bucketful until the fire was completely out, leaving the scroll half-burned in the ashes. Then it stopped as abruptly as it had begun. The centurion drew out his sword and poked at the charred scroll a few times, convincing himself that the document was adequately destroyed. He then barked out an angry order and the praetorian guards formed up in ranks and marched out of the courtyard.

As the Roman soldiers left the courtyard, the Christians heard the sound of a dog barking furiously out in the street, accompanied by the loud cursing of several of the praetorian guards.

"That sounds like Caligula," blurted out Mardonius.

"Go get him, Caligula!" Marcellus shouted out the window before Vivia could restrain him. "Bite his whole leg off this time!"

"How did Caligula get out?" Cassandra asked Gallus with embarrassment as they exited the building. Her husband shrugged.

As the Christians emerged from the meeting hall, Gallus and Juba looked at each other and could not help but smile, even though the situation was deadly serious. Caligula could still be heard several streets away, nipping at the heels of the haughty praetorian guards and barking incessantly at them, yet apparently always staying quick enough to dodge the sword of any enraged guard who lost his patience with the annoying dog.

Antonius stood at the gate and looked down the street. "Watch yourself, Caligula," he said softly to his dog.

chapter fourteen

Καὶ ἐπέστρεψα βλέπειν τὴν φωνὴν ἥτις ἐλάλει μετ' ἐμοῦ,

THE GUILD

καὶ ἐπιστρέψας εἶδον ἑπτὰ λυχνίας χρυσᾶς καὶ ἐν μέσῳ

At midmorning the next day, Gallus and Antonius left their house to go to the guild meeting hall. The sky was overcast, and a stiff breeze greeted them in the street.

"We may get rain," Gallus said as he led the way into the busy street.

Antonius nodded, glancing toward the gate to Monica's house. "Isn't Juba going with us?" he asked, pausing in the street.

"No. He had some business to attend to before the meeting. He will join us at the meeting hall." Gallus walked away briskly, and his son hurried to catch up, wondering if there was any other significance to Juba's absence.

"Do you think the guild will force the issue of supporting the Imperial Temple and swearing allegiance to Domitian today?" Antonius asked.

"That is the rumor. Things are moving very quickly."

"What will Juba do? How will he vote?"

"That's his decision, not ours. Vivia is worried. Cassandra had a long talk with her yesterday."

"Is that what you and Mother were discussing late last night?"

"Yes. Did we keep you awake? We thought you were asleep."

"No, I had trouble getting to sleep."

"I don't think any of us are sleeping well these days."

"And Mother was unusually edgy this morning. She snapped at me during breakfast and was sharp with Caecelia. That is not like her."

"I think that she is also worried about our decision to keep the Apocalypse at our house."

Antonius nodded, remembering the discussion they'd had yesterday after the service with Flavius regarding the scroll. The senator was concerned that Creon might inform the guard about the scroll and the copies he had made. Gallus felt sure that Creon, as a respected scribe, would keep his client's business private. Antonius had his doubts. Even if Creon kept silent, there were lots of other ways that the knowledge of what he had copied could leak out to the Imperial Temple. Servants talked. Wives talked.

Despite Antonius's reservations, they decided to keep the original and the extra copy hidden at Gallus's for a few more days. After Isaeus returned from Ephesus they would meet again and reevaluate. They all agreed that they needed to send the copy to the province of Galatia, probably to the city of Iconium. Flavius offered money and the use of a horse for the trip. Also, they agreed that another copy should be made, but at the moment, hiring a professional scribe like Creon would be difficult.

Antonius and his father walked in silence for the rest of the trip, each man deep in his own thoughts. Antonius thought of Monica and her father, Juba. He knew that both Monica and her mother had been trying to persuade Juba to reject the compromise with the Imperial Temple. Surely the former legionnaire would stand with his centurion! They had been through so much together.

Soon Antonius and his father reached the guild meeting hall. They entered and headed for their usual seats. The merchants inside the hall were conversing with each other nervously. Word had traveled quickly, and most of the members knew what would happen today if Gallus refused to support the new Imperial Temple. Gallus's friends addressed him politely. Several of them had sorrowful looks in their eyes; they wanted to say something in consolation or to try to explain their situation, but instead all of them just greeted him with the standard afternoon greeting.

After a few minutes Juba entered the meeting hall and silently took his seat beside Gallus.

Simeon was there, too. He and his father, Ephraim, had always sat next to Gallus and Antonius at guild meetings. Now he sat across the hall next to two other Jewish merchants.

Archelaus, the guild president, called the meeting to order. "Members of the Laodicean Wool Merchants' Guild, greetings! As you know, the religious and political situation in the province of Asia has been changing. To maintain our preeminent role in the province as the merchants of Laodicean wool, we must react and adjust to the changing situation."

Antonius scratched his ear nervously and shifted his weight on the wooden bench. He stared down at his feet. Gallus and Juba sat completely still, looking ahead at the president without emotion.

"Caesar Domitian has commissioned a new Imperial Temple for Laodicea. This is a great honor for our fair city. It entitles us to numerous economic advantages that cities in Asia without a temple do not have, and it casts us in a favorable light not only with Caesar but also with the proconsul and the Imperial high priest in Ephesus.

"In celebration of this great event, and to honor the birthday of our emperor, a festival will be held here in Laodicea one week from today. To show our total support for this new Imperial Temple, I, the president of the guild, pledged a considerable sum of money from the guild to help finance this festival; indeed, I have already transferred a sizable amount of money to the Imperial Treasury. This was guild money, under my control. The secretary has an accounting of all expenditures.

"However, this is only a fraction of the support expected from the guild. It is important to the Imperial Temple that each guild member support the Imperial Cult wholeheartedly, with all members participating. This backing involves not only financial donations to support the temple operations and festivals but also public proclamations affirming the deity of Caesar Domitian. I have promised the high priest that all guild members would give this support or face expulsion from the guild. Such action, however, requires a guild vote. What is your pleasure?"

For the next several minutes the guild members discussed the issue. Questions were raised from the floor to which Archelaus provided rational, logical answers. One member asked what the specific consequences would be for one who was expelled from the guild.

"Because of our support for Domitian's Temple," explained Archelaus, "each guild member will receive a certificate from the Imperial Temple. This certificate will allow each one who holds it to trade in wool throughout the Empire with special tariff reduction status. Without a certificate, trading will be nearly impossible. For example, no merchant without a certificate will be allowed to ship his merchandise through the harbor of Ephesus."

The members of the guild murmured to each other. This type of tight harbor control in Ephesus was unheard of. The Ephesian port had always been open to all who paid the standard harbor fee. All of them realized that without this certificate, their livelihood as wool merchants would come to an end.

"Furthermore, a merchant without the certificate will pay triple tariffs at the gates of all cities in the province of Asia." Again the members shook their heads in amazement.

Very little discussion followed. Gallus and Juba were silent. A few of Gallus's friends tried to raise some mild objections about letting the Imperial Temple manipulate and dictate policy to the city's most powerful guild. However, to most of the members the issue was clear, and so was their logical course of action. The vote was nearly unanimous. Only Gallus and Juba voted against Archelaus's suggested proposal. Antonius, who did not yet have full membership status, did not vote.

"So," continued the guild president as he unrolled a papyrus scroll, "in light of our vote, each guild member will be required to sign this document." He held the scroll up for them to see. "The scroll says, 'I, the undersigned, a member of the Laodicean Wool Merchants' Guild in good standing, do hereby pledge my total support to Caesar Domitian, proclaiming him to be both our lord and god, protector of the Roman Empire, and giver of all blessings and prosperity. To further the honoring and worshiping of our lord Domitian, I pledge to support, protect, and revere the Imperial Temple of Laodicea.'"

Archelaus paused for a moment to allow his words to sink in, then continued. "Exempt from signing this pledge are the Jewish members of our guild. I have a certificate from the elders of the synagogue listing all Jews in our guild who are members of the synagogue and thus exempt from signing this document." He unrolled a small scroll and read out the names: "Ruben, Phinehas, and our newest full member, Simeon.

"The rest of you are required to come forward and sign this pledge. Failure to sign the pledge will result in automatic expulsion from the guild. I know that old Aurelius is sick in bed. We will take the scroll to his house after the meeting for him to sign."

Silently the members of the guild each rose, walked to the front, and signed the document. Few of them could look at Gallus. After a few moments of internal struggle, Juba also rose to go forward.

"Juba!" exclaimed Antonius, grabbing the Berber's sleeve. "What are you doing? You can't sign that scroll. You will receive the mark of the beast."

"It's for the best, Antonius," he answered solemnly, gently pulling his sleeve loose. Juba walked to the front and waited in line for his turn. Antonius looked at his father, still puzzled over Juba's decision. He felt betrayed and confused. *Why doesn't Father do something, talk some sense into him? What is Monica going to think?*

Gallus stood and put his hand on Antonius's shoulder. "Let's go home, son."

The two of them rose and walked out the back of the meeting hall, both realizing that they probably would never be allowed to come back.

On the way home, Gallus said, "Antonius, Juba is in a different situation than we are. He has not only Vivia but also Monica and the twins to worry about. Furthermore, I do not think that Juba ever really grasped the meaning of the Apocalypse. He truly believes that he can compromise with Caesar and still be faithful to Christ."

Antonius just shook his head. First Simeon, now Juba. It made him doubt his own determination.

As they turned onto their street, Antonius saw Monica in front of her gate, apparently waiting for the men to come home. When she saw Gallus and Antonius, she ran down the street to meet them.

"What happened?" she asked, trying to catch her breath. "And where is Father?"

Gallus and Antonius looked at each other. Apparently, Monica did not know of Juba's final decision. Gallus nodded at Antonius.

"Monica," Antonius said, "your father stayed behind to sign the pledge in support of the new Domitian temple. We left."

"Father signed the pledge?" she exclaimed. "No! It's not possible. Earlier I was afraid he might, but I thought that Mother had convinced him to stand firm. Why did he do it? Doesn't he know what it means?" Her lower lip quivered. Antonius stepped forward to put his arm around her, but she pushed him away.

"Are there no men in my life I can trust anymore?" she asked, sobbing. Then she turned, ran back down the street, and disappeared into her house.

Antonius watched her run away. He hurt for her, knowing how disappointed she was in her father. He wondered what this would do to their own relationship. *Would Juba now want Monica to marry the son of a guild member in good standing?* Antonius knew several young men in the guild who thought highly of Monica and would be interested in such a marriage. What should he do? Gallus let out a weary sigh, and the two men continued down the street toward their house.

"Antonius," his father said as they entered the gate, "I think it is time for you to visit Galatia for us. I want you to travel to Pisidian Antioch and perhaps even Iconium. Survey the situation. Find out if we can buy wool there. Can we export wool through the ports in Pamphylia? Can we trade with Cappadocia or Pontus? What about Syria? In addition, you can carry a copy of the Apocalypse to the Galatian churches. It might be safer there, and no doubt, some of them will need it as well in the coming days."

"But, Father, don't you think you should be the one to make this trip? I don't know how to find out this information. And I am too young for anyone there to take seriously. You should go—or we could go together."

"No," said Gallus. "It has to be you. I must stay here in Laodicea for the next few weeks, especially through the festival. Many of our fellow Christians will be faced with the same terrible decision we had to make today. They need me here to encourage them—someone to be strong when many are falling away. Your mother and I, along with Pastor Epaphras and Elder Shabako, will soon start visiting each Christian family and encouraging them. I must stay here. You will be the one to go."

"When do I leave?" Antonius asked.

"Tomorrow. At dawn."

"What about Monica?"

"She will be here when you get back," replied Gallus.

τῶν λυχνιῶν ὅμοιον υἱὸν ἀνθρώπου ἐνδεδυμένον ποδήρη

LOOKING EAST

καὶ περιεζωσμένον πρὸς τοῖς μαστοῖς ζώνην χρυσᾶν.

Antonius rose before dawn. He ate a light breakfast with his mother and father, followed by a short time of prayer. He wrapped the extra copy of the Apocalypse in a wool cloth and placed it carefully in his travel sack, along with some light provisions.

As Antonius was packing, Gallus entered the room. "You might need this," he said, handing Antonius his Roman infantryman's sword.

"You know what happened the last time I took this sword on a trip?" Antonius said with a smile.

"Keep your sense of humor, son." His father placed his hand on the young man's shoulder. "We're going to need it. Come, I'll walk with you as far as Flavius's villa. Hopefully his offer of a horse for this trip still stands."

Cassandra followed the two men to the gate. Teary-eyed, she hugged Antonius and kissed him on both cheeks.

"We're so proud of you, Antonius," she told him as he and Gallus went out the gate. "And I will be praying for you every day."

The sky in the east had turned from black to light blue, and only a few stars still shown. The air was crisp. Antonius was excited about the trip.

As they stepped out into the street, the gate to Juba's house opened and Monica stepped out. Antonius stopped, wondering what to say.

"I thought you might be leaving this morning," she said. "Where are you going?"

"Galatia," he answered. "Pisidian Antioch. Perhaps Iconium."

"How long will you be gone?"

"Ten days; perhaps two weeks."

"That's a long time. A lot can happen in two weeks."

"Monica . . . Listen . . . I . . . ah . . ."

Suddenly she ran across the street and threw her arms around him. Antonius dropped his travel bag and embraced her tightly. She sighed and then moved but a few inches away. She looked into his eyes and tried to smile. The look in her eyes, Antonius realized, was not the flirtatious sparkle that he had seen in Julia's eyes but rather the look of one who cared deeply for him. The eyes showed worry and concern—for him.

"Be careful," she whispered.

"I will."

"I'll be here when you get back."

"I know."

"God be with you, Antonius."

"And with you, Monica."

Antonius and his father walked east, toward the Iconium road. When they reached the end of the street, Antonius turned and looked back. Monica still stood by the gate of her house, illuminated now by the pale, clear light of dawn.

As they walked across the city, Gallus reviewed with Antonius the many details of the trip—friends and relatives they had along the way, dangerous locations along the highway, places to visit and places to avoid, questions to ask, people to seek out.

Laodicea was coming to life. Roosters crowed. Merchants and vendors were carrying their wares through the streets. An irritated donkey brayed in the distance. Fires were burning in many courtyards as families throughout the city cooked breakfast.

Gallus and Antonius entered the main colonnaded street that would lead them to the Eastern Gate. As they drew near the gate, however, Gallus suddenly pulled Antonius aside into one of the many shops that lined the street.

The shopkeeper looked up in surprise and exclaimed, "I am not open for business yet! Please come back later."

Gallus ignored the shopkeeper and whispered to Antonius, "Look! There are several praetorian guards at the gate, checking people as they go in and out. They are likely to recognize us and ask to inspect your bag. I'm afraid they will confiscate the scroll and destroy it, perhaps even arrest us."

"What do you think we should do?"

"Give me the scroll and I'll take it back to the house. You go on to Flavius's by yourself to borrow his horse. Isaeus should return from Ephesus in a day or two. He should be able to smuggle the scroll out of the city. I'll send him on to meet you in Pisidian Antioch. Besides, he knows the business well and he can be of assistance to you."

"I would be delighted to have Isaeus join me. You are going to make Caecelia mad, however, sending her husband off on another dangerous mission as soon as he returns."

Gallus and Antonius both laughed, but it was true. Caecelia didn't care whether Gallus was the master of the house or not; when she disagreed—especially about something that affected her family—she could be very articulate.

Antonius removed the scroll and gave it to his father. They embraced one final time, and Antonius set out alone toward the gate. There were four praetorian guards there, checking everyone who went in or out. He hoped that none of them would recognize him, and that he could simply pass through without incident. He approached the gate, trying to look nonchalant, keeping his head down to avoid eye contact. Suddenly one of the praetorian guards stopped him, grinning devilishly.

"Well, well, well. Look who we have here. Where's your cursed dog?" The other three guards gathered around him.

"Is this the one who tangled with Maximus at the wool guild?" one of them asked.

"The very same. Too bad Maximus isn't here. He has a score to settle. Perhaps we should send for him—or simply settle the score for him."

Antonius shifted his travel bag to his left hand, freeing up his right. He wondered if his father was nearby watching. He glanced around. Besides the four praetorian guards, there were also four regular gate guards, now coming over to see who was so interesting to the praetorians. If a fight began, Antonius was hopelessly outnumbered. He kept quiet.

"Give me your bag!" the guard who had first stopped him demanded. Antonius handed him his travel bag. The guard opened it, and a loaf of bread fell out, landing on the dusty road.

"I am so sorry, sir!" He stepped on the loaf with his sandaled foot as he leaned over to pick it up. He tossed the soiled loaf of bread back into the bag, rummaged through it a few moments more, and then tossed it back to Antonius.

As he did, his eyes fastened on the Roman infantryman's sword hanging from Antonius's waist.

"Why is a boy like you wearing a sword?" he asked contemptuously.

"I'm traveling to Galatia. Travel is safer with a sword."

"We can't allow a child like you to carry a Roman infantryman's sword," the guard snarled. "It would be an embarrassment to the army. Give me the sword."

Antonius dropped his travel bag to the ground.

"No!" he answered defiantly.

The praetorian guard stepped back, putting his hand on the hilt of his sword. The other guards did likewise. All of the other people at the gate grew quiet, slowly backing away from Antonius and the guards, giving them plenty of room in anticipation of a fight.

"Give me your sword!"

"No!"

Suddenly an old man stepped between Antonius and the guard. He was gray-haired and his face was lined with wrinkles, but he still stood straight and tall, with broad shoulders.

"You're Gallus's son, aren't you?" the man asked.

"Yes, sir," Antonius answered.

"Have you boys from Rome not heard of the Bloody Centurion?" the old man asked the praetorian guards. "This lad's father is the most famous legionnaire in the entire province of Asia. Have you not marched to his songs? Show some respect for a legionnaire who fought for the glory of Rome while you were still nursing in your mother's arms."

Several other gray-haired men stepped out of the crowd and came to stand beside Antonius, eyeing the praetorian guards critically.

One of the local guards stepped close to the praetorian guards and whispered, "If we kill the son of Gallus and a score of retired legionnaires, we will be in serious trouble. And over what? What excuse will we give? Let him go."

The praetorian guard standing in front of Antonius thought for a moment, glancing back and forth from Antonius to the crowd, which continued to grow larger.

"Go on!" he ordered Antonius. "Get out!"

The son of Gallus picked up his travel bag and walked cautiously through the gate and out of Laodicea, breathing a sigh of relief as he left.

An hour later Antonius stopped at the senator's villa to see Flavius and to borrow a horse. It was still early, and both Julia and Sabina were still asleep. Antonius met Flavius and Demetrius in the garden, where they discussed his trip. Flavius had heard what had taken place at the guild meeting the day before, but he still asked a few pointed questions, specifically about Gallus, Juba, and Simeon. Antonius answered honestly.

"I am very sorry about Juba and about Simeon," said the senator. "I know that you and your father were very close to these men. It must be difficult."

Antonius only nodded.

Since he no longer carried the scroll, Antonius was reluctant to ask about borrowing a horse. He assumed that he would now walk to Galatia. But Flavius insisted that Antonius take the beautiful Arabian mare he had ridden before.

"Take it," Flavius encouraged when Antonius balked. "You will be treated with much more respect on your trip if you arrive on a horse like that."

Antonius accepted the horse gratefully but refused the money Flavius tried to give him for the feed and care of the horse on the trip. He said his farewells and rode out through the villa gate onto the Iconium highway. Julia, he noted with irony as he headed east, was apparently still asleep.

ἡ δὲ κεφαλὴ αὐτοῦ καὶ αἱ τρίχες λευκαὶ ὡς ἔριον λευκὸν ὡς

WHO ARE THE ONES IN THE WHITE ROBES?

χιὼν καὶ οἱ ὀφθαλμοὶ αὐτοῦ ὡς φλὸξ πυρὸς καὶ οἱ πόδες αὐτοῦ

Eight days later, a frustrated Antonius walked through the streets of Pisidian Antioch just as the sun came up. Nothing was going right. Many cities throughout Galatia were discussing whether to dedicate temples to Domitian. Everyone was in an uproar about the temples. Rumors spread like wildfire, and people were afraid. Most wool guild members were reluctant to talk to him. Friends of his father's that he was supposed to see were either out of town or tight-lipped. Only the relatives of Isaeus, primarily servants, but also a few freedmen, would talk freely to him. The word on the street was that Imperial Temples were scheduled to be built soon both in Pisidian Antioch and in Iconium. The wool guild in Pisidian Antioch had also heard rumors of what had occurred in Ephesus and Laodicea, and they were concerned.

The proconsul of Galatia remained silent; no one knew whether he had enough political clout to oppose the expanding Imperial Cult. According to the rumors, only Cappadocia was far enough away to escape the growing power of the Imperial Temple and the cult that worshiped Domitian.

Furthermore, Isaeus had not come yet. Antonius had expected him days ago. He had heard no news from Laodicea, and he was worried.

He was on his way to the stables to check on Flavius's Arabian mare when he heard a familiar voice behind him shout, "Antonius!"

He turned and was pleased to see Isaeus riding toward him. "Isaeus! Old friend!" Antonius cried. "I expected you days ago. What happened? I hope that nothing bad befell you in Ephesus."

Isaeus dismounted wearily. He was covered with dust; obviously he had been riding hard. Antonius began to grow alarmed. Isaeus's face confirmed his fears.

"Antonius," he said. "I do not know what to say . . . or how to begin. Yes, I had trouble in Ephesus. After I delivered the scroll, I was arrested by praetorian guards and then questioned about the scroll and beaten for my silence. I continued to say nothing, and the Christians in Ephesus were able to hide the scroll from the guards. Finally I was released, but when I arrived back at Laodicea, your father ordered me to rest for a few days.

"But, Antonius, my problems and my suffering are nothing." Isaeus hesitated. He looked around for a moment. "Let's find a place to sit down."

"No," Antonius insisted. "Tell me now. Tell me everything."

"The worst has happened. The beast or the antichrist or whatever the evil one in your book is called . . . he has struck a deadly blow against Laodicea, and the blow has struck your family most severely."

"Speak, Isaeus! Speak! Don't leave me guessing at the worst. Tell me what happened!" Antonius demanded.

"The day before yesterday, at dawn, dozens of praetorian guards from Domitian's Imperial Temple broke into our house and arrested your father and mother. Gallus restrained himself and did not resist, for he believed that they wanted only him, and he did not want to endanger Cassandra or us servants. But after they had tied him, they took Cassandra as well. I followed them to the Domitian Temple. As I stood outside waiting, another group of praetorian guards arrived at the temple, with Senator Flavius in custody. Caius himself was leading them; he recognized me and sneered."

"The others?" Antonius interrupted. "Monica? Juba and Vivia? Julia and her mother?"

"No, only these three. Later they brought our pastor, Epaphras, and Shabako the Ethiopian elder, and their two wives. From my cousin, a servant within the temple, I heard of their brief trial before Caius. They were ordered to profess allegiance to Caesar Domitian as their lord and god. All of them refused and were condemned to death."

"To death?" Antonius exclaimed. "Condemned to death in the temple! What legal authority does the Imperial Temple have to condemn to death Roman citizens, brave legionnaires who served the Empire heroically? We will appeal to Caesar! We will hire the best lawyer in Rome! They have no legal authority to do this!"

"Antonius, Antonius," Isaeus said. His voice broke on a sob. "We can't appeal. They are already dead."

"Already dead? How can that be? What about Roman law? It cannot be!" But he knew from Isaeus's tears that he spoke the truth. "Mother, too?"

Isaeus only nodded, tears streaming down his face.

Antonius wept bitterly. Isaeus put his arms around him and the two men wept together for several minutes. Antonius sobbed and shook. Isaeus held him, patting him on the back.

After a time, Antonius asked, "How did it happen?"

"I will try to tell you everything as it happened," Isaeus promised, wiping the tears with the sleeve of his robe, "but I don't know if I can get all the way through the story. They kept the condemned Christians at the temple until late afternoon and then took them to the stadium for the circus."

"Caius took my parents and Senator Flavius to the *circus?*" Antonius asked with anger.

"He did. He and the new Proconsul Sulla, who had arrived from Ephesus. I ran to the Poorman's Gate of the Stadium and entered with the old retired soldiers. They recognized me and allowed me to sit with them. After a few minutes, Monica came in by herself and sat beside me. The old veterans all know that she is Juba's daughter, and they treated her with respect, making room for her beside me—she wanted to come with me here to tell you . . . you know that, don't you? She thinks of no one but you. But I insisted that I could travel much faster alone, and that her family needed her strength at home.

"The two of us watched together. For the first hour, it was the regular circus—gladiators fought, and there were some races. The crowd was rowdy and loud. Then after a loud trumpet fanfare, Caius ordered the condemned members of the heretical Christian sect to come out. Your parents, along with the senator, Shabako, and the others came out of the gate—the gate of the condemned—slowly, led by stadium guards. Your father and Flavius had already been beaten badly. Gradually the noisy crowd began to recognize Gallus and a deathly pall fell over the stadium, such as I have never heard there in all my life. The old soldiers could not believe that their hero Gallus could be among the condemned. Caius called out to your father by name and then shouted out pompously that if he recanted of his heresy and professed allegiance to Domitian, then he and his wife could live." Isaeus stopped and wiped his eyes again with his sleeve.

"Go on," Antonius demanded.

"Your father, Gallus Marius Quintus, shook off the pain from his beating and stood straight and tall. He marched across the stadium field with a legionnaire's marching cadence. Step, step, step. Each retired legionnaire around me counted the cadence. Gallus marched until he stood before the center platform that held Caius, Sulla, and Plautus, the young high priest. There was dead silence in the stadium, except for the gentle breeze and the flapping of the flags around the center platform. I thought for a foolish instant that maybe your father would recant. He stood at attention before them for a brief moment, then spun around as if in formation, with his back to Sulla and his face toward the legionnaires. He pointed upward to the sky, made the sign of the cross, knelt, and then bowed his head in prayer to God, with his back and his heels insultingly pointed toward Sulla, Caius, and Plautus.

"Caius was infuriated. He jumped to his feet and ordered the lions released. Across the field they released five terrible lions from their cages. As the lions bounded out onto the field, Gallus finished his prayer, rose, and immediately began the legionnaire's march toward the lions. Not running, mind you, but marching . . . the same measured tread all legionnaires use when marching to battle.

"A one-armed retired veteran behind me suddenly broke out into a legionnaires' marching song. Soon all the old soldiers joined in. It was the Bloody Centurion's song, Antonius. They sang Gallus's song. The stadium reverberated with it. They sang of his valor in the forest of Athanel and of Sulla's cowardice. They sang of how he slew his enemies right and left and won the victory for Rome and for honor. He stopped when he heard them. I think the emotion of it overwhelmed him for a moment. He saluted his retired comrades and they answered with a roaring cheer, then sang even louder.

"Gallus continued his march toward the lions. Soon one of the lions noticed him, roared, and ran to attack him. As the lion approached, your father broke into a furious charge. All the legionnaires shouted a battle cry, and the stadium shook with that cry. Gallus the centurion sprinted at the lion, lowered his shoulder, and hit the surprised lion with all his might, locking onto the lion's neck with all his strength. The lion clawed furiously in defense, inflicting unimaginable wounds on your father, who nonetheless continued to grip the lion by the neck. The two fell to the ground in a cloud of dust. For a brief moment we could see nothing, but soon the dust cleared . . . and your father staggered to his feet. He had broken the lion's neck. The legionnaires cheered wildly, and your father, now mortally wounded and bleeding badly, saluted them once again. The legionnaires roared and began singing his marching song again. Gallus, however, collapsed and fell to his knees as the other lions attacked.

"The legionnaires shouted and cursed as the lions did their grim work. The old soldiers cursed the lions; they cursed Sulla, Caius, and Plautus; they even cursed Domitian himself. They cursed by the gods of Rome and the gods of Gaul and Britain and Africa, and by the names of some gods I have never heard of—from all of the regions where they had fought. They hissed and threw their trash on the field. I thought that perhaps Caius or Plautus would stop the event and save the others, but no, their cruelty and lack of compassion—indeed the very evil that seems to flow from them—are beyond our comprehension. In horror we watched as the lions then attacked the others, including Senator Flavius, Shabako the Ethiopian . . . and your mother, who all waited patiently on their knees in prayer until the end came. As the lions finished, the stadium grew deathly silent. It was eerie.

"Then an incredible thing happened. You know that toothless old woman Zenia who sings at our worship gathering sometimes? She writes good songs, but really can't sing very well?"

"Of course," Antonius said. "She is the one who had been a temple prostitute and then turned from it to follow Christ when the apostle Paul came to Laodicea years ago."

"The very same. She must be eighty at least. She was sitting in the central section. Do you remember the song she sang in our worship gathering two weeks ago? The one with the chorus, 'Who are those in the white robes?'"

Antonius nodded.

"Well," Isaeus continued, "after all were dead and the crowd was silent and ashamed, she stood and sang that song. It's from the Apocalypse, isn't it?"

Again Antonius nodded.

"Do you remember the words? 'Who are the ones in white robes? They are the ones who have come out of the great tribulation. They have washed their robes in the blood of the Lamb. Never again will they hunger; never again will they thirst. And God will wipe away every tear.' She sang loud and clear. Everyone in the stadium could hear her. She sang it over and over.

"An amazing thing happened. People started to join in and sing with her. Men and women who have never visited our meetings joined in. Even the old hardened veterans around us sang, tears streaming down their faces. Monica and I tried to sing, too, but we were weeping too hard and couldn't. Finally, in fury, Sulla, Caius, and Plautus stormed off the dignitaries' platform and left the stadium. Zenia sang for another ten minutes or so, then bowed her head and prayed, dismissing the crowd. She had turned the circus into a worship service, and now she dismissed us. After praying she slowly walked down the stairs and out of the stadium. In silence the crowd followed. The only sound to be heard was that of muffled crying.

"Later, Juba and several of the legionnaires came and wrapped up the bodies. They carried them outside the city and buried them properly in spite of the prohibition against such burials."

Antonius stood before Isaeus with tears still streaming down his face. He tried to wipe the tears away with the back of his hand, then with his tunic.

"Isaeus," he said between sobs. "I must return to Laodicea as soon as possible. Your horse is exhausted and will need several hours of rest. I will start out now, and you can follow me in a few hours."

The two men embraced again, and Antonius ran to the stable. He paid the stable manager for the horse's keep, then mounted immediately and rode out of Pisidian Antioch at a gallop, with tears still in his eyes.

ὅμοιοι χαλκολιβάνῳ ὡς ἐν καμίνῳ πεπυρωμένης καὶ ἡ φωνὴ

HIDING THE
APOCALYPSE

αὐτοῦ ὡς φωνὴ ὑδάτων πολλῶν, καὶ ἔχων ἐν τῇ δεξιᾷ χειρὶ

The day after Isaeus found Antonius in Pisidian Antioch, Monica rose early, prepared a quick breakfast for her father and two brothers, and then slipped out through the gate into the street. The paving stones of the street were wet from the rain that had fallen throughout the night. The sky was still overcast, with thick clouds hanging low over the city like a shroud. She looked toward the mountains to the east, where the bright sun should have been rising, but the mountains themselves were wrapped in gray mist. She murmured a quick prayer for Antonius, out there somewhere to the east, and she hoped that he had sunshine to travel by instead of these depressing dark clouds.

She walked across the street in the dim light. The air was so thick and the city so quiet! She could smell the wood smoke of morning fires, and there were even a few people on the street already, but all sound seemed muffled by the clouds and mist. The roosters, the birds, the neighbors, even the people walking in the street—all seemed to be silent.

She shivered, then knocked softly on the gate. "Mother!" she called quietly.

"Monica?" came Vivia's voice from inside. "Is that you?"

"Yes, Mother."

Vivia opened the gate and Monica hurried in. Her mother embraced her warmly.

"Have you fed Juba and the twins already? Is everything all right at the house?" Vivia asked.

"Yes, Mother. Father and the boys are fine. But how are you? And how is poor Caecelia?"

Vivia glanced quickly around the courtyard. "She has had so much thrown on her; I don't know how she bears it all. I don't know if she slept. Gallus and Cassandra were like family to Caecelia; indeed, Cassandra had been her closest friend, more like a sister even. And now she finds herself with many added responsibilities and uncertainties. With Antonius in Galatia . . . she desperately needs Isaeus, but he hasn't returned from Galatia either. In the meantime, she's responsible for managing Gallus's household and his affairs. And her own two children to care for. Yesterday she needed to purchase things in the market, but she was reluctant to use Gallus's money. I told her to go ahead and use some of Gallus's money to buy food. Certainly Antonius would want them to use that money. She won't take any money from me either. I am worried about her."

Monica patted her mother on the arm. "And while you are consoling Caecelia, who comforts you, Mother? Gallus and Cassandra were close to us, too. Who comforts us?" A tear trickled down Monica's face. Vivia embraced her again, both of them crying softly.

"We will comfort each other," Vivia said. "And the Lord will comfort us as well."

Caligula bounded over to Monica, happily wagging his tail and repeatedly sniffing her ankles and feet with his wet, cold nose. In spite of the tears, both of them smiled at the dog, and Monica reached down to pet him on the head.

Caecelia came out into the courtyard from one of the side rooms. "Thank you for coming." She hugged Monica. "I don't know what I would do without you and your mother." She sighed, then led Monica and Vivia across the courtyard to the table, where she had begun to prepare breakfast. Her two children were awake; Monica could hear them talking in one of the rooms. An instant later they raced into the courtyard with Caligula on their heels.

Caecelia sighed again. "At least the children seem all right. I wonder how much they understand of what has happened." She watched them for a moment as they played with Caligula across the courtyard. "Vivia?" she asked.

"Yes?"

"What will become of us? Will they confiscate this house? Don't the magistrates sometimes confiscate the estates of convicted criminals? Or will the Imperial Temple manipulate the law to seize this house? One of Isaeus's cousins told me yesterday that the olive orchard that belonged to Elder Shabako has been seized by the praetorian guards and the servants there forced to leave. Do you think that they will do the same thing to us?"

"Caecelia, we will trust in God, and everything will work out. If you lose the house, then you and your family can come stay with us, at least until Antonius and Isaeus return. They will know what to do."

Caligula ran to the gate, wagging his tail furiously. A series of rapid knocks came. The women looked up nervously.

"Mother? Monica? Caligula?" shouted Marcellus.

Monica rushed to the gate and opened it quickly. Her twin brothers bolted in. Caligula barked with delight.

"Father has gone to the guild storehouse. He told us to come over here," Mardonius announced as they ran across the yard to Caecelia's two children.

The children's play seemed to brighten everyone's spirits. After breakfast, the three women sat around the table and talked of happier days, remembering the fun they had known with Cassandra, who had been close to all of them. The four children had discovered a small green lizard on one of the trees in the courtyard, and had all climbed the tree trying to catch the speedy reptile. They laughed and giggled and shouted to one another as the lizard raced from branch to branch. Caligula ran around the tree on the ground, barking happily.

Suddenly, Caligula ran once again to the gate and began sniffing excitedly. A rapid knock sounded.

"Caecelia! Caecelia! Open the gate . . . quick!"

Caecelia sprang up and ran to the gate as the children dropped from the tree. She threw open the gate to see Rufus, the ten-year-old son of Isaeus's cousin who worked at the Imperial Temple. Rufus, covered with sweat, was gasping for breath. Caligula bounded out and sniffed him.

"What is it, Rufus?" Caecelia asked.

Rufus was still trying to catch his breath. Between gasps, he blurted, "My father sent me . . . to tell you . . . that the praetorian guards . . . are coming."

"Here?" she asked. "What for?"

"They are looking for . . . the new scroll . . . the new one by the apostle John . . . the one with the strange things about Rome in it." Gradually, he regained his breath and began to talk smoothly again. "They want the scroll and all copies of it. That's the message. I need to run. They will be here any moment and I don't want them to see me. Farewell." He fled down the street in the direction away from the Imperial Temple.

"Quick!" ordered Vivia as she ushered Caligula in and closed the gate. "Get the scrolls."

The three women ran to one of the back rooms. Caecelia quickly removed one of the stones in the wall, revealing a hiding place. She removed two large scrolls and one small leather bag.

"What's in the bag?" asked Monica.

"It's Gallus's money," answered Caecelia. "It's all he has here in Laodicea. If they search the house they are likely to find the money. Who knows? They will probably take it, too. But what are we going to do with this? Where's Juba?"

"Juba is at the guild storehouse. We can take the scrolls to our house for the time being," suggested Vivia. "We can hide them there. It may take them a day or two to connect our two families together."

Caligula ran to the gate again, but he was no longer barking happily. He sniffed at the gate nervously, then started his low, threatening growl.

"Oh no!" said Caecelia. "They are already here."

Immediately there came a strong, solid knock at the gate. A man's voice called, "By the order of the High Priest Plautus and the Imperial Temple, open this gate immediately!"

Caligula barked angrily.

"Here," Monica said. "Give me the scrolls and the money. I can climb over the back wall and down the fig tree. I'll circle to the next block, go up the broken section of wall at Ophelia's house, walk along the wall, and drop into our house from the back."

"How on earth—," started her mother.

"Antonius and I used to do this all the time when we were younger," explained Monica. "But quick, there is no time."

The knocking at the gate was louder and the guard repeated his demand for immediate entry. Monica grabbed the two scrolls and the moneybag and dashed for the back of the courtyard. She placed the scrolls and moneybag up on the wall, stepped up on a large water jug, and then boosted herself up on the wall alongside the scrolls. She placed the moneybag inside her work dress, wrapped her left arm around both bulky scrolls, and then reached out with her right hand to grab a branch from the fig tree that grew outside of Gallus's house in the street behind. She swung over to the tree and then dropped to the ground. Immediately she darted into the street and quickly walked away, with sweat forming on her forehead and her heart pounding.

Vivia and Caecelia stood frozen in the center of the courtyard, watching as Monica left. Vivia recovered first. "Children," she ordered quietly. "No one says a word to these men about Monica and the scrolls. If they ask you, tell them Antonius took the scrolls to Galatia."

She walked to the entrance, called on Caligula to calm down, and opened the gate.

"It's about time," the guard said rudely, pushing by Vivia into the courtyard. Four other guards followed him. The last was Maximus, still limping slightly. He and Caligula recognized each other at the same instant. Caligula went after him just as he drew his sword.

Maximus kicked at Caligula, warding him off for an instant.

"Here is that cursed cur from Hades! Come here, you devil of a dog, and I'll lop off your flea-bitten head."

Caligula barked furiously, but stayed out of range of Maximus's sword. One of the other guards, however, shut the gate, picked up a small pot from the courtyard, and gave orders: "Shut all the doors! We'll keep him trapped in the courtyard. Either we'll corner him and finish him with our swords or else we'll pelt him with rocks and water pots until he slows down. Then we'll cut him up and feed him to the buzzards."

Panic ensued. Caecelia shuttled her two children to a corner of the courtyard, out of the way. Vivia's two boys huddled next to her against the wall, not far from the gate. The guard with the pot hurled it at Caligula, barely missing him. It hit the wall behind the dog and shattered. The other guards quickly closed all of the doors that led from the courtyard into the house. Maximus picked up a small stone and fired it at Caligula, hitting him hard in the side. The dog let out a sharp yelp of pain, but stayed on his feet and resumed his angry barking. The five men backed Caligula into the far corner of the yard and began slowly closing in on him.

Marcellus slipped away from Vivia and raced to the gate. In a flash he unbolted the gate and threw it open, crying, "Here, boy! Caligula! Run!"

The wily dog darted between two of the guards and dashed out of the gate, with Marcellus right behind him. The guards followed, but by the time they reached the street, Caligula was rounding the corner at the next street and Marcellus was disappearing over the wall of a neighbor's house.

The praetorian guards came back into the courtyard. "Where are the scrolls?" Maximus demanded of the women.

"They are not here," answered Caecelia meekly.

Maximus slapped her sharply on the face, nearly knocking her down.

"Leave us alone!" Mardonius shouted in anger, much to Vivia's alarm. "My father will be here any minute. You'll be in big trouble!"

"Two smart-aleck kids that look identical," said Maximus, walking over to Mardonius. He pulled out a dagger and grabbed the boy by the arm. Vivia gasped.

"Perhaps your fearsome father would like to have a quiet son rather than a loudmouthed son like you. I think I'll cut your tongue out; that will cure you of being smart-mouthed with the praetorian guards."

"Wait!" interrupted Vivia. "I'll tell you where the scrolls are. Antonius, the son of Gallus, took the scrolls to Galatia, where they would be safe. He left over a week ago. By now the scrolls are probably in Iconium."

Maximus grabbed Vivia by the hair with his left hand, and with his right he held the point of his dagger against her throat, just barely cutting the skin.

He whispered in her ear, "If you're lying to me, we'll find you and I'll personally cut your throat and the throats of both your smart-mouthed kids." He shoved her toward the gate. "Get out!" he ordered. "Both of you women, leave! And take these snotty-nosed kids with you! We'll take this place apart and see if you're lying."

Vivia, Caecelia, and the children hurried out the gate, thankful to get away from the guards. Out in the street, they could hear the soldiers smashing water pots and banging on the walls, searching in vain for the Apocalypse.

Across the street, Monica immediately threw open her gate, and everyone scurried into Juba's courtyard before the guards could see where they went. Monica and her mother embraced.

"Mother, I was so afraid. I could hear shouting and barking. I saw Marcellus and Caligula run out. Marcellus had enough sense to run somewhere else and not lead them to our house. I think he has gone to get Father.

"Oh, Caecelia!" exclaimed Monica. "Your nose is bleeding. Did those animals hit you?"

"I'm all right," Caecelia answered. "Just let me sit down for a moment."

They led her to a chair. Both of Caecelia's children, crying, climbed into her lap.

Monica thought for a moment and then said to her brother, "Mardonius, climb over the back wall and run down to Agathon's lamp shop. Wait there and watch for Father. If he comes from the guild he should pass by that way. Tell him to come here and not to Gallus's house. And stay out of sight! Don't let those men see you."

Monica's mother was still shaking, but she nodded her approval. Mardonius quickly climbed up and over the back wall and disappeared.

Vivia gave Caecelia a wet cloth for her nose. The women sat nervously in the courtyard and waited. After a short time, they heard someone run up to the gate, and with relief, they recognized Juba's voice calling quietly to his wife. The three women raced to the gate and unlatched it. Juba quickly stepped inside. Caecelia closed and latched the gate while both Vivia and Monica threw their arms around him. He hugged them both.

After a moment Vivia pulled away. "Where are the twins?" she asked anxiously.

"I sent both of them, along with Caligula, to Flaminius's house. I told them to stay there until I came for them later today. What happened?"

"Father," Monica said, "the praetorian guards are at Gallus's house searching for the scrolls. Perhaps we should move inside to talk."

Juba nodded and they all hurried into one of the sleeping rooms on the far side of the courtyard. Once inside, Vivia related to her husband all that just happened.

"Did they see any of you come in here?"

"No," Vivia answered. "I don't think so."

"Where are the scrolls?"

"I put one of them in the storage room, under the grain sacks," Monica answered. "The other I put in our hiding place, under the paving stone in front of your sleeping room. I couldn't fit both of them in the hiding place, and I thought that they might not know that there are two copies. So if they find one, they may think they have all of them."

"Smart girl," Juba said approvingly. "I am proud of you. I am proud of the twins, too. They were very brave. All of you were very brave." He hugged his wife again.

"But we are still in danger," Juba continued. "Vivia, the guards may not wholly believe you about the scrolls being with Antonius in Galatia. And it won't take them long to connect the twins with us and this house. Once they do, they are likely to come here to search for the scrolls. Somehow, we need to move the scrolls somewhere else. However, I hesitate to ask any of our friends or anyone from the church to hide the scrolls; it is simply too dangerous. It would be good if we could get them out of the city."

Monica thought for a moment. "Father, I know a cave up in the mountains that Antonius and I used to visit when we were children. I could take the scrolls and hide them in the cave. No one knows about that cave except Antonius and me."

"That sounds like a good place," said Juba. "But I won't allow you to be the one to carry them there. It is too dangerous. I will do it."

"But, Father, you would never find the cave on your own, even with my directions. And since everyone knows that you are close friends with Gallus, don't you think the praetorian guards might be watching for you at the city gates, expecting you to try to smuggle the scrolls out? I think that you might be recognized. And they have seen Mother, Caecelia, and the twins. I am the only one they haven't seen."

Juba was listening but shaking his head. "No," he said. "I don't like it."

"It has to be me," Monica insisted. "I'm the only one they won't recognize. I can walk right out of the city gates without raising any suspicion. We can put the scrolls in a grain sack and I will be just another farm girl returning to the farm after a day at the market."

Reluctantly, Juba agreed.

"And, Father, I should probably go immediately. The guards could come at any time."

Again he nodded reluctantly.

"But I will wait at least until early afternoon before trying to pass through the Eastern Gate. There will be hundreds of people loaded with bundles and bags of merchandise heading out of the city to the surrounding villages and farms. One girl with a half-filled grain sack will not look suspicious."

"What will you do in the meantime?" her father asked.

"Just walk around in the agora. No one will be looking for me."

"I don't like this," Juba said. "If there were any other way . . ."

"I'll be fine, Father," answered Monica with a weak smile.

"I still don't like it."

"I don't either," Vivia added.

"Let's get the scrolls ready," suggested Monica, and she hurried out.

Vivia found an empty grain sack. Juba and Monica retrieved the two scrolls and placed them in the sack. Monica then tied up the end of the sack with a small piece of rope. They prayed together briefly, then Vivia kissed her daughter on the cheek. Monica climbed up on the back wall, and Juba handed her the sack. Without a word, she took the sack and disappeared over the wall. She landed on the street, drawing a few inquisitive stares from the people passing by. She set out immediately for the agora. She forced herself to walk slowly, for she had plenty of time to waste.

Monica spent the next several hours at the agora, walking from one side to the other, trying to look nonchalant. She saw several people she knew, but fortunately none of them asked her what she had in the bag. She was afraid that everyone would see how nervous she looked. Her heart continued to pound. She imagined that everyone was looking at her. The time crawled by. She looked at oranges and apples, brass pots and lamps, cloth and ropes, always keeping her sack tightly clenched under her arm. When she noticed that more and more people were loading up their purchases and making their way toward the exits, she joined the stream leaving by the exit that led to the Eastern Gate of the city and the Iconium road.

She melted into the crowd silently, trying to avoid all eye contact but still observe everything happening around her. When she drew near the Eastern Gate, she was relieved to see that the gate was indeed very busy. Streams of people were going in and out. Two oxcarts had been stopped, and the guards were inspecting the carts and determining the tariff requirements. There were four local city guards and only one praetorian guard. Monica proceeded through the gate as nonchalantly as she could, keeping her eyes on the road before her.

Suddenly the praetorian guard called, "Hey, young woman! Stop!"

She froze, then slowly turned. The cocky praetorian guard strolled over.

"Where's a pretty girl like you going today?" he asked, eying her up and down.

"I ... ah ... I'm just going home. I've been to the agora."

"Want some company? I could go with you and make sure that nothing happens to you along the way," he suggested, moving closer to her as he spoke.

"No thanks. I'll be all right by myself." Monica whirled away and walked quickly through the gate.

"Hey! You can't just walk off while a praetorian guard is interrogating you!" He caught up with her and grabbed her by the sleeve. "What's in the bag?"

"Rolls of tanned leather," she mumbled. "For my father to use on the farm." She continued to look down, trying to conceal the panic in her eyes, not daring to look at her interrogator.

"Let her go," one of the local guards said. "We have plenty of work to do without flirting with every pretty peasant girl that passes by. You stop every pretty face that comes through this gate. What's the matter? Haven't you seen pretty girls before? Are all of the girls in Rome homely?"

The other guards laughed and joined in the teasing.

"Shut up!" the praetorian guard ordered, without effect. Monica hurried away, never daring to look back, praying that the guard could not hear her heart pounding. With each step, she listened for his dreadful voice, fearing that he would call her back to examine the bag. But the voice never came, and she widened the distance between herself and the gate as rapidly as she could. Finally she realized that she had made it; they weren't going to stop her. She felt like crying; she had been so terrified. But she fought back the tears—they would surely attract attention—and kept plodding down the Iconium highway away from Laodicea.

Only after several hundred paces did she relax a bit and allow herself to think about which road she would take to the hiding place. Soon she turned off the Iconium highway and followed a smaller dirt road into the forest at the foot of the mountains. No one else took that road, and she was joyful to be alone.

In the quiet of the woods, she finally began to feel safe. As she walked, she remembered the many times she had come down this very road with Antonius. She remembered the last time they came here together, nearly a year ago. He had kissed her; she smiled at the memory. But she had been too shocked by the kiss to know how to respond, she thought with regret.

After an hour's walk, she looked up and down the road to be sure no one was watching her, and then quickly darted off the road onto a small hidden path that led up toward the mountain on her right. *I wonder if he will ever kiss me again.*

αὐτοῦ ἀστέρας ἑπτὰ καὶ ἐκ τοῦ στόματος αὐτοῦ ῥομφαία

DECISIONS

δίστομος ὀξεῖα ἐκπορευομένη καὶ ἡ ὄψις αὐτοῦ ὡς ὁ ἥλιος

Monica climbed the mountain quickly, following faint trails and taking shortcuts that few people other than she and Antonius knew about. After some effort, she reached the cliff near the top, then the ledge cut into the cliff. She found their secret cave—a small, narrow opening into the bottom of the cliff, hidden by bushes. She wished for a lamp, for the cave was dark and foreboding. She tossed a rock into the cave to rouse any animals that may have been in there. She listened and heard nothing.

To enter the cave she had to lie on her stomach and crawl, pushing the scrolls ahead of her. She inched her way into the darkness, praying that there were no snakes. Once inside, she was able to sit up. Slowly her eyes adjusted to the darkness. Just enough light trickled in through the narrow opening to allow her to make out the bare outlines of the cave. She went on all fours to the far side of the cave. There she moved some rocks, creating a small hole. She placed the scrolls in the hole and then piled the rocks back on top. *When I come back to get these,* she thought, *I'm bringing a lamp.*

Monica crawled out of the cave, glad to be back in the sunlight. As she stood, she noticed with irritation that she had gotten her work dress dirty. She brushed it with her hands to remove the dirt. She didn't remember getting dirty the last time she'd gone into the cave. She smiled, remembering the many times she had come to this spot with Antonius—although neither of them had actually been in the cave for several years. *I must have been only twelve when Antonius took my dare and the two of us first entered the cave. I probably didn't even notice the dirt back then.* Brushing more dirt off her dress, she reflected on how significantly things can change.

She gazed out at the valley below her, reminded once again of how beautiful the view was from this lookout point. She sat on the rock where she and Antonius had spent so many hours talking in their childhood. She wanted to think, to pray, to find some answers. She was angry with her father, and she admitted, angry with Antonius, too. Yet she loved them both. What would happen to Antonius now? Would his house be confiscated? Would he be banned from Laodicea? Where would he go? Galatia? Would he take her with him as his wife? Or would he take Julia instead? The thought of living in Laodicea without Antonius was almost more than she could bear.

She frowned down at the beautiful villa and gardens below her in the valley. This was Flavius's villa now. Julia was there. As much as she disliked Julia for trying to steal Antonius, she hurt for the senator's daughter. It would be terrible to lose your father—especially like that, in the circus. What would happen to Julia and Sabina now that Flavius was dead? Would Antonius feel obligated to marry Julia to take care of them? Perhaps Antonius wanted to marry Julia anyway.

She's beautiful. Everyone says she's the most beautiful girl in the province. How can Antonius resist that? All the young men in the city gawk at her and fall apart when she flirts with them. How can I expect Antonius to be any different? Why would he choose me, in my simple—and now dirty—working dress and my plain hair when he can have her, in those gorgeous gowns and that beautiful hair?

She felt her stomach churning and knotting up. Her heart ached at the thought of Antonius married to Julia. What would she do? How could she stand it? Who would she marry instead?

She tried to put these thoughts out of her mind, but she failed miserably. She looked at the road below and remembered the game she and Antonius had played as children, creating stories about the people on the road. *That old man in the oxcart, for example, might have just murdered the magistrate and is now sneaking away to Iconium. And that rider on the horse . . . wait! That rider . . . it is . . . yes, it is him! Antonius! He must be returning from Galatia!*

She jumped to her feet and shouted, "Antonius!" Immediately she felt foolish, calling to him from this distance. She tried to judge how far away he was and how fast he was riding, thinking that if she ran back down the trail she could intercept him just before the creek crossing. But to her dismay, he stopped at the gate to Julia's villa. He sat motionless on his horse for a moment outside the gate, as if thinking. *No!* Monica screamed in her head. *Don't go see her! Don't propose to her! Hurry home, Antonius! Hurry home to me!* Yet he rode up to the gate. A few moments later, she saw a servant open the huge gate, and then she watched in agony as Antonius spurred his horse and trotted in through the gate. Her heart sank. *He has decided. He is going to accept their proposal and marry Julia.*

But maybe, she thought, *he is just returning the horse.* She grabbed eagerly at this straw, this new glimmer of hope. She started back down the trail, trying to walk calmly, but breaking into a run from time to time. Her heart was pounding, but not from the physical exertion. *I will wait for him on the roadside and find out. I will find out now. I need to know where his heart is and what he has decided.*

As Antonius rode the Arabian mare along the tree-lined road that led into the big open courtyard of Flavius's villa, his thoughts wandered back through all the reasons and arguments regarding marriage he had pondered over the past two days. He still had many unanswered questions, and his future was still largely uncertain, but he had made his decision. In the midst of his grief, he could see clearly now his course of action. He no longer had any doubt; in fact, now that he saw clearly, he was amazed that he had remained indecisive for so long.

A servant ran out into the courtyard to meet him. Antonius dismounted and handed the reins of the horse to the servant, who eyed him and the horse suspiciously. Antonius and the Arabian mare were both covered with dust and sweat. The horse was near exhaustion. Antonius looked up to see Demetrius scurrying out of the house toward him, looking worried and distressed.

"Antonius! I am so sorry about your parents. You have my deepest sympathies."

"Thank you, Demetrius. I am likewise heartbroken about the death of Senator Flavius. We have both experienced great loss, have we not?"

"True, Antonius, we have." Demetrius glanced over at the servant leading the mare to the stables. "Good, I see you brought the mare back. How was your trip?"

"I need to see Julia," Antonius interrupted. "Where is she?"

"She is not available at the moment," Demetrius responded. "Perhaps you could come back later . . . tomorrow afternoon, perhaps?"

"No," insisted Antonius. "I will see her now."

"It's not a good time, Antonius," Demetrius said firmly.

"I don't care," the young man answered, pushing past the steward. "Julia! Julia!"

The main door to the big house opened, but it was Sabina who came out.

"Antonius!" she exclaimed, apparently startled and definitely displeased. "What are *you* doing here?"

"I am returning the horse the senator loaned me."

His mention of Flavius jolted Sabina. She stood still for a moment, fighting back tears.

"I am terribly sorry about the loss of your husband, Sabina."

She nodded and then looked at him with sympathy. "Thank you. Losing a husband is nearly as tragic as losing your parents. You have my sympathies as well, Antonius." It was the first time Antonius had seen any sign of friendliness or compassion in her.

"I need to talk to Julia," Antonius repeated gently. "Please call her for me."

"No." The sympathetic look was immediately replaced with a scowl. "She is occupied at the moment. You must leave."

Ignoring her, Antonius shouted again loudly toward the house, "Julia!"

"Antonius?" came Julia's startled voice from the edge of the garden. She came out of the garden walking quickly, glancing inquisitively back and forth from Antonius to her mother. "We thought that you were in Galatia."

"I was . . . the day before yesterday. Isaeus found me and told me about your father . . . and my parents."

They both stood silently, feeling their recent loss. Julia wiped away a tear that trickled down her cheek.

"I am deeply grieved over your father, Julia. Flavius was a great man. I feel honored to have known him."

"We are deeply grieved, too, Antonius, about your parents." Awkwardly Julia looked back and forth from Demetrius to Sabina to Antonius. "What is it you want, Antonius? Have you come just to pay condolences?"

"Not really," began Antonius. "This may not be the proper place or time, but the situation has become urgent, and there is no longer any time for niceties and social convention."

"Yes?" she asked, showing the faint trace of an amused smile.

"I am declining your father's offer of marriage. You are a beautiful girl, Julia. However, I have always loved Monica. I know that now. She is the only one I can ever marry. I'm sorry."

Julia's smile vanished. She looked confused, then hung her head slightly and blushed. Sabina smiled sardonically.

"I fail to see the humor here," Antonius said to Julia's mother.

"Perhaps I can clarify it," came a man's voice from the edge of the garden. "Or at least point out the irony."

Startled, Antonius turned to see Plautus strolling out of the garden.

"Plautus!" exclaimed Antonius. "What are you doing here?"

The handsome high priest walked up beside Julia and put his arm around her. "We were just discussing the arrangements for our upcoming wedding. You see, I proposed to Julia less than an hour ago; she—with her mother's blessing—has joyfully accepted. Thus you can see the humor and the irony . . . for now you, the wool merchant's son, have come barging in to decline her hand in marriage."

"But . . . Julia. How can you marry *Plautus?* This snake is responsible for the murder of your father and my parents—and many others!"

"I would advise you to be careful with your accusations, Antonius," warned Plautus. "I have explained my role in this unfortunate business very clearly to Julia and Sabina. I knew nothing of any of these events. My father and Sulla planned it all without my knowledge. I had no idea that they would be brought out in the circus. I opposed it vigorously and did all I could to stop it."

"Besides," interjected Sabina, as she stepped off the veranda and crossed the courtyard to approach Antonius, "without this marriage we would lose the villa. Furthermore, Plautus has generously offered us an extremely valuable piece of property as a wedding gift. He has given us a beautiful olive orchard that lies on the Hierapolis road, just across the Lycus River. It is a very profitable orchard and it will greatly add to our income. What could *you* have possibly offered as a comparable gift?"

Antonius glared at Plautus with disgust. "That orchard belonged to Shabako, elder of the church and former legionnaire. So not only have you murdered a righteous man, but you have stolen his land from his children. You are not just a snake, but you are a lying, thieving snake."

"And that's enough of your impertinence!" responded Plautus angrily, now red-faced. "I should have you flogged for such disrespectful and wild accusations. If my praetorian guards were here I'd flog you right now, here in this courtyard. If I see you in Laodicea, I'll have you beaten on the spot. Come, Demetrius, let's throw this lying, uncivilized sheep farmer out of this house."

Demetrius glanced at Sabina, who nodded her approval. Plautus stepped rapidly and authoritatively toward Antonius, with Demetrius close behind. Suddenly Plautus jumped back, startled. He was staring at the point of a Roman short sword.

"Not so fast, reptile," Antonius warned. "I ought to kill you now, while I have the chance."

"Antonius! Don't!" shrieked Julia.

Antonius looked at Julia in pity. "I grieve for your father," he said. "But he died for his faith in Jesus the Christ. I likewise grieve for you, Julia, and even for your unpleasant mother, for you have both sold yourself blindly to the very beast who killed your father, who killed my parents, and who seeks to kill other Christians. You have not just compromised; you have denied the faith completely. Have you understood *nothing* of John's Apocalypse?"

"Can you leave now?" Julia pleaded.

"Thank you for the use of your horse," Antonius said curtly. He turned and marched away quickly, sheathing his sword as he left.

He walked rapidly down the tree-lined lane that led from the courtyard to the main gate of the villa. The servant nodded at him in silence and opened the gate. Antonius stepped onto the Iconium road feeling as if an enormous burden had been lifted from his shoulders. He knew that Plautus was dangerous and powerful, and that it had been foolish to enrage him. But it would have happened sooner or later anyway.

If I stand as firm as Father stood, then the Imperial Temple will have to come after me sooner or later. All I did today was speed things up. And it felt good to end the speculation about marriage to Julia. Hopefully, Monica hasn't given up on me in the meantime.

After days of agonizing about Monica and about Flavius's proposal, Antonius had finally realized that he was attracted to Julia primarily because of her beauty and her flirtatious manner. All men were attracted to her in this way. But that was not love; it was mere infatuation. In truth, what he and Julia felt toward each other was shallow and superficial. Furthermore, she was fickle and spoiled. Her character was weak. Indeed, her faith in Christ was weak. She was more than willing to compromise her faith to make life easier. Marriage to such a woman would be disastrous.

Monica, on the other hand, he mused with a smile, was solid as a rock in all aspects of her character, but especially in her faith. She would stand strong for the Lord. They could face this persecution together. It would be so much easier to stay true and faithful to the Lord if your wife stood strong beside you—like Mother stood with Father.

Antonius fought back tears as he reflected on his parents and their love for each other and how the faith of each had strengthened the other. Monica had many of the same virtues his mother had possessed. In contrast to his feelings for Julia, Antonius realized that he felt something deep for Monica. He had thought at first it was just friendship, since they had been so close as childhood friends. *But*—and he smiled again at the thought—*if you really want to put your arms around her and hold her and kiss her, then . . . you are probably not just friends anymore.* At some point, the friendship merges into love; indeed, he thought, the friendship enhances the love. He was unsure of many things at the moment, but he was certain that he would marry Monica if the Lord permitted. Besides—it was exactly what his mother and his father would have wanted.

And then suddenly, miraculously, there she was! Standing by the road, looking lost and forlorn. Antonius stopped and stared at her, wondering if this were some strange dream. He walked toward her slowly.

"Monica?"

She was quivering, struggling to remain composed. Antonius could see that she had been crying; her eyes were red and her cheeks still wet. He looked tenderly into her eyes, reading traces of pain, anxiety, and concern. Suddenly she threw herself into his arms and began crying and shaking. He held her tightly and fought the tears that were welling up in him as well.

"Your parents, Antonius . . .," she sobbed and continued to hold him. "It was so awful . . . You must hurt so badly . . . I feel so sorry."

Antonius could no longer restrain the tears; they streamed down his face. The couple stood for several minutes, holding each other tightly and weeping. Antonius was vaguely aware that several people passed by on the highway, eyeing them curiously.

Finally, Monica pulled away slightly and looked up at Antonius fearfully.

"What happened in there? At Julia's? I have to know."

He took her gently by the hands, still standing face to face. He lifted her left hand up and softly kissed the back of her fingers. "I told them that you were the only girl I could ever love . . . and that you were the only one I could ever marry."

She burst into tears and threw her arms around him again. He embraced her tightly; she sobbed uncontrollably. After a few moments she laid her head gently on his shoulder, still quivering and weeping, but not releasing him. People on the road continued to walk by and stare. Antonius ignored them and held her until the sobs subsided. Finally she lifted her head and smiled at him, trying to wipe away the tears.

"I got your cloak all wet," she said, touching the damp spot on his shoulder.

He wiped a trace of dirt off her chin, and then stood back to look at her dirty dress. "What have you been doing?"

"Come," she said. "Let's walk back into the city. I have a lot to tell you, and we have some serious decisions to make."

The two of them walked together down the Iconium highway toward Laodicea. The terrifying things in the city were still there— the praetorian guards, the Imperial Temple, the persecution of the Christians, Caius and Plautus, the circus—but somehow, now that they walked together, both of them inspired by and committed to following the Lord, they believed in the depths of their souls that with the Lord's help they could overcome all that stood before them.

φαίνει ἐν τῇ δυνάμει αὐτοῦ. Καὶ ὅτε εἶδον αὐτόν,

THE SWORD OF
THE ENEMY

ἔπεσα πρὸς τοὺς πόδας αὐτοῦ ὡς νεκρός, καὶ ἔθηκεν

"How many children do you want, Antonius?" Monica asked shyly as they approached the city. The sun was disappearing behind the city walls, casting soft shadows along the road.

"I don't know. A dozen?" He laughed and she elbowed him in the ribs.

Monica had already told Antonius about the tumultuous events that had taken place in Laodicea while he was gone, starting with the arrest of his parents and ending with her scare at the gate that afternoon and her visit to their cave with the scrolls.

"Seriously, do you want lots of children?"

"I suppose. Whatever you want. I guess we will take them one at a time."

"Unless we have twins, like my brothers."

"Heaven forbid that we have twins *like* your brothers," Antonius responded.

She smiled. "Where will we live? At your house? Will you be able to keep it? Caecelia is worried that the Imperial Temple may try to confiscate it."

"They may. They apparently stole Shabako's land."

"Will we live with my parents, then?"

"I don't know. When we get back, we need to sit down and talk seriously with your parents. I'd also like to hear what Isaeus thinks, at least about the business and the house. He should arrive tomorrow morning at the latest, perhaps even tonight. Nathan the banker is holding quite a sum of money for us in Ephesus. We have to at least consider leaving the province of Asia. I fear that I have enraged Plautus. The Imperial Cult may not tolerate my presence in Laodicea. It may be best if I flee."

"Leave Laodicea? What about my parents and my brothers?"

She frowned for a moment, thinking hard. Finally she sighed and stopped him in the middle of the road.

"Antonius," she said firmly. "If you have to flee, then we will flee together. If God leads us to leave Laodicea, then we will do what we have to do. I will go with you anywhere—Alexandria, Antioch, Cyrene, anywhere. And if God leads us to stay here and face the persecution, then I will stay with you and face it. Antonius, I am not naive about our future. I realize that this is not a children's game we are playing. This is real, in all of its harshness and tragedy. I know that. I have come to grips with the danger we face. I was there at the circus. I saw what the lions did to those we love. I still have nightmares about it. It was horrible beyond words. I am terrified at the thought of facing the same death. But if God calls on us to face such a danger for the sake of Christ, then I am ready to do so—with you."

Antonius saw the fire in her eyes. Faith that overcomes fear, he realized, and determination that produces courage in the face of death are not things that come only with age. He admired Monica's courage. He also noticed that she was beautiful when her eyes flared like this. He loved her—and he was proud of her. His heart pounded. He leaned over and kissed her softly on the lips. She quickly threw her arms around him and returned the kiss warmly. People stared at them as they walked by, but Antonius and Monica ignored them.

They reached the Eastern Gate as darkness descended on the city. They passed through the gate without incident. The gate was staffed with local guards only; they saw no praetorian guards there. The young couple walked quickly through the streets of Laodicea. They approached Monica's house cautiously, not sure what to expect. But Vivia rushed out from the gate, joyfully embraced Monica, and then gave Antonius a quick hug as well. Then she quickly pulled them into the courtyard and closed the gate.

"Juba!" Vivia called. "Monica's back!" She hugged her daughter again, clinging to her as if she would never let go. Juba ran across the courtyard, followed by the twins and Caligula. While Juba hugged his daughter, Antonius dropped to one knee and petted his barking dog to keep him quiet.

"Let's move away from the gate and into the courtyard," Juba suggested. As they moved away from the wall, Juba also embraced Antonius, expressing his grief about Antonius's parents. Vivia and Caecelia expressed their sympathy, too, and as tears formed in their eyes Antonius fought to keep his own tears away.

Juba led them across the courtyard to the main table.

"What happened at the gate, Monica?" her mother asked. "Did you have any trouble smuggling the scroll out?"

"I thought you were in Galatia, Antonius," Juba said.

"And have you seen my Isaeus?" asked Caecelia. "Did he find you in Iconium?"

"Everyone, please, please," Antonius said. "Isaeus is fine, Caecelia. He is on his way here and should arrive later tonight or early tomorrow. We will try to answer all of the rest of your questions, but time is short. Please sit. Monica and I have several things we must discuss with you all, and we must make some decisions quickly."

They circled the table. Juba, Vivia, and Caecelia turned the chairs toward Antonius and sat down. The children sat on the ground. Monica stood beside Antonius. Vivia leaned across the table and lit an additional lamp for more light.

"Uh . . . first of all . . .," Antonius said, looking first at Monica and then at Juba, "I would like to ask for Monica's hand in marriage." Monica took his arm and looked at her parents, beaming. Vivia and Caecelia smiled joyfully, too.

Juba looked concerned. "You both are aware that these are dangerous and uncertain days. Antonius will probably have to flee Laodicea soon if he refuses to sign the guild pledge for Domitian."

Antonius and Monica nodded. "We won't sign or swear any kind of allegiance to Domitian . . . either of us," stated Monica firmly.

The two of them could see the pain on Juba's face. "Where will you go?"

They looked at each other for a moment. Antonius spoke. "We're not sure. Probably Cappadocia, perhaps Pontus."

Juba sighed. "Have you considered North Africa? We have relatives in Cyrene and even in Carthage. The Imperial Cult has limited power in those cities, and you should be safe there. Also, many people in the mountains there raise sheep. The wool business should be good."

The couple looked at each other again. "We really don't know where to go," confessed Antonius. "Everything has happened so quickly. Cyrene sounds all right."

"Juba, Cyrene is so far away. Do you think that is best?" asked Vivia.

The conversation was interrupted by the low growling of Caligula, followed by a rapid knocking on the gate. Everyone looked at the gate with alarm.

But the visitor cried out, "Hail, Juba. I bring a message from Archelaus, the president of the Wool Merchants' Guild."

Everyone breathed a sigh of relief. Antonius opened the gate.

Maximus rushed through, sword drawn and pointed at Antonius's heart.

Caligula immediately attacked, but Maximus was ready and kicked the dog hard in the side of the head, sending him tumbling to the ground, yelping. Marcellus grabbed Caligula and held him back. The dog barked viciously and struggled against the boy's grip. As Antonius backed from the gate, four other praetorian guards rushed in with swords drawn, followed by their centurion, wearing his flashy uniform, complete with shiny breastplate and feather-crested helmet. Finally, Plautus stepped in with an evil smile, latching the gate shut behind him.

"Well, well, well," he said to Antonius. "We meet again. And so soon, too. You should have kept the horse, Antonius. You needed the time."

Everyone else in the courtyard was silent. Juba, Antonius, and Monica were standing; the others were still sitting. Juba had moved back toward one of the open doors of the house as the guards had entered. He now stood only a few paces away from the door. A gentle breeze blew through the courtyard, causing the lamps to flutter slightly, casting an eerie yellow light around the courtyard and reflecting off of the praetorian guards' helmets and swords. The guards cast on the walls of the courtyard huge grotesque shadows that moved with the flickering of the lamps.

"Who else do we have here?" asked Plautus, looking around. "Oh yes, Juba the Berber and his wonderful family . . . including his pretty little daughter."

Plautus stepped closer to Monica. He touched her face with the back of his hand. She slapped it away. Antonius bristled, but Maximus held his sword up in front of the young man's face as a warning.

"She is rather pretty, Antonius," Plautus continued, still standing in front of Monica, uncomfortably close. "Of course, she's nothing like Julia, is she? So your decision puzzles me. But you and your father have acted foolishly ever since I arrived in Laodicea."

One of the praetorian guards stepped closer.

"Is this the one?" Plautus asked him.

"Without a doubt," the guard answered. "She left through the Eastern Gate this morning carrying a large grain sack. I spoke with her. She said it contained rolls of tanned leather for her father to use on the farm."

"Hmm. Here's the problem," explained Plautus. "I want the scroll ... the so-called Apocalypse. I want *all* copies of it. And I want to know right now where all the copies are."

"We told you Antonius took them to—," Vivia began.

"Shut up!" Plautus shouted. "Antonius? I'm going to give you one chance to avoid the lions. Where are the scrolls?"

"I took them to Iconium." He instantly felt guilty for lying. It was not part of his character, and he knew that Christians should always be honest. However, to protect the scrolls and possibly also the women and children, lying seemed to be the right choice. Especially to these snakes.

"I don't believe that for a moment," Plautus retorted. Then turning back to Monica, he asked, "And what about you, pretty thing? You know where the scrolls are, don't you? You didn't have rolls of tanned leather in that bag. Tell us or we'll flog the skin right off the back of your young man."

"He's telling the truth," she stated without flinching. "He took the scrolls to Iconium for safety."

Antonius wondered if she were struggling with the blatant lie as much as he was.

"You are all lying!" shouted Plautus, now red in the face.

The praetorian guard standing beside Plautus grabbed Monica by the arm and turned to Plautus. "Why don't you let me and Maximus take this girl to one of the rooms in the house and make a woman out of her. Maybe that will loosen some tongues."

Maximus sheathed his sword, grinning. "Sounds like a good idea to me."

Plautus glanced at the centurion, who simply shrugged and nodded. With an evil smile, Plautus stroked Monica's face again. "I like that idea. So long as you share her with all of us."

Maximus grabbed Monica by the other arm, grinning hideously. He pointed toward the nearest door. "In there!"

As they dragged her toward the room, she screamed and kicked. At the same instant, Antonius drew his sword and charged Maximus. Juba reached around the corner of the nearby door and retrieved his sword from a hook on the wall. Marcellus released Caligula, and the courtyard erupted into a battlefield.

Maximus saw Antonius coming, and immediately released Monica and drew his sword. The huge guard spun just in time to parry Antonius's thrust. Without hesitation, Maximus countered with a powerful backhand slash. Antonius barely blocked Maximus's blow, and the impact knocked him back on his heels. He had never experienced a blow that powerful. Maximus rapidly stepped forward and drew back his arm to thrust his sword into the stunned Antonius—but Caligula suddenly attacked him from behind, sinking his teeth once again into the praetorian guard's calf, reopening his old wound. Maximus cursed, shook his leg loose, and swung his sword downward toward the dog, who quickly darted away. It gave Antonius time to recover.

The rest of the dimly lit courtyard had exploded into chaos. Caecelia screamed and ran for the nearest doorway, shouting frantically for her children to join her. Vivia bolted to the outer edge of the courtyard. Monica shook her arm loose from the grip of the other praetorian guard just as her father crashed upon him, striking the stunned guard with two devastating, lightning-fast slashes, sending him crumpling to the ground.

Two of the nearest guards instantly moved quickly toward Juba, swords drawn confidently, ready for close combat. Juba charged the two soldiers with a bloodcurdling war cry, as if he were back in the forest fighting the barbarian hordes. He swung his sword ferociously and powerfully. The two shocked praetorian guards tried desperately to block his blows, but Juba cut them both to pieces in an instant. They went down before they ever made a serious thrust or counter-stroke.

He stepped over the dead soldiers and faced the remaining three men. Plautus held up his hands to show that he was unarmed and wanted no part of this. The centurion of the praetorian guards, flanked by another experienced guard, approached Juba cautiously, sword in hand.

Across the courtyard, the panic-stricken Antonius was fighting for his life. He had attacked Maximus with his best moves, slashing and thrusting with all the skill that his father had imparted to him. Maximus, however, blocked his blows easily, countering each time with massive strikes that sent Antonius reeling backwards. Caligula continued to bark ferociously, nipping at Maximus's legs with every opportunity, and only the pestering of the dog kept Maximus from overpowering the younger man.

Enraged, Maximus was finally able to kick Caligula in the side, knocking the dog completely off his feet and rolling him over on the paving stones of the courtyard. Maximus then roared and swung his sword with all his might once again, aiming at Antonius's head. The young man blocked the blow just in time, backing against the court-yard wall as he did so. But just as Antonius blocked the blow Maximus stepped up close to him, grabbing the wrist of Antonius's sword hand at the same instant. Antonius did likewise, and the two combatants locked up together against the wall. The larger, more powerful Maximus then began forcing Antonius downward, bending his sword hand slowly backward.

Caligula jumped quickly back to his feet and raced once again into the fight, biting Maximus with all his might in the back of the guard's calf. At the same instant Antonius exploded forward, pushing the guard with all of his remaining strength. Maximus fell backwards, tripping over the dog, and the two men crashed to the ground, still locked up together.

Vivia and Monica stood in the doorway of the house, frozen in terror. Everything had happened so quickly. They now watched the centurion and his companion attack Juba systematically, putting him on the defensive. They saw Antonius and Maximus struggling on the ground. Vivia was white-faced. Across the courtyard she saw her small son Marcellus prying up a large paving stone from the courtyard.

Monica regained her senses and raced across the yard to pick up the sword of one of the guards Juba had killed in the first moments of the fight. Vivia followed close behind her, retrieving the other sword. They turned first toward Juba and watched as he slashed the leg of the guard in front of him, sending the man screaming toward the ground, and then struck him again, fatally, as the guard fell.

Juba then thrust powerfully at the centurion, catching him right below his breastplate. But as Juba withdrew his sword, Vivia and Monica watched helplessly as Plautus attacked him suddenly from behind, plunging a dagger into his back before they could do anything to help.

Both women screamed and sprinted across the rest of the courtyard to try to save him, but they were too late. Juba cried out in surprise and pain, looked for an instant at Vivia, and collapsed to his knees. Plautus struck him again in the back and Juba fell forward on his face.

Monica raised her sword with fury and charged the startled Plautus, who did not even have time to pick up the dead legionnaire's sword. Plautus backed up against the wall, holding his dagger out threateningly. Monica hesitated, uncertain whether to strike the wretched man. Plautus began to slide slowly along the wall toward the gate, but Vivia ran to cut off his escape. The two women, holding their swords firmly in both hands, approached the frightened high priest cautiously, slowly backing him into the corner away from the gate.

Meanwhile, across the courtyard, Maximus and Antonius had dropped their swords and were grappling hand-to-hand on the ground. Using his superior strength, Maximus rolled Antonius on to his back and emerged on top. With the big praetorian guard pinning him to the ground, Antonius found himself fighting frantically for his life. Caligula continued to bark and to nip at the guard from behind, but Maximus ignored the dog and concentrated on finishing off Antonius. The praetorian guard was too big and too powerful. With one huge hand, the praetorian guard pinned one of Antonius's arms to the ground. Antonius flailed wildly at the guard's face with his free hand, but Maximus easily warded off the weak blows. Then the guard punched Antonius hard in his ribs, knocking all the air out of him. Antonius thought that his ribs must surely have cracked.

Maximus had just drawn his arm back to strike again at Antonius's ribs when he looked quickly to the side—one of the twins, Marcellus, was sneaking up on him. But Maximus was too late; he turned to look just as Marcellus swung the paving stone with all his might against the side of the guard's head. The blow stunned him. It probably would have killed a normal man, but Maximus just shook his head for a moment to clear his blurred vision.

But from the other side, Mardonius, who had picked up the centurion's sword, whacked the guard in the back of the head with a powerful two-handed swing. Maximus's Roman helmet prevented Mardonius's blow from splitting his big head wide open, but the power of the blow, landing squarely at the back of his head and following so soon after the impact of Marcellus's paving stone, knocked Maximus unconscious, and he collapsed on top of Antonius.

Antonius immediately threw the limp praetorian guard off him and jumped to his feet. Sword in hand, he ran across the courtyard to help Monica and Vivia. At the moment, however, they were not in desperate need of help. They had backed Plautus into a corner and stood in front of him, swords in hand, struggling with their rage, trying to decide whether to kill him.

"Put your swords down, women," Plautus advised, "before one of you gets hurt. I don't want to have to kill a woman, but I will, if I have to."

"Drop your dagger, you snake, before I take your head off!" shouted Monica without hesitation. She held the sword in both hands, cocked back behind her head, like a coiled spring ready to be released. As Antonius approached, he saw Plautus look from Monica to Vivia and back again. Both held their swords as if they meant business and could inflict some serious damage.

"All right," he said, dropping his dagger. "Lower your swords."

Monica held hers even tighter. "You evil, cold-blooded, treacherous, cowardly killer," she snarled at him, taking a step forward. "You stabbed my father in the back. You would have raped me if you'd had your way. You probably were responsible for killing Gallus and Cassandra, too. I think I'll do all of Laodicea a favor and end your miserable life right here. Justice would be served."

Plautus cringed. "Please!" he begged, dropping to his knees. "Please, I beg you."

Antonius stepped beside Vivia, sword in hand, and placed his hand on her shoulder. Vivia dropped her sword and ran to Juba, lying unconscious on the ground. She rolled him over and felt his face. "He's dead!" she wailed.

"Marcellus!" Antonius called.

"Yes, sir?" answered the boy.

"You and Mardonius keep an eye on that big unconscious guard. If he so much as moves his little finger, clout him on the head with that paving stone again. Understand?"

"Yes, sir," they answered. "Is Father really dead?"

Their mother's sobbing told them all that it was so. Caecelia came and put her arm around Vivia. Antonius glanced at Caecelia; she caught his eye and shook her head, confirming Vivia's conclusion—Juba was indeed dead. Monica fought to hold back the tears, but they started to trickle down her cheeks. She still gripped the sword with all her might. Her knuckles were starting to turn white.

"I've got him, Monica," Antonius said softly. "Go see your mother."

Monica dropped the sword and ran to Vivia. The three women sat on the ground beside Juba, holding each other and weeping softly.

"Vivia," Antonius interrupted after a moment, holding his sword inches away from Plautus's throat.

Plautus cowered to the ground and curled up in a ball. "Please!" he begged.

"What do you want me to do with this vile creature?" Antonius continued. "Give me the word and I'll kill him."

Vivia continued to cry softly. After a few moments, she looked up at Antonius and said, "No, Antonius, don't kill him."

Slowly she stood. She wiped at her tears with her sleeve and then pulled Monica up as well. She looked around the courtyard at the carnage.

"There's been enough killing today." She sighed deeply and continued, "The Apocalypse says that we do not overcome evil by killing; that remains in the hands of God. We overcome by steadfastly enduring the persecution. No, Antonius, don't kill him, although God knows he deserves it."

Vivia walked to Plautus, leaned over him, and looked him directly in the eyes.

"Some day," she said, "you will stand before God Himself and answer for what you've done to His people."

Another quick knock came at the gate. Monica gasped. But Caligula ran to the gate, sniffed once or twice and wagged his tail.

"Open up. It's me, Isaeus!" cried the familiar voice.

Caecelia raced to the door, followed by her two children. Weeping uncontrollably, she opened the gate and threw herself into the arms of her surprised husband. The children joined their mother and hugged their father tightly around the waist. Isaeus leaned in from the darkness and looked at the bodies lying on the ground of the dimly lit courtyard. He shuffled in through the gate with his wife and children still clinging to him and surveyed the carnage. "Mother of the gods!" he muttered, turning quickly to close the gate behind him.

As they all caught their breath and their hearts gradually slowed to normal, they began to think more clearly. They were still in great danger.

They bound and gagged both Plautus and Maximus, placing them in one of the interior household storerooms. Moving the massive unconscious Maximus proved difficult, but Antonius and Isaeus were able to manage it, with considerable effort and with help from the women and the twins.

With Plautus's listening ears well out of range, they huddled around the table to discuss their options.

"Without doubt, we will all have to leave Laodicea immediately," Isaeus said.

Everyone agreed.

"My family and I will go to Cappadocia, where we have relatives," Isaeus continued.

"Let me write you a letter of manumission, Isaeus, giving you your freedom," Antonius suggested. "It will be much easier for you to establish yourself if you have freedman status."

Isaeus smiled and pulled out a pouch that hung around his neck. "Your father wrote me such a letter over three months ago," Isaeus explained, "anticipating such a time as this."

"Some money, then. You will need money," Antonius offered.

Isaeus held up the pouch again. "Already taken care of, Antonius."

"Cappadocia? Should we go there too?" asked Vivia.

"I think we should get farther away from the influence of the Imperial Cult," Antonius answered. "Juba had just suggested that Monica and I ought to go to Cyrene on the North African coast. That sounds like as good an option as any. Why don't you and the twins come with us to North Africa?"

"We do have distant relatives there. What do you think, Monica?" Vivia asked.

"I think it's the best choice," she answered as she put her arm around her mother. "But we should leave immediately."

"How will you ever get through Ephesus?" asked Isaeus. "How will you find a ship?"

"They won't be expecting us to go west to Ephesus," said Antonius. "They will expect us to go to Galatia. You are the one heading along the more dangerous route. You might want to take the long route to Cappadocia, Isaeus. Go north through Sardis up to Bithynia and Pontus. From there go east to Cappadocia."

Isaeus nodded.

"We will travel discreetly and carefully to Ephesus," explained Antonius. "We will find some Christians there to hide us. I hope Nathan the banker will help to smuggle us out of Ephesus by sea."

"What about the scrolls?" asked Monica.

"We will take the scrolls with us," Antonius said. "Isaeus and his family can take one scroll to Cappadocia, and we will take the other to North Africa. Each of us should try to have copies made as soon as possible after arriving safely."

All of them nodded. Their plans were made.

"All right," Isaeus said somberly. "Let's finish up as quickly as we can and get going."

They placed the dead praetorian guards in one of the other storerooms. They pulled up paving stones in the courtyard and solemnly buried Juba beneath the courtyard in a shallow grave, placing the paving stones back on top. Isaeus said a few words over his grave, then led the group in prayer while Monica and Vivia wept. Isaeus also said a few words for Gallus and Cassandra and prayed for them as well. Antonius stood beside Monica with his arm around her. It was not much of a funeral. He knew that these who had died deserved so much better, but he also knew that there simply was not time to do more.

After the brief funeral, Vivia retrieved Gallus's moneybag as well as a small amount that Juba had stored. "Here, Antonius," she said, handing the money to him. "You keep this."

They quickly gathered some light provisions for the trip. As they prepared to leave, Caligula ran back and forth in excitement, anticipating a trip somewhere.

"What will you do with Caligula?" Isaeus asked Antonius. "You can't really take him with you to Cyrene, can you?"

"Of course we can," said Marcellus.

"I don't know that it would be wise, Marcellus," advised Antonius. "We may have to hide along the way."

"But he saved your life!" argued the boy. "How can you leave him here? That big guard will kill Caligula if he finds him."

Antonius looked at Vivia, but she just shrugged. "All right," Antonius agreed. "Caligula will sail for Cyrene with us."

When all was ready, they paused for a moment, saying their silent farewells to Juba and to Gallus and to Cassandra and to their homes and lives in Laodicea. Vivia gave one final tearful look at the house where she had spent so many happy years, then ushered the twins out of the gate and into the dark street. They split up by families—Isaeus's family and Antonius's family—to avoid attention. Each group carried a lamp, a small pot of extra oil, and one traveler's bag filled with provisions. They were afraid that anything more might draw attention.

Each family exited the Eastern Gate without incident, and all of them breathed a sigh of relief as the city gate and its guards disappeared behind them. The two families met again along the highway and walked together on the main road for a while. Monica then led them down the same side road she had traveled earlier that day. After a short distance, she led them onto a path that took them to an isolated quiet place in the woods.

"All of you wait here quietly and rest while I climb the mountain and retrieve the scrolls," Antonius said as they stopped.

"Can you find the cave in the dark with just this lamp?" Monica asked him as she handed him the small flickering lamp.

"I think so. It might take a little while longer than usual."

"Be careful," she said and she kissed him on the cheek. He quickly disappeared into the darkness with Caligula on his heels. Soon even the faint glow of his lamp could not be seen.

Two hours passed, and they all began to worry. Finally, however, they saw the faint light descending through the forest toward them, and soon Antonius stumbled in out of the darkness, carrying the scrolls, Caligula still trotting along behind. Monica greeted Antonius with a hug.

"Were you glad you had that lamp when you crawled into the cave?" she asked.

"What for?" he lied. "What could possibly be in the cave to frighten me?"

"Hmmph!" she said, wiping dirt off his chest.

Antonius handed the copy of the scroll to Isaeus, who placed it carefully in his traveling bag. Antonius kept the original Apocalypse, holding it securely under his arm. It was still wrapped in the goatskin bag that had protected it from the sea.

Both groups embraced. Isaeus's family would travel north, taking an isolated path that bypassed Laodicea until they were clear of the city, where they would then cut across and intersect the road that led to Hierapolis, and beyond to Philadelphia and Sardis. Antonius and his group would travel through the woods, first to the south and then westward, avoiding the main highway until they had circumvented Laodicea and connected to the road going west from Laodicea to Ephesus.

Everyone was tense. No one knew how long it would be before someone discovered Plautus and Maximus. Isaeus agreed to persuade one of his relatives in Hierapolis to take a message back to Laodicea where they would discreetly deliver the message to the Imperial Temple to let them know where to find their illustrious high priest and oversized praetorian guard.

Isaeus led them in a brief prayer. Antonius then unrolled the scroll, and by the dim light of the lamp he read a few words from the Apocalypse:

"'Then I saw thrones, and the people sitting on them had been given the authority to judge. And I saw the souls of those who had been beheaded for their testimony about Jesus, for proclaiming the word of God. And I saw the souls of those who had not worshiped the beast or his statue, nor accepted his mark on their forehead or their hands. They came to life again, and they reigned with Christ for a thousand years.'"

They said farewell and parted.

τὴν δεξιὰν αὐτοῦ ἐπ᾽ ἐμὲ λέγων, μὴ φοβοῦ· ἐγώ εἰμι ὁ πρῶτος

THE CITY
OF THE BEAST

καὶ ὁ ἔσχατος καὶ ὁ ζῶν, καὶ ἐγενόμην νεκρὸς καὶ ἰδοὺ ζῶν εἰμι

Antonius and his new family groped along throughout much of the night, skirting Laodicea on back roads and farm paths. Both Monica and Antonius were fairly familiar with the network of farm roads around the city, but things looked different in the dark. Marcellus and Mardonius had also roamed this area, and more than once they were able to pick the right path when Antonius and Monica were uncertain. Monica carried the lamp and walked in front with Marcellus. Mardonius and Vivia followed them, with Mardonius carrying the scroll and Vivia carrying the clay pot of extra lamp oil. Antonius, carrying the traveling bag of provisions, brought up the rear.

After several wearisome hours of walking, their oil ran out and total darkness enveloped them, forcing them to stop and to rest until dawn. They spent the remainder of the night trying to sleep, huddled together on the cold damp ground wrapped only in their cloaks.

They rose before dawn and began walking as soon as it was light enough to see the path. They stopped briefly to eat a meager breakfast of bread and to drink from a cold stream, but soon they were back on their feet and traveling again. Before long, their path emptied onto a substantial dirt farm road. A short time later, just as the sun crept over the mountains, they ventured cautiously out onto the main highway that led west from Laodicea to Ephesus.

They now walked in two groups, thinking that they would not be so easily identified that way. Vivia and the boys walked in front, taking turns carrying the traveling bag. Antonius and Monica walked several hundred paces behind, as far back as they dared, and carried the Apocalypse. The roads in Asia Minor were not always safe, and a woman traveling with only two boys might present an easy target for thieves. Antonius wanted to be close enough to Vivia to come to her aid if anyone troubled her. Caligula stayed with the twins most of the time, although occasionally he would run back to Antonius and Monica.

As the sun rose, the highway became busy, and there were almost always other travelers in view, as well as many oxcarts. Vivia and the boys often followed right behind one of these oxcarts; to another traveler, they would appear to be the oxcart driver's family.

Antonius and Monica talked to each other constantly as they walked, pouring out both their dreams and their sufferings to each other. Antonius talked a lot about his father and mother. Sharing his thoughts with Monica seemed to help him work through his grief. Monica likewise shared her feelings about Juba—her anger at him for signing the guild pledge to Domitian, but also her pride in him as he sacrificed himself bravely for her. They talked of Cyrene and Carthage. Juba had told Monica tales of his home country and of his childhood. She told Antonius as many of these stories as she could remember. They were both excited and afraid: joyful to be together, but still deeply grieving over the loss of those so dear to them.

Because of the danger, they could not relax. Antonius kept a close watch behind him for horsemen. Three times that day, lone horsemen came galloping down the highway from Laodicea. Two were Imperial dispatch riders; one was a private messenger. Twice Antonius and Monica saw the riders approaching in the distance and were able to dart into the woods unseen. Each time, the riders had passed by Vivia and the boys without so much as a glance.

The third rider, however, had been screened by a curve in the road. He came around the corner behind them quickly, surprising Antonius and Monica. Now that he had seen them, it would have been foolish to flee into the woods. The two of them continued to walk, trying to look unconcerned. As the rider passed them he slowed the horse, turned in his saddle, and looked closely at them. Their hearts pounded and their throats went dry. The rider smiled at Monica and then spurred his horse on. He passed Vivia and the boys without a look.

"Whew!" declared Monica, her heart still pounding. "That was scary. Why did he look at us like that?"

"I don't think he was looking at *us*," said Antonius. "He was looking at *you*. He probably slows down and smiles at all the pretty girls on the road. It makes his trip more interesting."

Monica blushed. "After a night on the ground in the woods, I probably look frightful. I certainly don't feel very pretty."

"Well, he thought you were. Didn't you see that big smile?"

"Yes, I saw it. He had a handsome smile too, didn't he? Especially with that big nose and those two missing teeth." They both laughed, and it felt good to laugh together. However, they soon grew silent, reflecting on how easily they could have been discovered.

They spent the next night sleeping on the cold ground in the woods again, and by their third day on the road they were growing weary, especially Vivia and the twins. Several horsemen passed them that day during their long walk. Antonius and Monica were able to hide from the riders only once, but they were thankful that they heard that particular rider coming in time to hide; they watched from the woods as the rider passed, and they recognized the red uniform of the praetorian guard.

On the third night they reached the city of Tralles, and Antonius led them to a respectable inn, where they ate a good, hot meal and then slept in comfortable beds formed by interlaced leather strips hung from sturdy wooden frames. By the next night they were in Magnesia, like Tralles a substantial city with numerous inns. As they cautiously checked into one of the inns for the night, they all hoped the city was large enough to absorb five weary travelers without anyone noticing.

They left Magnesia before dawn, hoping to make it to Ephesus before dark. From Magnesia, the road took them up and over a small mountain range. The road was often steep and the going slow. Several hours after dawn, Vivia, the twins, and Caligula were walking several hundred paces in front of Antonius and Monica as usual. Vivia saw a large road repair work crew of perhaps fifty men ahead in the road. It appeared that a creek had flooded recently, washing out part of the highway. The crew had restored the roadbed and was now replacing the paving stones. But the large number of rough-looking workmen on an isolated stretch of highway made Vivia uncomfortable. She slowed her pace, allowing Antonius and Monica to catch up. They passed through the work crew together, trying not to interrupt the construction. The overseer of the work crew stood on the far side of the construction site, watching them intently as they passed by the work crew.

"I don't like the way that man is looking at us," whispered Monica to Antonius as they passed him.

"Maybe he's just looking for pretty girls," suggested Antonius, under his breath.

"I don't think so."

As they approached him, the overseer stepped in front of Antonius, stopping him in the road. "May I have a word with you, sir?" He spoke quietly, even though they were out of hearing range of the workers.

"Certainly," Antonius answered, not knowing what else to say. They all stopped and looked at each other anxiously. Caligula sniffed the overseer, but soon lost interest in him and lay down beside Marcellus.

"Yesterday a rider from Ephesus, a soldier in the praetorian guard from the Imperial Temple, stopped to ask us whether we had seen a certain party traveling on this road."

"Which party would that be, sir?" inquired Antonius.

"Either a group of nine, or perhaps a group of five . . . a pretty girl with her mother and twin brothers, accompanied by a young man, probably armed with a soldier's short sword." He saw the look of panic in their eyes, and added with a smile, "But they didn't say anything about a dog, so they must be looking for some other group."

As if on cue, Caligula rose to his feet and trotted over to the overseer, who leaned over and patted the dog on the head.

"Are you the son of Gallus the centurion?" he asked Antonius.

"Yes, sir, I am."

"I am sorry to hear of your father's death; he was a great man, respected by believers and unbelievers alike. And the Ethiopian Shabako died with him?"

Antonius nodded. "And Senator Flavius. And Pastor Epaphras, his wife, Shabako's wife, and . . . my mother."

"We have lost many faithful ones here in Ephesus as well. The senator's cousin Severus was beheaded two days ago. I am part of the church here, although these days we meet secretly in our homes with only those we trust. Terrible things have happened in our city. You must be extremely careful. I would advise that you split into small groups, so that you won't be so obvious. Now hurry on before my work crew grows any more suspicious."

"Thank you, sir, and may the Lord bless you," said Vivia. "Perhaps we will see you in Ephesus."

"It is more likely that you will next see me at the foot of the throne of God, worshiping with the rest of the martyrs from this province. You are heading right into the arms of the beast. Be careful, and may God bless you and watch over you. I will be praying for you."

Soberly, they walked away, splitting back into two groups, but this time, Mardonius stayed back with Antonius and Monica. The mention of twins had alarmed them.

A few hours later, they looked down on Ephesus from a secluded resting place in the woods, just off of the highway. There they made plans for entering the city. They would leave one by one, at intervals of ten to twenty minutes. Antonius would go directly to the secret church elder Isaeus had told him about and ask about a place to hide until he could contact Nathan about passage out on a ship. The rest of them would go to the main agora of Ephesus, the busy lower marketplace, where they would wait for Antonius. He would find them in the market one by one and tell them where to go next.

All of them were uneasy about the plan, but no one could come up with anything better. Vivia was beside herself at the thought of letting her boys go into Ephesus alone. In fact, Antonius was worried that she would not actually let them go. He drew a map of Ephesus in the dirt, and went over the layout of the city with the boys several times.

Vivia and Monica had each purchased a bundle of firewood from one of the many woodcutters who sold wood along the road near Ephesus. Hundreds of women went out of the city each day to buy wood for their cooking fires. Two more would not be noticed.

In addition, Antonius was alarmed at the words of the road maintenance overseer about a young man with a soldier's short sword. He realized that he could not be seen in Ephesus with his father's sword on his belt. He agonized over what to do with it.

Vivia suggested that she take the sword into the market and then deposit it with a loan merchant, taking out a loan on the sword.

She could say that it belonged to her deceased husband, and that now she was in financial difficulty and needed a loan. When they got ready to leave Ephesus they could then repay the loan and retrieve the sword.

Antonius agreed. He untied one of the firewood bundles and placed his father's sword inside, wrapping it in Marcellus's cloak. He then carefully retied the bundle, ensuring that the wrapped sword could not be seen. Vivia insisted on carrying this bundle, overruling Monica's protestations.

Soon it was time to go. Antonius went first because he had to make the arrangements for them. It was hard to leave. Monica held him tightly and then gave him a quick kiss.

"Be careful," she whispered. "I need you."

"I'll see you in the agora in a few hours."

Antonius walked out onto the highway with the goatskin bag containing the Apocalypse tucked firmly under his arm. Soon he fell in behind an oxcart loaded with cowhides. He told the driver that he was weary of walking, and after a brief negotiation, he paid two copper coins and climbed up on the oxcart beside the driver. The driver paid the same two coins to the local guards in the tollbooth at the gate, and they passed into the city without incident. Antonius noticed, however, that there were six praetorian guards at the gate, observing all who entered. He was sick with anxiety for the others, and he wanted to stay and watch the gate to see whether they got in safely, but he knew that he must start immediately on his errand. Thanking the driver, he set off on foot across Ephesus.

Mardonius was to follow, leaving shortly after Antonius. Vivia hugged and kissed him, and then with hesitation, let him go. He fell in with some shepherd boys who were bringing their small flocks into the city to sell. The praetorian guards did not notice him.

Monica left next, loaded down with a bundle of firewood on her back. Her heart was pounding as she approached the gate. She kept her head down, but she still noted five . . . no, six praetorian guards standing around the gate, watching everyone who went in. *I can't stop now,* she thought. She walked into the gate, trying to look tired—which was not difficult—and bored, which was extremely hard. As she drew alongside the praetorian guards, one of them stopped her. Her heart jumped into her throat. Sweat began to form on her brow. Panic was creeping in. *Stay calm. Keep your wits. Help me, Lord.*

"Here's a pretty girl I haven't noticed before," the guard said to her, blocking her way into the city. "Why not?"

"Because Olivia, our good-for-nothing Scythian slave, normally gets the firewood," Monica said, trying to act disgusted. "Only today she is too sick . . . or so she says. So Mother decides that I can get the wood. As if I don't have enough to do already. Hmmph! Good-for-nothing slaves." She then gave the guard a quick smile. He smiled back and stepped aside.

"I hope she stays sick for a long time so that we can see you some more," he called after her as she walked away.

"A pox on you!" she shouted back. The other guards all grinned. Monica thought she might faint, but she continued to trudge through the gate and into the city, forcing herself to keep her head down, ignoring the beautiful colonnaded streets and the fascinating shops on both sides.

Ten minutes later Marcellus and Caligula wandered in the gate without drawing any attention. Just another kid and his dog. Vivia was not far behind. She could not stay in the bushes and let Marcellus get out of sight. In fact, he had barely entered the city when she reached the gate. A middle-aged woman with a load of firewood should not attract attention, and Vivia thought that she would pass through easily. But two of the local guards got into a scuffle, laughing and shoving each other. They tumbled away from the gate and stumbled right into Vivia, knocking her down. The load of wood likewise fell to the ground with a crash! *What if the bundle breaks open and they see the sword?* Vivia scrambled up to her feet and bent over to inspect the bundle. The guards stopped their scuffle and apologized to her. The youngest guard grabbed the bundle for her before she could stop him.

"Here, ma'am," he offered. "I'll help you with this. Whoa! This bundle is heavier than it looks. Do you have a plowshare inside this?"

"No," she mumbled nervously. "I think they sold me some wet wood."

The guards helped her load it back on to her shoulders and she continued into the city. She saw Marcellus just up the street, watching for her. As she cleared the gate he turned and continued into the heart of the city. Just inside the gate, Vivia noticed a newly erected statue of Domitian. Not a gigantic one, like the one in the temple, but a life-size replica of the emperor, with an inscription that read: "Caesar Domitian, our Lord and God, Protector of Ephesus, His Grateful City." Vivia shuddered as she walked by.

εἰς τοὺς αἰῶνας τῶν αἰώνων καὶ ἔχω τὰς κλεῖς τοῦ

THE BRIDE

θανάτου καὶ τοῦ ᾅδου. γράψον οὖν ἃ εἶδες καὶ ἃ εἰσὶν καὶ

The main street leading from the Western Gate across Ephesus passed in front of the Imperial Temple dedicated to Domitian. Antonius did not want to go near the temple, but there was no other logical route. As he approached, the street became extremely crowded, packed with pilgrims, worshipers, and curious onlookers, in addition to the normal crowd of shopkeepers and shoppers. Clutching the goatskin bag tightly, Antonius was jostled against an elderly man trying to move in the same direction.

"Excuse me, sir," Antonius said.

"It's all right," the old man replied. "The streets are extra crowded today. Everyone wants to see the statue. They think it may speak again."

"It may . . . what?" asked Antonius.

"It spoke—the statue of Domitian spoke. At least that's what everyone says. You must be the only one in Ephesus who hasn't heard."

"When did this happen?"

"Yesterday. At the time of sacrifice, just about now. The priests and praetorian guards brought in several people who would not bow down to Domitian. They placed them in front of the statue and ordered them to bow and worship. When they refused, lightning crashed down and killed them all, striking terror in the hearts of everyone there. Then the statue spoke, commanding faithful worship and sacrifice to the emperor and warning of death and judgment on anyone who refuses."

"Do you believe it?" asked Antonius.

"Everyone else seems to. I'm going to the temple today to see for myself. My son is sick; perhaps if I sacrifice to Domitian he will be healed. Strange things are happening. Many people are frightened."

Antonius was amazed at the thousands of people trying to crowd in through the temple entrance. Looking through the open gates, Antonius could see the huge statue of Domitian, with thousands of worshipers bowing before him, proclaiming his power and authority over all creation, pleading with him to speak again.

On the sacrificial platform directly in front of the statue, Caius, the great high priest, was sacrificing a large goat. The priest was dressed in a bloodred toga, with a long flowing crimson outer robe that fluttered in the wind. He was assisted by a dark-haired priestess who kept a long snake draped over her neck and shoulders. The snake was alive! It was constantly moving, turning its head from side to side, observing all that was around it. She petted it as she poured the blood from the slaughtered goat all across the altar.

Antonius shivered; his skin was crawling. Several merchants in front of the temple were selling miniatures of the statue. Hordes of people crowded these stalls, buying the small statues as fast as the merchants could make change. *Madness!* Antonius pushed on through the crowd.

The crowd on the road thinned out slightly as Antonius moved farther from the temple, and he hurried to the house of Nathan the banker. After knocking, he was met at the gate by the steward of the house, who recognized Antonius and politely informed him that Nathan was at the harbor on business and was not expected back until late that evening. He suggested that Antonius come back in the morning. Antonius's heart sank—but he knew that it would not be prudent to wander along the harbor asking for Nathan the Jew; if he were recognized, he could endanger both Nathan and himself. Reluctantly, he agreed to meet with Nathan in the morning.

Antonius hurried to find the house of the elder whom Isaeus had recommended. Isaeus had met with this man on his visit to Ephesus earlier in the month—he had, in fact, been the one to whom Isaeus had given the copy of the Apocalypse.

It took Antonius nearly two hours to locate the elder's house. As each hour passed, his anxiety rose about Monica and her family. He desperately wanted to run to the agora to make sure they were all there, safe and sound.

He knocked at the gate of the elder's house. No response. After a moment, he knocked again.

A woman's feeble voice called from the other side, "Who is it?"

"A friend," Antonius answered.

"What do you want?" she demanded.

"I would like a word with Pheidon, elder of the church."

"Go away," she said.

"Just a word with the elder, please!"

"He's dead. They beheaded him yesterday. Go away." The woman sobbed softly on the other side of the gate.

What do I do now? Antonius slowly turned away, confused and frightened. He had brought Monica and her family here to Ephesus. He was responsible for their safety. And now, he did not know where to go or what to do. They desperately needed a place to hide until Nathan could arrange to smuggle them out, if indeed Nathan would take such a risk. But where? The inns were dangerous. Yet where else could they stay? He walked slowly down the street, crying out to God, pleading for guidance and wisdom.

"Young man!" a voice called.

Antonius turned to see a thin, middle-aged, balding man hurrying toward him.

"I am Lysias, the servant of Elder Pheidon," the man said as he approached Antonius. "Formerly a slave of Pheidon, now a slave of Jesus Christ. Greetings! Please excuse Pheidon's wife. She is distraught over the death of her husband. Can I help you?"

"I am Antonius, from the church at Laodicea. I am the son of Gallus, who was recently martyred in the circus at Laodicea."

"We heard. I am so sorry. I know Isaeus, the servant of Gallus. What has become of him?"

"Isaeus and his family have fled to the east. The woman to whom I am betrothed and her family are here with me. Her father, Juba, killed some praetorian guards defending her and protecting the original copy of John's Apocalypse, which the high priest was trying to seize and destroy. The high priest is also seeking to arrest me. We fled Laodicea and came here, hoping to arrange passage on a departing ship. But we need a place to hide for a day or two."

The servant stared at Antonius for a moment, apparently thinking. He glanced down at the goatskin bag Antonius held, and then said quietly, "Come with me. I'll show you the place."

Lysias led Antonius back across town to an expensive house on Curetes Street, not far from the Imperial Temple. The gate and courtyard fronted the street, but much of the house itself was carved into the mountainside. Lysias did not go in; rather, he casually strolled past it, with Antonius close behind him.

"That's the house," Lysias said, under his breath. "We are hiding several families there now. Come at night. See that bathhouse ahead on your right?"

Antonius nodded.

"Go to the back of the bathhouse. There you will see a trail leading up the side of the mountain. Take the trail until you come up behind this house. Can you see the big fig tree behind the house on the side of mountain?"

"Yes."

"Just below that tree is the entrance to a cave, hidden by some bushes. Just inside the cave, you will find a bolted wooden door. Knock five times."

Antonius thanked him repeatedly. He wondered whether he should trust this man, but realized that he had little choice. *It is a greater wonder,* he thought, *that Lysias trusts me.*

Lysias was gone in an instant.

Without hesitation, Antonius turned and practically ran through the streets to the large lower agora. The market was huge, covering acres and acres. There were perhaps twenty or thirty thousand people here at any given time during the day. Antonius roamed through the market, searching for familiar faces. With joy he found each member of his new family—first Marcellus and Caligula, then Vivia, Mardonius, and finally . . . Monica, who was examining silk scarves from Persia. He wanted to hug each of them, especially Monica, but he refrained. He spoke softly to each, explaining their next maneuver.

They waited in the market until dusk, keeping each other in sight. Vivia and Monica had sold their firewood and had purchased fruit and vegetables in order to look like regular shoppers. When the time came, Antonius left the agora first, leading the way. Monica followed, staying behind him a hundred paces or so. Next came Mardonius, Marcellus and Caligula, and then Vivia, each likewise separated by about the same distance.

They passed through the streets of Ephesus without incident, then gathered on the trail behind the bathhouse, embracing each other and whispering about their individual adventures during the day. Antonius led them cautiously along the trail toward the house of refuge. They stopped in a sheltered place, waiting for night to completely set in, and then proceeded slowly, hampered by darkness. Antonius found the fig tree, but for a few panic-stricken moments he could not find the cave entrance. Fortunately, Caligula found it, darting suddenly out of sight behind some thick bushes. They all squeezed past the bushes and into the low and narrow entrance to the cave.

The door was there, just as Lysias had said. Antonius knocked five times and waited anxiously. After a moment the door opened, and a voice in the darkness invited them in. They all quickly filed into the cave, which was nearly as dark as the night outside.

But after the door was closed, someone uncovered a lamp, and Antonius and his companions could see their surroundings. The "cave" was actually one of the back rooms of the house, carved into the mountainside. The room had been plastered, and the walls had been decorated with beautiful paintings. There were mosaics on the floor as well. A solid wooden door, bolted firmly, appeared to lead to the rest of the house.

Soon several other lamps were lit, and the room became a warm, friendly place. There were two other families in the room. Everyone introduced themselves. The families were both from Ephesus, prominent citizens until recently. Both of them had lost family members during the last few days and had been forced to flee upon hearing reports that they also were to be arrested.

There was also a lone young man from Smyrna. As he rose to introduce himself, Antonius recognized him. "Polukarpos!"

Antonius led Monica across the room to meet the young man. "Monica, this is the pastor from Smyrna I told you about. He is the one I met at Severus's house here in Ephesus, when we were first reading the scroll and trying to decipher it. Polukarpos, this is Monica, my betrothed. And this is her mother, Vivia, and her brothers Marcellus and Mardonius."

"Hail, Antonius! Finder of the Apocalypse!" greeted the young pastor with a smile. "And warm greetings in the name of the Lord to you, Monica, and to your family. It's good to see you again, Antonius, although the circumstances are not the best."

Antonius and Polukarpos sat together and shared the events that had so dramatically shaped their lives in recent days. Antonius told him briefly about his parents. Polukarpos truly seemed to understand and to grieve with him.

After talking for a few minutes about the recent traumatic events, Antonius suddenly changed the subject. "Pastor Polukarpos, do you have the authority of the church in Smyrna to marry people?"

Monica looked at Antonius with a start. Vivia's mouth dropped open.

"Yes, I do. Who is getting married?"

Antonius pulled out a leather pouch that hung around his neck. He opened the pouch and pulled out a roll of delicate red cloth, which he carefully unrolled to reveal a crimson veil. He placed it ceremoniously over Monica's face.

"Antonius!" Monica exclaimed, throwing her arms around him. "When did you get a wedding flammeum veil?"

"We were stuck in that market for a long time today. It looked to me to be providential. Also . . ." He retrieved a small piece of papyrus. "Paper for the official wedding contract . . . to make the marriage legal even in the eyes of Rome."

"Amazing," announced the pastor with a smile. "I didn't expect to perform any marriages in Ephesus, but the Lord has his ways and his purposes. None of us are dressed in wedding clothes, but surely the veil is enough. The contract will certainly formalize it. Let's get started."

Polukarpos and Vivia organized the room and the current occupants into a traditional Christian wedding party. The other families gladly joined in the celebration. They even located some candles and lit those, as was the custom. Polukarpos wrote out a traditional marriage contract on Antonius's papyrus. Antonius signed on behalf of his family. Polukarpos signed for Vivia on behalf of Monica's family. Several of the others signed as witnesses. The group next sang several hymns and a traditional wedding song. Polukarpos muddled through most of the ceremony. He was not eloquent, but he was warm and sincere. The simple service was short. Before the bride and groom knew it, Antonius had lifted the veil, completing the ceremony, and they were man and wife.

"We are forbidden to leave the room," Polukarpos reminded them. "So you are not going to have much of a wedding night."

Yet no one seemed to be listening. Antonius, Monica, Vivia, Marcellus, Mardonius, and all of their new friends were hugging each other and crying. Caligula, too, caught the excitement of the moment, circling the new couple and wagging his tail furiously.

Eventually everyone calmed down. The lamps and candles were snuffed. Thin straw mattresses and blankets were provided for the new family, and everyone lay down to sleep. With no privacy, Antonius and Monica merely cuddled together on a straw mattress and talked softly late into the night, when they finally drifted off to sleep as well, overcome at last by weariness.

chapter twenty-two

ἃ μέλλει γενέσθαι μετὰ ταῦτα. τὸ μυστήριον τῶν ἑπτὰ ἀστέρων

MARTYRDOM OR ESCAPE?

οὓς εἶδες ἐπὶ τῆς δεξιᾶς μου καὶ τὰς ἑπτὰ λυχνίας τὰς χρυσᾶς·

Morning came quickly. Most of the adults had risen early and started breakfast. Polukarpos was reading aloud softly from the Apocalypse, which Antonius had shared with him shortly after they woke. Marcellus and Mardonius remained on the floor with their blankets pulled over their heads, trying in vain to catch a few more minutes' sleep, and wishing that the young pastor could wait awhile longer before he read the scroll.

Suddenly a rapid five knocks came at the door leading to the house. Polukarpos instantly handed the scroll to Antonius and hurried to the door. He unbolted it immediately and pulled it open.

A young woman, apparently a servant girl, stood in the hallway, her face deathly white. She spoke quietly but quickly and nervously. "Someone must have betrayed us! The praetorian guards have entered the courtyard and are starting a search of the house. There are no guards behind the house, so they do not seem to know about the outside exit. Quickly! You must all flee! Run!" She raced away down the hall.

Polukarpos closed and bolted the door. Antonius already had the scroll rolled up and was placing it inside the goatskin bag. Vivia had jerked the sleepy boys to their feet. The other two families were already exiting through the outside door into the early morning light.

"Where will we go?" Vivia asked anxiously, as she moved the twins toward the exit.

"We will all scatter across the city as we did before," Antonius said, trying to think. "Then at midmorning we will all meet in the agora, as we did yesterday. Don't speak to each other; I'll contact you. Hopefully, Nathan can help us."

They rushed out through the door and pushed past the bushes. Polukarpos came out last. He closed the outer door and then suggested to Antonius that they wedge several large rocks between the door and the outer cave wall.

"Go!" Antonius ordered the others. The boys took off down the trail with Caligula running beside them. Vivia and Monica hesitated. "I'll see you in the marketplace," he promised.

"I'll be waiting," Monica answered. She and her mother raced away.

Polukarpos and Antonius took only a few moments to carry the rocks and place them tightly behind the door, making it nearly impossible to open.

"I wish that I had my sword," Antonius muttered to himself as they completed their work.

"The sword is not the answer to this attack from Satan," the young pastor counseled. "Christianity will defeat Rome, Antonius. Make no mistake about it. But we will not defeat it by the sword. Let go of your sword. Cling to that scroll under your arm instead."

"What will *you* do?" Antonius asked the pastor as they finished.

"I'm a rather slippery fellow. I will sneak out over the walls and return to Smyrna."

"Farewell, friend," Antonius said. "May the Lord bless you."

"And may He be with you always!"

Antonius flew down the trail and then slowed to a trot as he approached the bathhouse. He tried to walk calmly out on to the street, but he was sweating profusely. Anxiously he glanced down the street at the house where they had been hiding. He saw a dozen or more praetorian guards standing along the wall outside the house on the street. As he looked up at the hillside he saw other guards climbing over the back outer wall of the house onto the mountainside. He turned quickly toward Nathan's house and rushed down the street. As he went, he prayed fervently that Nathan would be able to help; they were running out of options.

Nathan's house was not far from the agora. As he walked, Antonius thought once that he saw Mardonius in the distance. Perhaps it was Marcellus, although Antonius did not see Caligula. Soon he arrived at the gate of Nathan the banker. He took a deep breath and knocked.

Secundus the steward opened the gate and invited Antonius in. He led the young man into the courtyard where Nathan was just finishing his breakfast.

"Antonius!" he exclaimed. "I am delighted to see you. I have been worrying about you. Through our sources at the Imperial Temple, we hear all kinds of horrible things about you and your family. Is it true about your father?"

"Yes, sir."

"In the circus? Lions?"

"Yes, sir."

"I was grieved to hear it. They are barbarians, Antonius. Worse than barbarians. They are inherently evil. It is as if they come from Satan himself. At least that's how it looks to this old humble Jew." The banker looked at Antonius with compassion. "Your father was a good, honest man. As good and as honest as they come. We knew each other for many years. How can I help you?"

"Our situation, as you know, is urgent. We need to catch passage on a ship to North Africa, or to a location from which we can transfer to North Africa ... and we need to do it discreetly."

"*We?*" asked Nathan. "Who else is with you? Isaeus?"

"No, Isaeus has fled to Cappadocia. But my father's closest friend Juba killed a few praetorian guards back in Laodicea before he was killed himself. I have his family with me. As a matter of fact, I just married his daughter."

"In the midst of this, you got married?" asked the banker with a slight smile.

"Yes, sir . . . last night."

"You got married last night? Incredible! You Gentile Christians never fail to amaze me."

"Can you help us?"

"Antonius, I have always felt that the God of Abraham smiled on your father. Not only did he survive that terrible battle by the Elbe when he shouldn't have, but in all of his business dealings with me, God always seemed to bless him."

Antonius nodded. Business with Nathan had always gone well.

"And today—whether it's my God or whether it's your God or whether it's the same God—someone up there is looking out for you."

"How is that?"

"I just purchased a ship. It sails for Alexandria and Cyrene within a few hours."

"That's wonderful! Miraculous even. Can you sneak us aboard? Can the captain be trusted?"

"The captain is completely trustworthy. He is also anxious to leave Ephesus, at least for a while. I'm sure that we can book passage for you and your family."

"You don't know how thankful I am for this."

"One other thing, Antonius," continued the Jew. "As you know, you have a considerable sum of money deposited with me. I can give you all of this money now if you want to. Or . . . I was thinking—as I said, I just bought this merchant ship. I was hoping to ship grain from North Africa here to Ephesus, or perhaps Miletus—even in

Athens the price for grain is high. Then we return to Cyrene or Carthage with goods from Greece or Asia. The profits should be good."

"I'm listening."

"Well, I would like some partners in this venture. The captain of the ship has agreed to buy a quarter share in the enterprise. You have enough money deposited with me to purchase a quarter share as well, and still have a small amount left over to help establish you in Cyrene. You could then run the North African side of the enterprise."

"Nathan, this sounds wonderful. I would be honored to enter into partnership with you."

"It's a deal?"

"It's a deal."

"All right," the Jew said with a smile. "We must hurry. The ship must sail in the next two or three hours, or else it will miss the tide. I must also draw up a contract and withdraw some money and do a few other things. We have a lot to do in a short time."

"We will be ready. We are anxious to leave," Antonius declared.

"Let's do this," the banker said thoughtfully. "The ship is in the sixth stall along the main wharf—a two-masted, midsized cargo ship. I'll send my steward to the captain to alert him that he has some important passengers coming. Gather your people and go directly on board. The captain will hide you in his cabin. I'll meet you there to sign the contract, and with God's blessing, you could be at sea within three hours!"

"Thank you so much," Antonius said gratefully.

"Thank the God of Israel," encouraged the Jew.

Antonius and Secundus left immediately and walked together as far as the agora. The steward headed for the harbor while Antonius entered the market, looking hard for his loved ones and hoping they all were safe.

He spotted Marcellus and Caligula first. He strolled over to them casually and explained the plan to Marcellus. They would leave the agora as they had yesterday, staggered by only a hundred paces at most. They were going to a ship, on the main wharf, in the sixth stall.

"Which one is the main wharf?" the boy asked.

"Just keep me in sight and follow me. I'll lead you to it."

Antonius then circulated throughout the agora, finding his family members one by one, quietly explaining the plan. All of them were greatly encouraged and excited to be leaving. The tension they had been facing the past few days had been almost overwhelming.

Antonius found Monica last. He walked up beside her, gently squeezed her hand, and quickly explained Nathan's plan. She sighed with relief, then smiled at him. He thought that he had never seen a more beautiful smile anywhere.

Suddenly her smile faded and her face darkened.

"What is it?" Antonius asked.

"Don't turn around. Caius and some praetorian guards have just entered the agora . . . and there is that snake Plautus, along with that big goon that Caligula bit."

"Plautus?" exclaimed Antonius with alarm. "He can recognize all of us!"

"Just keep your back turned. Maybe they will leave quickly."

Monica watched fearfully as Plautus and Caius walked into the market. She glanced across the stalls and caught the eye of Vivia, who had also noted the entrance of Plautus. Vivia was scanning the crowd, searching frantically for the boys.

Monica grabbed Antonius's arm. "Oh no! I think he sees Marcellus!"

Marcellus and Caligula had been walking nonchalantly through stacks of cowhides and goat hides, Marcellus acting as if he might be interested in buying one. Suddenly, he stopped and looked up in horror. Not more than fifty paces away was the evil man who had killed

his father! Next to him was the gorilla Marcellus, whom he had clob-
bered with the paving stone. The big soldier had a huge bruise on
one side of his face. His eye on that side was nearly swollen shut.

Caligula growled and began to bark. The man who'd stabbed
Marcellus's father in the back must have heard the bark, because he
turned in their direction—and saw them! Caligula continued to bark
angrily.

"There!" the man shouted, pointing at them. The big guard and
the other praetorian guards started toward them. Marcellus spun and
bolted away, zigzagging through the stacks of hides with Caligula
right behind him.

Antonius had turned to watch, regardless of the danger. The
guards sprinted after Marcellus, stumbling over the merchandise in
the aisles and rudely shoving people out of the way, determined to
catch him. Many of the people in the market noticed the chase and
watched with amusement as the agile boy and his dog eluded the
praetorian guards. Marcellus flew past the spectators, running for his
life, with Caligula close on his heels.

Monica clutched Antonius's arm tightly and stood on her tiptoes
to try and see better. Vivia was standing not far from them, as white
as a new cotton dress. Mardonius was slowly drifting toward them
and away from the chase. Somehow he was able to walk calmly.

Marcellus took a sharp turn to the right, sprinted between several fruit stalls, and then headed for the northern entrance to the
agora.

"He is leading them away from us," whispered Antonius. "At least
he has kept his wits."

Suddenly Nathan was standing beside Antonius and Monica.

"You must leave, Antonius," he insisted. "And you must leave
now. The ship is ready and is expecting you. But the tide is fading.
And you seem to have alarmed the entire city. The ship must depart
before the guards shift their chase to the wharf."

"But Marcellus . . .," Antonius protested, pointing to the boy as he scampered out of the northern gate to the agora.

"It can't be helped. If you stay here, you will all be caught for certain. They now know that you are here. They will soon search the entire market. You must flee."

It was true. Antonius could see that Plautus had ceased chasing Marcellus, and was now staring across the market, trying to locate the rest of the family. Caius likewise was moving rapidly past the stalls, peering at everyone he encountered.

"Come," urged Nathan. "We can easily exit through the western portal before they see us. I will try to locate the boy later and send him on to you."

Monica looked at him in horror. "We can't just leave him here!"

"He knows which stall on the wharf the ship is in," said Antonius. "With luck he can circle around and make it to the ship."

"We need to go now!" insisted the Jew.

"No!" argued Monica.

"Go with Nathan to the ship," Antonius told Monica. "I will try to bring Vivia. Mardonius knows to follow. Marcellus will find us after he shakes the guards. It's the only way."

"Antonius!" Monica cried as Nathan pulled her away and ushered her toward the western gate of the agora.

Antonius moved quickly through the market to Vivia, who was almost in shock. He had feared that she would be impossible to move, but she was strangely passive. He led her gently but firmly toward the gate. She shuffled as she went and kept turning her head to look back. Antonius checked behind them once, and saw Mardonius following a short distance behind.

Antonius and Vivia passed the loan stall where she had deposited Gallus's sword. Antonius hesitated for a moment. The sword meant much to him, and he hated to be without it during their final flight.

He felt safer when he had it with him. He started to pull out his money purse—then noticed Monica and Nathan disappearing into the crowd up ahead. He did not want to lose sight of them. Also, Polukarpos's words came back to him: "We will not defeat Rome by the sword." Antonius turned away from the stall and guided Vivia quickly to the agora gate.

Just as they were about to leave the market, Vivia came out of her daze. "We must wait for Marcellus."

"He will meet us at the ship," Antonius assured her, hoping he was not wrong.

"No," she insisted. "We must wait. What if he comes back here?"

"He knows where we are going. He is a smart lad. He will find us. It is the only way."

Antonius placed his hand on her arm and gently led her out through the gate of the agora. They walked the short distance to the harbor without speaking, but Antonius could tell that Vivia was in agony. He kept Nathan and Monica in view, maintaining about two hundred paces between them. Mardonius stayed fairly close behind Antonius and Vivia. Once on the wharf, Antonius watched Nathan and Monica board the ship. He began to breathe a little easier, although he was still worried about Marcellus. Vivia was frantic, turning frequently to look behind them and wringing her hands.

As they approached the ship, Antonius suddenly stopped and stared. *It couldn't be ... No, surely it is not ... There has been a mistake ... It is ... It's the* Orion*!* His stomach turned over. Vivia stepped onto the deck, greeted by Nathan. Monica was already in the captain's cabin near the stern. But there beside Nathan was ... *Heron! How could it be?* Antonius froze.

"Come on, Antonius!" Nathan urged. "Are you going to stand here on the dock until someone recognizes you?"

Heron stepped forward and said, "Someone does recognize him. Welcome aboard, Antonius. We meet again."

"You!" was all that Antonius could say.

"You two already know each other?" asked the puzzled banker.

"On my last voyage from Athens," explained the captain, "I and my crew—a different crew than I have now, I assure you—tried to murder him . . . and Senator Flavius as well."

"Oh, dear," said Nathan.

"I am a different man now, Antonius," the captain explained. "I have become a Christian. My whole life has changed."

Antonius wanted to believe him, but he was still cautious. *How long could Heron have been a Christian? His conversion must have been very recent indeed. Could it be a trick?*

"How did it happen?" asked Antonius.

Heron looked up and down the wharf to see if he had time for a short explanation. Nathan was fidgeting, but there was no indication of anything alarming on the wharf yet, so he continued.

"I was drunk with some friends in Laodicea. We went to the circus to see an old acquaintance of ours fight. But while we were there, I saw several Christians killed by the lions. They faced death rather than worship Domitian. I returned here, haunted by the way they had died, by their convictions, and by the eerie song an old woman sang after they died. Here in Ephesus I happened to meet a very unusual man from Smyrna who told me all about his God, Jesus Christ, the same God those people in the circus had died for. After a long night of talking, I found myself weeping, overcome by the realization of the wretched life I have lived. With this man's help, I confessed my many sins and accepted Jesus as Lord and Savior. It's only been a few days since I made this decision, and I know you have no right to trust me, but—"

"Polukarpos," Antonius interrupted. "Was the man's name Polukarpos?"

"It was," answered Heron. "But how did you know?"

Antonius stepped on the ship and embraced Heron. "Welcome to the family," he said with a smile.

"Antonius," the captain said, "I see you still have the goatskin bag with the scroll, but where is your fearsome sword?"

"I left it behind. Polukarpos told me that I didn't need it anymore. I guess I have traded my father's sword for this scroll. The word of God is more powerful than the iron of a Roman sword."

Mardonius came bounding onto the ship, breaking the moment, and bringing them all back to the current crisis.

"Where's Marcellus?" he demanded. "Did Marcellus make it yet?"

"No," Antonius answered. "But he will be here soon."

"You must quickly get into the cabin," Heron ordered. "And we must set sail within the next hour or the incoming tide will begin and we will be stuck here for several hours. There is also a storm rolling in," he said, looking at the dark gray clouds creeping over the edge of the mountains, just beyond the city. Lightning flashed in the distance. Several seconds later, thunder rumbled.

The travelers hurried into the captain's cabin at the back of the ship. Heron followed them. Inside the cabin, Antonius, Heron, and Nathan quickly signed the contract that Nathan had prepared. Nathan tucked it under his arm and quickly left the ship, promising to look high and low for Marcellus and also promising to send him on to Cyrene if he found him.

To the anxious travelers, it seemed as if it were only minutes till Heron said, "We've got to leave."

"No!" answered Vivia, adamantly. "We will wait for Marcellus."

Heron looked imploringly at Antonius. The minutes crawled by.

Suddenly Heron pointed to the road along the shore that led to the wharf.

"Look!" he said. "Praetorian guards are coming."

He ran outside the cabin and shouted at the crew, "Cast off!"

"No!" shouted Vivia, running after him. Antonius grabbed her from behind. Three crewmen were untying the ropes that held the ship. Two of the mariners were releasing the front sail. The praetorian guards were now on the pier, marching in their direction. Maximus led the way, accompanied by ten other soldiers. Plautus and Caius followed at a distance, eyeing carefully everyone they passed.

"Marcellus!" screamed Vivia, looking hopelessly toward shore.

"Get her inside!" ordered the captain.

"No," she pleaded. "We must wait. Marcellus!"

"Come on, Vivia," Antonius coaxed. "We must get into the cabin."

"Wait!" she demanded. "Listen!"

"Mother! Antonius!" They could faintly hear the voice of Marcellus. All of them looked around in wonder. Marcellus was not in sight.

"Marcellus! Where are you?" shouted Vivia.

"Down here! In the water."

They ran across the deck away from the wharf and looked over. Below, in the water beside the ship, was Marcellus, with Caligula paddling alongside him.

"Get a rope!" the captain commanded his crew. To his passengers, he added, "And get in the cabin, so they don't see you!" Antonius and Vivia returned to the cabin. The guards were getting closer on the dock. Heron threw the rope over the side of the ship and quickly slid down the rope to retrieve Marcellus. He returned to the deck with the wet boy on his back, clinging to his neck. Heron shouted to the crew, "Now! Cast off! Lower the sail!"

"No!" Marcellus demanded, now on his feet and leaning over the rail. "You must get Caligula!"

"We can't," shouted the captain. "There is no time." The ship was starting to move.

"Get Caligula or else I'm going back in after him," threatened Marcellus, climbing up on the rails.

"Mother of Zeus," muttered Heron. He slid back down the rope and pulled in Caligula just as the ship began to pick up speed. It was now moving steadily away from the wharf.

"Get in the cabin, boy. Quick!" Heron ordered, once back on deck. "And take your dog with you."

Marcellus scurried down the deck and into the cabin, where his mother smothered him with a tight embrace. Caligula, however, ran excitedly around on the deck, sniffing everything.

"Caligula! Come here, boy!" Mardonius and Antonius called from the door in a whisper, but the dog ignored them.

Maximus saw the ship slowly pulling away from the wharf, and he sprinted down the dock toward it. He ran up beside the *Orion*, now no more than twenty paces from the dock and moving steadily away. Antonius caught a glimpse of the giant praetorian guard through a crack in the wood of the cabin. His heart was pounding. Monica was squeezing his hand tightly.

"Halt! By order of the Imperial Temple, stop that ship!"

"We can't stop this ship, soldier!" the captain shouted back. "Once in the tide and with the sails out we are under way. Stopping is impossible. But we'll be back in a month or two."

"Do you have passengers on board?" Maximus cried.

"No!" answered Heron. "Only wool and garments from Laodicea."

Caligula heard the voice of Maximus and caught his scent. The dog placed his front paws on the railing of the ship and barked a warning at Maximus.

"You must have them!" shouted Maximus. "You have their cursed dog."

"I found this dog wandering along the pier," shouted Heron as the ship moved farther and farther away. "It's not a crime to take a stray dog on a voyage, is it? Is it now the occupation of the praetorian guards to chase stray dogs?"

The crew of the ship laughed. Caligula continued barking. Maximus cursed at the dog in a great rage. The ship moved steadily on. Antonius could see Plautus and Caius standing and shouting at Maximus, who was pointing out at the ship. Yet as he watched, Antonius noted with joy that the wharf and the soldiers on it were getting smaller and smaller.

The dark clouds continued to pour down from the mountains as the ship fled across the harbor. Lightning flashed across the sky and a loud roar of thunder followed. Rain began to fall, slowly at first, and then in a torrential downpour. The shoreline faded from view.

Another blast of blinding lightning was followed instantly by a crack of thunder. Antonius opened the door of the cabin and looked out. Heron was standing by the twin rudders at the stern, smiling in spite of the pouring rain. Antonius looked at the sky with concern.

"Don't worry, lad!" Heron shouted. "The *Orion* has been through lots of storms, remember? We will overcome this one as well."

The ship headed out of the bay and into the open sea. The dark storm rumbled behind them, but the rain slowly grew lighter and then stopped. Antonius noticed that there was a trace of clear sky far off to the southwest. Monica stepped close beside Antonius, and he put his arm around her. She laid her head on his shoulder, sighed, and said, "I told you we would make it."

Heron smiled at them. He was humming as he steered the ship, altering the course to head southwest after the *Orion* cleared the harbor. He started singing, softly at first, then gradually louder and louder. Soon he was singing with zeal.

Antonius and Monica recognized the lyrics. They looked back at Heron, standing by the rudder, soaking wet, singing the song of Zenia as loud as he could: "Who are those in the white robes? They are the ones who have come out of the great tribulation. They have washed their robes in the blood of the Lamb. Never again will they hunger; never again will they thirst. God will wipe away every tear."

Vivia wept softly, but then joined Heron in singing the chorus. Monica began singing, too, and soon Antonius and the twins added their voices. "God will wipe away every tear," they sang together, as the *Orion* plowed through the stormy sea, headed for the coast of Cyrene.

οἱ ἑπτὰ ἀστέρες ἄγγελοι τῶν ἑπτὰ ἐκκλησιῶν εἰσιν

postscript: HISTORICAL ASPECTS OF THE NOVEL

καὶ αἱ λυχνίαι αἱ ἑπτὰ ἑπτὰ ἐκκλησίαι εἰσίν.

Although this story is fictional, we have attempted to place it in an accurate historical context. The story takes place around A.D. 95. While the main characters are fictional, the setting, many of the background events, and some of the minor characters are historical.

Domitian, for example, is a historical character—Titus Flavius Domitianus—who reigned as Caesar in Rome from A.D. 81 to A.D. 96. As described in our story, Domitian did mint coins proclaiming his deceased infant son's divinity. Likewise, the reference to the *Dea Roma* coin is historical. These coins are in the British Museum. Domitian instituted a cult of emperor worship, and most of our description relating to the Imperial Cult is historical.

This Imperial Cult was particularly influential in the province of Asia. Our description of the large statue of Domitian set up in Ephesus is historically accurate, and the rumors of supernatural phenomena accompanying the inauguration of that statue are likewise documented in ancient sources.

The description of the persecution of Christians by the Imperial Cult in Asia Minor reflects historical events. Likewise, the eviction of the Christians from the synagogue and the final break of Christianity from Judaism appear to have happened during this approximate time period.

Senator Flavius is a fictional character, but the story of his brother's execution is based on a true event. Domitian did execute a Roman aristocrat named Flavius Clemens and banish the aristocrat's wife, Flavia Domitilla, from Rome because of their Christian faith. Caius, Plautus, and Sulla are fictional characters, but their positions are historical.

The geographical and economic setting of the story is fairly accurate. Thus we have portrayed the cities (Ephesus, Laodicea, Magnesia, Iconium, and so forth) and the roads that connect them as accurately as possible. Likewise, the physical layout of Ephesus as well as the description of the buildings and streets (the theater, the agora, Harbor Street, etc.) in the story is based on the archaeological remains of the city.

Laodicea was famous for its black wool, and the wool industry was central to the city's financial well-being. Likewise, guilds were the backbone of the economic system in Asia Minor. They supported the Imperial Temples for financial reasons. Archelaus is fictional, but his title as president of the guild is historical.

Most of the names in the story are Greek or Roman names that were in common use at the time. However, Juba and Monica are Berber names (North African tribes) and Shabako is an Ethiopian/Cushite name—Shabako was an eighth-century B.C. Ethiopian/Cushite king who invaded Egypt.

Caligula the dog is named after one of the most infamous Caesars of the first century. Officially named Gaius Caesar Germanicus, he was known popularly as Caligula (literally, "little boots"). He reigned from A.D. 37 to A.D. 41, and nearly bankrupted the Roman Empire by his continuous extravagant parties and other excesses.

Many interpreters of 2 Thessalonians 2:4 believe that verse alludes to Caligula's imperial order to place his statue in the Jerusalem temple in A.D. 40. Before his order could be carried out, however, he was assassinated.

The Battle of Athanel is fictional. However, throughout the first century, the Roman legions were constantly fighting campaigns along the Empire's frontiers, and there are numerous stories and legends of heroic actions. There was a famous battle fought in the forests of Germany that resembles the battle we describe in some details. In A.D. 9, the Roman General Quinctilius Varus and three Roman legions were surrounded and ambushed by Germanic tribes in the Teutoburg Forest near Minden. As far as we know, however, the Roman column was completely annihilated, and there were few, if any, survivors. On the other hand, Shabako's description of the siege and fall of Jerusalem (A.D. 70) is fairly accurate, including the report of earthquakes.

Polukarpos is a historical person, a famous early church leader, known in English as Polycarp. He had been a personal disciple of John the apostle in Ephesus and later became the bishop in Smyrna. He was martyred in Smyrna at the age of 86 in A.D. 156.

Finally, although there are a few dissenting opinions, the majority of New Testament scholars date the composition of John's Apocalypse (the book of Revelation) to this general time period—the end of the first century.

We want to hear from you. Please send your comments about this book to us in care of zreview@zondervan.com. Thank you.

GRAND RAPIDS, MICHIGAN 49530 USA

WWW.ZONDERVAN.COM